SOUR
GRAPES

SOUR GRAPES

MARTIN SYLVESTER

VILLARD BOOKS

NEW YORK

1992

Library of Congress Cataloging-in-Publication Data

Sylvester, Martin.
Sour grapes / Martin Sylvester.—1st ed.
p. cm.
ISBN 0–679–40442-2
I. Title.
PR6069.Y43S6   1992
823'.914—dc20   91-24744

Manufactured in the United States of America
9 8 7 6 5 4 3 2
First edition

Book design by Debbie Glasserman
The text of this book is set in Bembo.

for Ann and Jeremy
and the Hyundai

Chapter opening epigraphs are extracts from
the notebooks of Joseph de Tournefort,
a cultivated young Frenchman commissioned
in 1718 by his secretary of state to visit
and report on the island of Crete, then a
Turkish possession. He was, in effect, a
gentleman spy, detailing fortifications and
military garrisons, but chose to include his own
observations on the people and their customs,
the landscape, the fauna and flora—a delightful and
perceptive account of Crete as it was nearly three
hundred years ago. Since then, bulldozers and
reinforced concrete have scarred the landscape he
described. But in the mountains, high above
the coastal tourist resorts, I found
de Tournefort's Crete again.

SOUR GRAPES

My Lord:—Pursuant to your Commands, I give you a
particular Account of what we obferv'd in Candia, that
fame'd Ifland, fo well known in former Ages by the name
of Crete.

he hand brake went on with a rasp that sounded final.
"What's up?"

Surely he could hear the question, if not understand the
words. But he ignored me, was groping for cigarettes. His
lighter clicked and flamed. Cancerous smoke invaded my personal space like an insult. Why do I always get taxi drivers like
this? And what about *xenophilía*, the love of strangers, that writers on Greece are always going misty about?

"Moustaki," he said through the poison cloud.

"What, *here*?" I leaned forward to see past his head and get a
wider view along the path cut by the headlights. The giant
angular arm of a bulldozer showed palely above a dark fuzz of

olive trees, beside a low, unlit barrier of planks guarding a trench across the road. Well, all right—this was as far as we went.

But there should be a town, a village at least. The three-pointed star on the bonnet was aimed at all-enveloping, uninhabited night.

"Can't be!"

He took a deep drag on his cigarette, opened the door, and got out. I followed.

Out of the car, the September night became transparent. I looked about me, the wind slipping cool fingers under my jacket.

Above, there was a blaze of stars such as you never see in England. Too many stars . . .

On each side, the black bulk of mountains. There's something ominous about mountains . . .

Behind, a distant glow of civilization from Rethymnon, down on the coast. Far behind. Planet Earth, as seen from the chill, inhospitable moon . . .

I could go back, check into a comfortable hotel, return in daylight. We're in the middle of nowhere, probably lost, and—

"Moustaki."

He'd found a sign lurking in the shadows at the side of the road. I read the translation under the Greek. So it said.

"But where? Is it far?"

My suitcase rattled on to the tarmac by my feet, followed by my carry-on bag.

"How far?"

He shrugged. My problem.

He took the sheaf of drachmas, counted them, and got back into the car. As he turned it, the headlights gave me a sweeping glimpse of more olive trees with ancient blackened and bulbous trunks, stone-walled terraces, a shepherd's hut with the roof covered in plastic sacks held down by rocks. Then he drove away. I watched the red taillights diminish and disappear round the next bend, listened as the rattle of the diesel engine faded and was gone. Then I took up the suitcase and bag, and began walking.

Fifty yards past the bulldozer, a narrow track lined with stone walls forked upwards from the road, worn cobbled surface glinting in the starlight. Was there a glimmer of yellow light up there?

I started up the track in the starlight, stumbling on the cobbles. A hundred yards on, the source of the yellow light appeared round a bend in the track—a streetlight, no less, faint but unmistakable. Houses, too—the straggling outskirts of a village. As I climbed, more buildings rose out of the hillside, dark shapes outlined by the pale sky beyond. Here and there, lit windows stared down at me. There was a faint humming of electricity, a distant rustle of water. A dog barked. There was also a smell, growing stronger with each step I took: an animal smell, warm and acrid, of dung and sweat. The yellow eyes, the sounds, the smells . . . the place was alive, a stone monster squatting on the mountainside.

Did Maud really live here, inside this beast? *The lovely Maud . . . ?*

No no, this won't do. Start at the beginning.

Normally I like the feel of Fridays—there's a weekend coming up. But this one was out to break the mold. "Oh Christ!"

"Well, don't take it out on me," Maggie said indignantly. "I just brought you the letter—I didn't write it."

I realized I was glaring at her. Emperors hang the bearers of bad news, but even they would have hesitated to string up such a faithful old retainer. "Sorry, sorry, didn't mean you. Just letting off steam."

"Humph," she said. The fire in her glasses receded somewhat.

"Hard to bear though, isn't it," I said. "Here's a restaurant

we've supplied with house wine for years, deciding to give up
our excellent Bordeaux for what? Bulgarian cabernet sauvignon,
that's what. *Bulgarian!* And who benefits? The KGB. They're
desperate to get rid of rubles in exchange for sterling, so they're
forcing the Bulgarians into giving the stuff away. A plague on
their politics, say I."

"You do say so," Maggie agreed. "Often."

"Am I unreasonable?"

"You say yourself it's good wine."

"Well, yes."

"And it's cheap."

"It's cheap."

"So—"

"Look! Whose side are you on, anyway?"

"The KGB's, apparently," she said, "according to you. Yesterday I was a loonie leftie because the dustbins weren't collected. The day before that—"

"Oh. Am I . . . ?"

"Yes, you are. *Outrage* is *middle age,* Mr. William. And the
sooner you go off on holiday, the better for all of us. *If* I may
say so without getting my head bitten off."

She left me to ponder this. She was right, I knew it. I was on
a short fuse these days—snappy, paranoid, and hard to please. I
knew why, too.

Most people would think I was a lucky man. Inherited business which, though under attack, still produced a comfortable
income. Beautiful wife, two darling daughters, and a studious
son. Count your blessings, they'd tell me briskly.

Well I did, of course I did. I looked round the room, my inner
sanctum. Paneled walls loaded with family mementoes: photographs of Father chatting to owners of famous vineyards, some
of myself trying to look equally at ease. On the carved pine
mantelshelf below the James Gunn portrait of him, a clutch of
cards summoning me to wine tastings, trade fairs, dinners (do

bring your wife!). I was sound of limb, secure at home, wanted in work. So what was missing, where was the worm in the rose?

Well of course, it's not where you *are,* but where you're *going* that counts. And I wasn't going anywhere. The business still filled a gap in the wine trade for quality and personal service: a limited gap, but with little or no room for growth. To expand I'd have to compete with giant chains and supermarkets for a slice of the popular market, and that would be financial suicide. So I was trapped. This room and all it represented would be here for years to come, with me in it, going gray, then grayer . . .

I shrugged and reached for the in-tray. I'd better pull my socks up, stop behaving like a spoiled brat. I was supposed to be the captain of this ship, and it was bad for morale to let my boredom hang out. Moreover, our planned fortnight in Crete was coming up soon: I had that to look forward to.

Oh yes!—two weeks more, and we'd be lolling on Maud's vine-shaded terrace, sipping iced drinks and watching the white sails drifting by on the sparkling Aegean. In the evenings, we'd stroll to the taverna, where jolly Greeks would be dancing arm in arm to the catchy bounce of *bouzoúki* music, to talk and laugh until the small hours . . . Then home by moonlight, arm in arm with Claudine, to the little white bedroom with the bright blue shutters and the honeymoon atmosphere . . .

Yes, I could picture it all. Though, in fact, it would be my first time in Greece—I usually take my holidays in France, combining business with pleasure, and it *is* a pleasure, I love France. But when Maud invited us, we thought it was time to widen our horizons. And it's so much better to stay with friends than in a hotel: you see the real country, not just the tourist façade.

I did my duty with letters and invoices, and was still in my office when, at about six-fifteen, I heard the side doorbell. The shop was shut, Maggie had just left to catch the bus home, and Claudine was already busy in the kitchen, so I answered it.

There was a girl on the doorstep, swinging a carrier bag to and fro. "Hello," she said in friendly fashion.

"Hello!" I responded with the warmth that wells up in me irresistibly on such occasions (and long may it last). I like girls, even when they're trying to conceal the evidence beneath someone else's castoffs. The black loose-knit sweater was three or four sizes too large, the baggy, long gray skirt made no concessions to the shape of the person inside. Below the skirt, pointed black lace-up shoes had been contributed by a passing witch. There was a lot of dark hair going in all directions, some of it tied up, some left loose. She was smiling. The smile reminded me of someone.

"You don't recognize me, do you," she said.

"I recognize the smile," I said. "I'll have the name in a moment."

"I'm Kate."

"Oh my God! So you are!"

"I wonder if I could . . ."

"Come in, come in. How lovely to see you. We'll go through to the kitchen, Claudine's there." She stepped over the threshold, and I closed the door. "That way." *Kate—daughter of the lovely Maud . . .* I was intrigued, also chastened a little. To have the daughter of an ex-girlfriend sprung on you, in all the panoply and power of full-grown femininity, is to be forced to recognize the passing of the years. Maud had been my last serious girlfriend before I met and married Claudine. She was then about the same age as her daughter Kate was now . . . Ouch.

"What are you up to, these days?" I asked.

"I'm in my second year at the Royal College of Art," she said.

"That's impressive—difficult to get in, isn't it?" I ushered her through the kitchen door.

"Oh, I don't know . . ." She gave a deprecating shrug.

"Look, darling, it's Kate Aspinall!"

Claudine turned from closing the oven door. "Kate, *ma petite!*
. . . Oh, but how long is it? Three, four years, I think. Too
long." She greeted her cheek to cheek, kissing the air to avoid
lipstick smudges, then leaned back to inspect her. "So, now you
are an *artist* . . ." Claudine, who believes in chic and whose
clothes all fit to within a millimeter, had rationalized Kate's *look*:
not simple scruff, but *La Bohème* . . . So everything was in order,
the world still right side up.

"We're looking forward enormously to seeing Maud and
Nick again," I said. "You know we're invited to stay with them
in Crete in a couple of weeks' time?"

"Yes, I know," Kate said. "Actually, that's why I'm here.
Maud phoned."

"Oh?"

"Yes, last night. I'm sorry I left it until this evening to contact
you, but, well . . ."

"What has happened?" Claudine asked. "Come, sit at the
table, my dear. Now, what is it?"

"I don't know quite where to start, it's a really odd situation . . ." Kate spoke from behind a sudden waterfall of hair. She
shook it back automatically. Claudine looked a message at me:
I understood it perfectly, and complied.

"I'll just get something to drink." As good an excuse as any.
I went down to the cellar for a bottle of muscat d'Alsace, taking
my time.

It was unnerving to have the chords of memory struck so
loudly by a simple play of muscles round a mouth. Here was
Kate, bearer of that awesome gift of Nature—Maud's smile.

That's why we called her *the lovely Maud,* a gentle irony to
balance her unfair advantage. It was famous, that smile. Not least
because it was rare—Maud was notoriously hard to please and
her smile had the increased value of scarcity. You had to work
for it. Her mouth, normally, was tightly closed and somewhat
sulky, to be honest. But when the downturn of discontent

softened and began to flicker at the corners, when the wide lips parted, drawing slowly back to reveal the crescent of white teeth within, *it was like the moon sliding out from between clouds.*

Pause for sardonic laughter . . . Finished? Then I'll resume this frank confession of youthful naïveté, commenting only that I wouldn't mind having that time over again . . . Anyway, so I was obsessed by her, and convinced that behind the smile there was a princess just waiting for the right man to turn up. Then disillusionment began to gnaw. Maybe I'd simply believed what I wanted to believe. Maybe we didn't have a future, after all . . . While I was having doubts, Aspinall turned up.

Guy Aspinall. He directed films, and was quite famous already. He had no doubts, and they were married a few months later, as soon as his divorce from a French actress came through. I hadn't got around to confessing my doubts to Maud, so she was able to be kind to me, sorry for letting me down.

And that's how it was left. After she'd produced Kate and was about again, I saw her occasionally at parties or over someone's dinner table. She treated me sympathetically, as the might-have-been. She remained as demanding as a duchess, but smiled more often in recompense: I was happy for her. Then came the split with Aspinall.

It must have hit her hard, as she disappeared for nearly two years. Then, as suddenly, she resurfaced with Nick.

Nick Cruickshank. Pale straight hair, pale eyes behind round John Lennon spectacles. Started as a copywriter with one of the big agencies—Finch & Finch? I forget, but it doesn't matter because he left after a few months. I heard he had, and next time we met at someone's party, I asked what had happened. He leaned closer and, after glancing round the room, murmured with an air of modest pride as if confessing to a recently conferred mark of distinction: "Actually, they realized I'm under surveillance . . ."

"Surveillance? You mean, *police*?" It flashed into my mind that Nick was always the one to produce the pot on those occasions. "Oh, come *on*! You haven't started *dealing*?"

"Shhh."

"Oh *Christ*!" Then I noticed the slight smile, and the way he was watching my reactions, watching to see the fish take the fly. "All right, all right. What, then?"

"Not now."

Typical, to spin out the mystery, make a serial of it. Nick of the easy charm and the quiet, confidential voice. You could never be sure which of the things he was confiding in you were true and which invention. He played games with people, and the odd thing was, they let him, so long as no real harm was done. He amused them. He amused Claudine.

"Listen, *chérie*, I think I invite Nick and Maud to the dinner next week. *D'accord*?"

"Okay with me, darling," I said, hiding my surprise—she knew that Maud had been my girlfriend. But she would have her reasons—curiosity, probably.

"I am a big fool, per'aps?"

"No, darling. Maud is prehistory. Before I met you."

"Mmmm . . . Nick is amusing, I think."

"Frightfully."

"Oh!—you don't like him?"

"He's good at parties. Ask them."

"All right. I will."

It went better than I expected, and we dined together on a number of occasions afterwards, a rather curious foursome, at which I was left in the passive rôle of observer as Nick worked at charming Claudine, Claudine worked at making friends with Maud, and Maud smiled kindly at me, the failed suitor. Then, about five years ago, Nick and Maud decided to drop out, and went to live in Crete. I hadn't seen either of them since, but we'd exchanged cards from time to time, and had finally got around to accepting a long-standing invitation to stay with them for a fortnight's holiday. I'd been looking forward to it.

But now, here was Kate, with a message. Surely Claudine would have her relaxed by now? I went up the cellar steps with the bottle.

As I crossed the hall, I could hear Claudine's voice raised in sympathetic horror. "Poor Maud!" she was saying. "Oh la! I am so sorry . . ."

I crossed the kitchen to the big pine table, where they were sitting side by side. "What have I missed?"

"I am so sorry, *chérie,* but when you hear this—"

"What's happened?" I went to collect the corkscrew from the drawer.

"There's a problem," Kate said.

I knew it. I knew it! Goodbye vine-shaded terraces, sparkling Aegean. "I'm sorry to hear that. What sort of problem?"

"Nick's disappeared," she said.

"Disappeared?" I'd expected a broken limb, a flood in the kitchen, a car off the road. "Since when?"

"He told Mum he was going to Athens. That was two weeks ago. But it turned out not to be true."

"How?"

"He's been seen on the island since."

"Poor Maud! Is that certain?"

"Yes. Someone from the village saw him, and it was at the same time that he sent a message saying he was held up in Athens, and would be there another week at least."

"What was he supposed to be doing in Athens?"

"Research. You know he's into archaeology and stuff."

"I didn't realize he was serious about it." Cork out, I began to pour. "I don't see Nick nose down in dusty diggings, some-how."

"He knows quite a lot about it," Kate said rather sharply.

I pulled myself up. To her, Nick was family—she needed to feel her mother hadn't made a mistake in taking up with him. I'd have to watch what I said.

"Well, it's five years since I last saw him, plenty of time to, er, settle down." That didn't sound too good. I ploughed on. "Look, I didn't mean to sound unsympathetic, Kate. It's just that, well, I have known Nick a long time, and he always liked to cultivate an air of mystery about his doings. My guess is, he'll suddenly reappear, with some amazing story or other. Don't you think?"

"Mum left it a week, thinking that," Kate admitted. "Then she rang me, to put you off going. She said to tell you she's very sorry about it, but you see how it is." She paused, looking down at the table.

"But of course," Claudine said. "Oh, I only wish there was something we could do."

I passed out glasses of wine. "How did she sound?"

"Livid," Kate said.

"*Livid?* Not upset?"

"Oh yes, of course she's upset. But you know Mum—she has got a bit of a temper, and she thinks Nick's up to something and ought to have told her."

"I'm afraid so," I said with relief. If Maud could say it, I must be allowed to agree with her.

"It leaves her very isolated," Kate said. "He's got the car, too."

"Oh, that is too bad!" Claudine said indignantly.

"Well yes, it is rather," Kate said, reluctantly.

"But certainly! To leave poor Maud so—no news, no car, nothing! *C'est abominable!*"

"It does seem fairly abominable," I agreed. "I'm not surprised that Maud's livid, frankly." She'd be incandescent by now, if I knew Maud. And Nick was going to have to pull out all the stops to play his way out of this one.

"Well yes," Kate said again, unhappily. I had a sudden mental picture of them together, Nick leaning over her in that confidential way he had, whispering in her ear, making her laugh. She wasn't just concerned for her mother, I realized: she was fond of him. "Something could have happened to him," she said.

"But he's been seen, alive and well?"

"Yes. All the same . . ."

"What then?"

"I don't know."

A silence fell. I found myself wondering why Maud hadn't rung us direct. Too upset? Or was there more to Kate's message than she'd told us so far? I said:

"Did Maud want you to do anything else, apart from putting us off?"

"She says she really must know what's going on. She says she can't go on living like this. But she doesn't really want to kick him out, if and when he turns up, not if she can help it."

"She's dependent on him."

"Yes. That's it. She is. There's no way she could go on living in Crete without him. Plus he's, like, her manager."

"Manager?"

"For the paintings. She's selling really well in the States and that's all due to him, the contacts and everything."

"Oh, is she? I hadn't heard about that."

"She's been trying for years, and it's a real breakthrough. Then she gets this." Kate's eyes, heavily rimmed with black liner, glowed earnestly first at me, then Claudine.

"I think Nick must have some problem, no?" Claudine said. "Something has happened to make him do this to Maud."

"That's what I think," Kate said.

"Very likely," I said.

There was a short silence. Then I added:

"You didn't say what Maud wanted you to do."

"Oh, no. I didn't, did I. Well, it's a bit difficult . . ."

"Go on."

"She needs help, that's obvious."

"Yes, of course. She could call in the police, I suppose."

"She said she didn't want to," Kate said.

"Unsympathetic?"

"She thought so. It's not that he's totally vanished. He just seems to be staying away."

"He's only been seen once?"

"Yes, but that proved he hadn't told the truth about going to Athens."

"She doesn't want to confide in a bunch of macho types with moustaches and revolvers."

"No. Not if there's any alternative."

"Quite. But is there?"

"Oh dear. This is awful," Kate muttered. The hair had fallen forward again, hiding her face.

"What is the matter?" Claudine said, putting an arm round her. "*Dit!* You must tell us."

"I feel such a fool . . ."

"Why?"

"I said I would, you see, but now I'm sitting here, it all seems . . . I mean, my mother does have the maddest ideas sometimes. If she wants something, she just goes for it, no matter what."

"As I remember, she usually succeeded," I said.

"Oh right, right. But I'm not like that."

"Kate, my dear, just tell us what she said?" Claudine urged.

"Oh well . . . she said: 'It's got to be done privately.' "

"Ah!" I said. "Well, no need for all this carry-on. She wants you to hire a private eye. And you don't know how to go about it. Right?"

"Well, sort of."

Her eyes were fixed on me alone now. She gave a nervous smile, had got stuck again. *O the smile, the smile!* A sudden, vivid flash of memory, Maud in the Notting Hill flat . . .

". . . but Mum said you just might."

"What?"

"Do it."

"Help her? Us?"

"Well, she really meant you." Kate's embarrassment looked about to overflow. Not her fault, poor kid. It was Maud, Maud Imperatrice. "She said, as you were due to go anyway . . . Of course, if you both wanted to go, I'm sure she'd be happy to . . . But she meant, to look for Nick."

"She wants me to look for Nick?"

"Well, you've been involved in this sort of thing before, haven't you. Everybody says so."

She meant that affair of the girl who went missing in Spain. "Never thought of it like that. All the same . . . I mean, I'd love to help her, of course I would, but . . ."

If it was up to me, I'd be packing the bags already. The longed-for holiday restored, with a mystery thrown in for added interest. All the while being smiled upon by the lovely Maud. Heigh ho. But there it was. I glanced at Claudine, and found myself under observation. Well, even if my enthusiasm had shown, nothing for it now but to fall into line. The thing was impossible.

"I'm terribly sorry," I said.

"William!" Claudine said. Or rather, remonstrated . . .

Remonstrated?

"Darling?"

"Surely you are not so *very* busy . . ."

I was struck dumb. But not for long.

"You mean, I should go? Oh, I see. Well . . . but what about you?"

"I think," Claudine said calmly, "I shall be all right, you know."

"Oh, really?"

"You do not think so?"

"Darling, I just want to be sure you're happy about it, that's all."

"I am happy."

"Well then—"

"Terrific!" Kate said, giving me a big smile. "I'm really, really grateful. You're sure?"

I glanced at Claudine. Last chance . . . but she nodded. I said: "Yes, we're sure."

"Well, it's really, really kind of you. Mum will be over the moon."

"I don't know that she should be," I said. "Listen, Kate, I've got very little to qualify me for this. Apart from two years in the peacetime army, and the Spanish episode you've heard about, my experience as action man and sleuth is nil. And I don't speak Greek."

But Maud had said: Send for William—he's the one . . . When it came to a crisis, she'd immediately thought of me—

"There isn't anyone else," Kate said artlessly.

Oh.

Well, that meant the same thing, more or less. Didn't it? "Tell her she can count on me," I said.

"I'm sure she can," Kate said politely. "And even if you can't *do* much, at least she'll have some moral support."

"I'll hope to manage a bit more than that," I said.

"Well, if you can . . . Is that all right, then? You really will go?"

"Yes."

"Well, terrific!"

"Tell me about flights and so forth. And then, all you can about Nick, and what he's been doing since they moved to Crete. Anything that might be useful."

"Yes. Well, you can get a direct flight from Gatwick to Heraclion, to avoid changing at Athens. When you get to Heraclion . . ."

So it was on. I really was going.

". . . then he was working on this dig somewhere up the east end, Zakros, I think it was."

"He takes it seriously, then?"

"Oh yes, he's really got to know a lot about it, the house is full of books on Minoan pots and all that. The really ancient stuff. It's what he spends his time on, when he's not pushing Mum's paintings . . . I don't know what else I can tell you, really."

"No need. That's fine—I can get the details from Maud."

"Yes. Oh, there's one more thing: Mum is desperate to have this." Kate picked the carrier bag off the floor by her chair, and held it out to me.

How like Maud, to coolly add this delivery to her cry for help!

"What is it?"

"Some paint she needs—Liquitex acrylic. She's run out and can't get it on the island. It's American—fabulous colors."

"I'll see she gets it," I said.

Later, as we were getting ready for bed, I called to Claudine, who was still in the bathroom:

"I didn't think you'd want me to go, you know. For various reasons."

"Yes, I know."

"I don't quite understand it, I must admit."

"My poor William! You look so excited, and then you look so sad. I think, if you want to do these things so much, you must do them."

"What things?"

"Your *p'tites escapades*."

"I suppose you think I'm *fou*."

"*Complètement, chérie*."

"But all the same, you understand . . . Maggie complained I was getting short-tempered."

"I know, I talked with her. And also, fat."

"*Fat?* It's my shirts, that's all. They've shrunk in the wash, they always do."

"Not only the shirts, the trousairs. Look!"

"Well, perhaps a little tighter."

"Trousairs do not shrink so much. So you see . . ."

"Oh, right. So I'm going for my health!"

"No, I do not think so . . . Listen, you look for Nick, *tout simplement, hein?* And that is all you do."

"Of course, of course . . ." *And now I feel a certain loosening of the libido at the thought of this . . .* "What did you call it? This trip?"

"*P'tite escapade, chérie.*"

"Yes, that's it." *How wise she is, my favorite Frog. And what a long time she spends in the bathroom . . .* "Surely you must have finished cleaning your teeth by now?"

"Yes, I just finish."

She emerged from the bathroom, and advanced towards me wearing *Mystère de Rochas* and an air of decision . . . I was in for a souvenir send-off, no doubt about that. I moved over to make space for her, feeling . . . well, why was I going away when we got on like this? She might seem formidable, what with the sharp eye for the bottom line on the accounts, and the color coordinated everything, but it's all for *us,* and I love it . . . most of the time. She also has this earthy side that you might not suspect from her careful appearance . . . "I'm going to miss you," I said, reaching for her.

"Show me," she murmured. Earthy laugh, too.

A colorful day!—acrylic and otherwise.

It were next to impoffible to have a happier or fhorter
Voyage. The Wind was conftantly in our Stern, and in
nine days we reached Canea.

"*I*t's rather difficult to explain," Kate had said apologetically. "But anyone in the village will direct you."

I pause for breath, and to change hands on the suitcase handle. Claudine was right—steaming slowly up this track, I can feel the extra weight around the midriff. The chairbound muscles creak and groan—but the calories must be burning off! There's a single, lonely streetlight ahead. When I reach it, I shall take a break . . .

Under the light, I let the suitcase clatter down on the cobbles, and take in the scene. Everything is whitewashed—buildings, walls, even a strip along both sides of the street surface. It's as if the paint had flowed down from the walls while still wet, solidifying just in time to leave a band of plain cobbles in the center.

The few small windows are mostly shuttered, but one on an upper floor is open: I can hear voices, an insistent rattle of words from a woman and the rumble of a man's reply. It doesn't sound the sort of conversation one should interrupt, and there must be a center to this village, a small square perhaps, with a bar or café where I can get directions: at five past eleven it may be closed, but if not, and if this is anything like France, the proprietor will know where Maud lives, as well as how, why, and with whom. Onwards and upwards, then.

I shall be scarred for life by the handle on this suitcase. Claudine returned from one of her Harrods expeditions with it, crying happily: "*Voilà, chéri!* Now I throw away that *frightful* old thing of yours . . ." I hadn't the heart to deny her, but I'm now paying for my weakness, for the Italian designer label, in *blood* . . .

What's that? A sigh, deeply felt, from the dark interior of a ground-floor room. There's a stable door, top half open, and a shadowy furry face, topped with tall ears, looking out. *A donkey!* I pause. His eyes, hugely convex, are bluish misty mirrors in which I can see myself reflected, upside down. Impossible not to put down the suitcase for a moment and give him a rub between the ears, enjoy the breathy warmth of his quarters.

On again, past more houses, a tiny barrel-vaulted white-washed church set back from the street behind blue-painted iron gates in an arched gateway. From the minature bell tower, a rope trails down, the end casually looped over an oleander bush.

Ah! Now, at last, I can hear voices ahead, echoing in a space that might be the village square. A moped engine is ticking over, is revved, moves away. Music now: a jukebox or radio. I've arrived by a back street, evidently, but up there, they'll direct me.

A movement catches my eye. It's from a side street, even narrower than the one I'm in. I stop, and turn. It's odd that, apart from the donkey, I haven't seen a living creature since the taxi left. I've heard sounds, but seen nobody. And it's only five past eleven. But here's someone—my first sight of a villager. At last I can ask where Maud lives.

It's a girl—I caught a gleam of raven hair and black eyes in the instant before she pulled a black scarf forward across her face. Do I look so frightening? Well, there's only the two of us, and the narrow street is badly lit, the sounds of life are a hundred yards away . . .

I must say something reassuring; there'd been time on the Airbus to study the phrase book bought at Gatwick. So here, to start the ball rolling, is Good Evening (I hope).

"*Kali spéra!*"

No response. And, pulling the scarf more tightly across her face, the girl slides past in the shadows, keeping close to the wall, and is gone. Somewhere nearby a door bangs shut.

Did I get it wrong? Or is there a rapist on the loose in these parts, six foot two, armed with Gucci suitcase?

Sigh, and check phrase book. Those sounds up there must mean café, or I've never heard one. Muttering *Pou éine Kyría Aspinall* (can I really believe that?) I give my rebellious legs the order to advance.

"William! Oh, how *lovely* to see you! So you found your way—I was worried about it. Look—leave your case there while I show you round." Maud closed the door behind me, and stood with her back to it, looking up at me.

"Oh, it was easy enough," I said, rubbing my hands to ease the creases, "once I got to the café . . . Maud, how *are* you? You look just the same as ever, but I was worried about you."

"Fine," she said, "I'm fine . . ." She put a tentative hand on my arm and, added shyly: "All the better for seeing you again. It's so *good* of you to come."

I bent to kiss her—*cheeks or lips?* In Claudine's presence, cheeks were appropriate, but hell, I can't be so formal here, not after what we'd once been to each other . . .

It was a brief, light taste of the past. "Well," she said, "well . . ." She seemed confused, nervous. *Damn!* I'd simply felt affectionate, no more.

"Show me where you're putting me," I suggested.

"Oh, yes. Of course." She flashed me a brief smile—*relief?*—and turned to lead the way. "I thought—I *hoped* you wouldn't mind if I put you downstairs. It's not *really* a cellar, and it's quite dry."

I followed, stumbling on the uneven stone paving. The door through which I'd entered opened directly from the street into a tiny central courtyard. Steep, narrow steps seemed to grow out of the courtyard wall, leading to an upper floor. The only light came from a bare bulb hanging from the concrete ceiling of what looked like a terrace above—I could see vine tendrils, and the bulging earthenware shapes of giant storage jars. *The vine-shaded terrace of my imagination.* Perhaps, after all, and in the daylight, my dreams would come true . . .

"Is the sea visible from up there?"

"The sea? Yes, just about," Maud said.

There! The shimmering Aegean . . .

"I'd better show you the loo," Maud said, pushing open a small boarded door. "No light, but I'll give you a torch."

"Oh. Thanks."

"In case of scorpions. They're tiny, but it's best to check before you—"

"Sit down. Quite."

"There's paper on the nail there. Let me know if it seems to be getting low. And that's the stone which holds the door shut."

"I see." I took a careful look round this shadowy death trap. An ornamental oil lamp, all fretted brass, hung on gilded chains in the corner. "Don't they have those in churches?"

"Nick got it," Maud said. "It gives a lovely soft light, when I remember to fill it."

"Don't you fear excommunication or heavenly retribution, using it in here?" I followed her back across the courtyard, past a stone trough with a tap over it, and a coil of plastic hose by the side.

"Well, we took the cross off . . ." She pushed open another door, and went through. Her voice came from the darkness inside: "Just a moment while I plug the light in."

What would be revealed, I wondered? Well, even if it wasn't the honeymooners' hideout with the blue shutters, it didn't matter now in my present state of celibacy.

"Oh, *delightful!*" I said. The light had come on, revealing a monk's cell, stone-floored, high-ceilinged, furnished with a single straw chair dangerously frayed, and a bed constructed of oddly shaped planks. "And a good, old-fashioned traditional bed, too. Where did you find it?"

"Nick made it," Maud said, "out of driftwood."

"*Really?*"

"Yes. Fascinating, isn't it, the way the wood gets worn into those shapes. And the rug was made locally. I adore the colors, don't you?"

"Yes, marvelous." I patted it, and my palm came away covered in fine, oily fluff. "Feels beautifully warm."

"Well, I *hope* you'll be warm enough. If not, there's a spare goatskin in the cellar next door you could throw over it."

"Splendid! Thank you very much."

"I think that's all, isn't it?"

"Yes, I think it is. Oh, except for washing."

"Washing? We passed it."

"We did?"

"In the courtyard. The tap and the—

"Stone sink. Oh yes, silly of me."

"There *is* a bath—"

"A *bath*? Is there?"

"I'm afraid you wouldn't be able to have one now. It's in the kitchen—you take the draining board off, and—"

"Oh no, I didn't mean now. Sometime."

"About four in the afternoon is best, when the water's had a chance to heat up."

"Oh, I see—solar heating!"

"Nick fixed up an oil drum on the roof, yes. Well, let's go upstairs. Can I get you anything? We've got bread, cheese, tomatoes—"

"I think I'll start with whiskey," I said.

There were no couches in Maud's barely furnished living room, just a pair of ordinary deck chairs with cushions. But the cushions were thick, with woven covers in red and black, and gave a surprising degree of comfort. I lay back and examined my feelings with the aid of half a tumbler of duty-free Famous Grouse.

Maud sat opposite me, with the glass of watered whiskey I had given her remaining untouched on a blue-painted wooden table by her side. In the light, I had seen the slight creasing at the corners of her eyes that had not been there five years ago. But she was still beautiful, and now, at forty, it was clear that hers was the lean, elegant beauty that lasts for life.

And though it wasn't my style, I could see that the house suited her exactly. There was little in it, but what there was had been chosen with care, placed exactly . . . No, it would drive me insane! A week of this asceticism, and reaction would set in. I'd be desperate for gross pleasures: pink champagne, lobster thermidor, fat ladies . . .

"So, here I am." Maud had been watching me as I surveyed the room and everything in it. "What do you think?"

"Perfect!"

"Do you really think so?"

"You seem to have found a way of life that suits you perfectly. How lucky you are."

"Mmm," she said. "I suppose I have."

"You're well out of London. Dirty, crowded, and ridiculously expensive."

"Mmm."

"You never cared for it much, did you. You were like an exotic bird in a grubby zoo."

Maud smiled.

O yes! How well I remember that . . .

"Well, I suppose I've changed," she said.

"Dear Maud, very little. Honestly. And your smile not at all."

"Oh William. Really?"

"Really."

She sighed. Then she said:

"I knew you'd come."

"Did you?"

"Oh yes. I knew."

This sounded a bit too meaningful for comfort. As I've explained, my rôle in Maud's life was Failed Suitor—every girl should have a few, and I was happy with it. But it needs a light touch; they mustn't overindulge the sympathy. I said:

"Claudine was very understanding. She sends her love, by the way."

"How *is* Claudine?" Maud said politely.

"Fine, absolutely fine."

"Oh good."

I swallowed some whiskey. Maud was absorbed in her own thoughts, and there was silence in the room.

"Shall we get down to it, then?" I asked. "Or would you rather not talk about Nick tonight?"

"No," she said. "I'm ready, if you are."

"Right. I suppose you'd have said if there was any news of him?"

"There isn't. Not for ten days now."

"When someone saw him on the island?"

"Yes."

"Who, where?"

"It was old Katerina, one of the village women. She lives just down the street from here, and she's got an olive grove down by the main road. She says she saw Nick drive past, heading up the valley."

"Up the valley . . . I'll have to get my bearings tomorrow, but what is there, up the valley?"

"Nothing, really. This is the last village before you come to the track across the mountains."

"No more villages?"

"No. Oh well, there's Kalikrati, but that's a long way up."

"Would he have any reason to go there?"

"Not that I know of."

"I see. Was this old woman . . ."

"Katerina."

"Yes—was she sure it was Nick?"

"Oh yes. We see her often, and Nick sometimes helps her with things, like the olive harvest, or if she's got something heavy she wants moving down at the house. Her husband's dead, you see."

"But she could have been mistaken, if he was just driving by?"

"I don't think so. It was our car he was in."

"Ah. What sort is it?"

"A white one, a Hyundai. It's not really a car, it's a pickup truck—they all have pickups round here."

"For farming?"

"Yes. And because the tax is less."

"I see. Tell me more about the village you mentioned, up in the mountains."

"Kalikrati. I've never been there, but Nick has: you have to go miles up a very rough track. And it's nothing much when you get there—mostly ruins, he said."

"Why did he go?"

"He likes exploring. It was not long after we came out here, and he'd been reading a book about the place, something to do with the war."

"So he was interested in what happened during the war?"

"Not specially. Mostly, when he had spare time, he used to spend it looking for ancient bits and pieces."

"Did he find any?"

"Oh yes. This island is the perfect place if you're interested in archaeology—you can hardly put a spade into the garden without turning up something interesting."

"Interesting, but not valuable?"

"Yes, there's not much of real value. Bits of pot, for instance, often look old because the designs have been the same for a thousand years or more, but they may have been made quite recently. It's hard to tell."

"Have you ever found anything really old?"

"Well, there are carved stones from Roman and Venetian ruins built into this house. The builders just used whatever was available, Nick says."

"Nothing older?"

"You mean, Minoan?"

"I don't know—when was that?"

"Earlier than 1500 B.C. That's when it was destroyed."

"Was it? I'm very hazy about that far back."

"There are lots of Nick's books here, if you want to read up on it," Maud said, looking a little impatient.

"Yes, well, I might . . . Anyway, back to the main issue. Have

you any other clues to where Nick might be? Just to start me
off?"

She shrugged. "I've lain awake over it, of course. No."

"I'm sorry. A constant worry like that . . ."

"If he walked in through that door now," Maud said, "I'm
not sure I'd be so very pleased to see him. But I must know
why . . ."

"Yes. I can see it would be easier for you to take if he'd had
an accident. Something clearly not his fault."

"William, Katerina is quite *sure* she saw him driving past on
the road up the valley," Maud said. "So I *know* he lied to me
about going to Athens. Even if he's had an accident since, it
doesn't wipe that out, does it?"

"It looks as though he wanted to get some time to himself,"
I said. "What for, that's the question."

"Yes."

There was a drop of whiskey left in my glass. I tipped it back.
"You haven't touched yours," I said.

"I hardly drink anything nowadays," she said. "I don't know
why—lost the habit."

"And I drink too much—but wine, mostly. What's the village
wine like?"

"We'll get some tomorrow. Then you can see Katerina for
yourself—she makes her own." Maud put her hand over her
mouth to cover a yawn. "I'm sorry. What next?"

"It's late. Let's call a halt for tonight."

"Breakfast will be on the terrace at eight," Maud said. "What
do you have?"

"As long as there's coffee, the rest is immaterial . . . I'm
looking forward to seeing the village in daylight. My impression
so far is somewhat through a glass, darkly."

"We'll do a tour," Maud said.

"Good, I'd like that. I'd expected the sort of warm welcome

travel books describe: Hello stranger!—drinks on the house! But it doesn't seem that sort of place. Am I wrong?"

"Mmm," Maud said. "It depends."

"What on? Don't they like tourists? When I arrived at the café to ask the way here, there were half a dozen chaps there, and they all, without exception, took one look and turned their backs. Perhaps I said the wrong thing."

"What did you say?"

"*Kali spéra*—Good Evening, according to the phrase book."

"Yes, that was all right."

"Wasted on them. But then, the proprietor came over to the door and pointed the way. Or I'd still be wandering the streets . . . Oh, and when I tried to ask a girl the way, she hid her face and vanished into the night at high speed. Made me feel a rapist."

"It was probably Maria."

"Extra shy, is she?"

"She's in trouble."

"Pregnant?"

"Yes."

"Well, girls do get that way . . ."

"She's not married."

"I understood that. But it happens, doesn't it."

"Up here," Maud said, "it's rather serious. She worked as a waitress down on the coast, but now that's all over. Her family are keeping her at home, and she's only allowed out after dark to visit an aunt round the corner. They're ashamed for her to be seen."

"My God, the poor kid!"

"Meanwhile, her brothers are looking for the man."

"Her boyfriend? Maud, this is *medieval*! What are they going to do? Does she get any say in this?"

"If they find him, they'll kill him," Maud said. "It's a question of family honor."

I stared at her. She looked quite calm, matter-of-fact. "Do you mean it? *Kill him?*"

"Yes."

"But . . . but . . . suppose she was willing? Most girls are when they let this happen, surely."

"She'll have certainly said she was raped," Maud said.

"Well, that's a bit hard on her bloke! So then, her brothers carve him up . . . How's she going to feel about that?"

"She's got to claim she was raped," Maud said, "or her father must save the family honor by shooting her himself."

"You're joking!"

"I'm afraid not."

I looked. *She wasn't . . .*

"Oh Maud, for God's sake!"

"They're rather behind the times up here," Maud said. "And proud of it."

"It's a far cry from Kensington," I said faintly.

She gave me a book on Crete to read at bedtime. I read about the birth of Zeus, about King Minos and the labyrinth, about the "lewd and lovely" Pasiphae who misbehaved with a bull . . . But it didn't do much for me. Symbolism is not to my taste—too often merely meretricious, a gloss on ideas too boring or silly to stand up for themselves . . .

The book wavered, and fell from my hands. With an effort, I groped for the light plug, pulled it from the socket, and fell back on the pillow in delicious darkness.

But then, as I sank towards sleep, a distant roaring nagged at the edge of consciousness. Something was out there, beyond the shutters, behind the mountains: it was coming this way, monstrous, bellowing, about to lumber into my dreams . . .

The Minotaur!

No no, you fool. The night flight back to Gatwick.

As for their Women, we faw fome very pretty ones at
Girapetra; the rest are but queer Pieces; their Habit
difcovers no Shape, which yet is the beft thing about them.

$\mathcal{I}$ was half awake when I became aware of the shuffling and
tapping outside. As I listened, trying to make sense of what I
heard, there was a slight darkening of the room as someone
arrived at the window, partially blocking the light.

I reared up in bed, fully awake now and prepared for confrontation . . . and saw the Devil looking in. His yellow eyes were
fixed on me in a level, intelligent stare. He dropped his horned
head to snatch a mouthful of green leaves from below the
window, and then trotted out of sight.

But the tapping and shuffling continued, and after a few
moments more the view through the window, into a sun-
streaked jungle of sprawling beans and man-high maize, was

again interrupted. A great-grandfatherly figure tottered past, bowed over his stick: he moved with the exaggerated care of the extremely old, as though each step threatened to unlock his joints and let his skeleton tumble to the ground in a heap of disconnected bones.

I had plenty of time to observe what he wore: a black fringed turban round his head, and a black braided waistcoat with mother-of-pearl buttons over a dark blue shirt. I saw his face in profile: large hooked nose, flamboyant white moustache, and jutting chin—still the face of a warrior, for all his age and decrepitude.

He passed without turning his head, and I sank back on the pillow, listening as the tapping of his stick and the bleating of the goat receded.

"I hope you slept well?" Maud asked. She sat at a scrubbed wooden table behind a collection of earthenware bowls, the sort that usually contain health food, meaning raw agricultural products, innocent of palatable processing, such as our ancestors were forced to breakfast on before the invention of croissants and Cooper's Oxford Marmalade. I like to be healthy, sure—but not at the cost of wearing out my teeth.

"It was beautifully quiet," I said. Best to be *positive,* and not mention the mosquitoes that had dived on me like Junkers 88's the moment I turned the light out, nor the missing plank that had let me and the cotton wadding mattress sag halfway to the floor.

In spite of all that, I was feeling upbeat this morning. I was enjoying it all—the goat, the old man, and now the view from this rooftop terrace down the valley to the distant silver triangle of sea. The shadows of vine leaves lay on the table, each one the shape of hexagonal France, familiar and comfortable. Across the steep valley, the mountains shimmered white in the clear air. I looked up, following the threads of sheep tracks in the thin vegetation.

"That bird looks gigantic—a trick of the light, I suppose."

Maud turned to see where the bird, and its shadow, slid across the pale backdrop of the mountain. "Griffon vulture," she said. "And they really *are* big—eight-foot wingspan, I think Nick said. Would you like to start with prunes and yoghurt?"

"Oh, er, thanks."

"Wheat germ? Sesame seeds?"

"I'd better own up, Maud, I'm not really a wholemeal person . . . Oh, but is that honey?"

"Yes, it's from near here: you can taste the herbs."

"Mmm, thanks. I'll have some bread and a blob of that."

"Whatever you want." She pushed a breadboard bearing a small yellow loaf towards me. "And coffee?"

"Ah!"

She poured it from an enameled pot. I took a first sip, strong and black, and felt my brain lift off the mud and tug at its moorings.

"So is he your landlord, then, the old boy with the goat?"

"Old Giorgi. No, he's our landlord's uncle. I don't think he realizes the house is let. Or chooses to ignore the fact. I'm sorry I forgot to warn you."

"No matter . . . He brings his goat through the garden every day, then?"

"Yes, at a considerable cost in vegetables. Nick threatens to shoot the bloody thing . . . There's nothing we can do about it, actually."

"Surely your landlord could . . ."

"Not from Athens."

"He lives in Athens?"

"Not from choice. He had to leave the village."

"*Had to?* Why?"

"It's a long story," Maud said. "More coffee? And there's

homemade marmalade, if you'd like to try it." She unscrewed the lid of a pot, looked inside, and frowned. "I'm afraid it's gone slightly moldy, but only on the top. I'll scrape it off."

"Don't worry . . . Yes, let's hear it. I want to know everything about the village."

"All right. Well, it happened about ten years ago. Our landlord was happily living here with his family when his son, aged eighteen, who'd just been sacked from his job and was at loose ends, borrowed the truck and took off with a friend from the village to go down to the beach. They picked up a couple of German girls, did a round of the bars, had a good time. Then, on the way home, no doubt the worse for wear, he crashed the truck. There's a notoriously sharp bend, and they went right off the road and over the edge. The boy's one of those who's always just avoiding disaster: his door burst open and he just stepped out of the truck as it was rolling down the hillside. The friend didn't."

"Killed?"

"Yes. So of course, our landlord had to leave the village."

I waited for more, but it didn't come. I said:

"No, I'm sorry. . . . Why 'of course'? It was an accident, wasn't it? Both boys were pissed—he just happened to be the one who was driving?"

"Is that how you'd feel?"

"Not *feel*, no. I'd probably feel murderous if that happened to be my son, but, well, it *was* an accident, wasn't it. And the boy was only eighteen . . . You'd have to keep telling yourself that, try to live with it."

"They're not *Guardian* readers here," Maud said drily. "They don't dissect their feelings and try to control them. If a boy from another family crashes a car and kills your son, the least you can do is drive them out of your sight."

"So your landlord lives in exile, in Athens? He can never live here again?"

"He occasionally comes for a day to see the house, arriving by the back lane, and avoiding everybody. If any of the boy's family—or their friends—see him, they look straight through him. He's a dead man, he doesn't exist for them. I don't know why he comes at all, now we're looking after the house, but he does, and it's a real pain: as no one else will talk to him we get it all, on and on about how he wishes he could come back, and what the village used to be like—all of which we know by heart, now. As for the boy, of course he's never been near the place since."

"Christ! And he lost his job as well!"

"No, that was before the accident, otherwise he wouldn't have been at home."

"What did he do?"

"Anything on offer. When he was sacked, he was a laborer on a dig at Zakros—that's up at the other end of Crete. After the accident, he became a taxi driver in Athens."

"It figures," I said, "from what I know of taxi drivers."

"Well now," Maud said. "You want to see round the village—just let me clear these things away, and then we'd better go, if you're ready."

"I forgot to pack my bulletproof vest," I said. "And after what you told me last night about the pregnant village maiden, and now this, I wonder if it's safe to go out without one?"

"Oh, as foreigners we're outside all that," Maud said. It sounded like one of the things people say to help themselves believe it.

The morning sun had bite to it. I stood in the street outside the house, blinking from the glare off the white walls, while Maud locked the courtyard door and hid the big rusty key behind a loose stone. "We'll go up the hill past the baker's," she said. "I need to reserve a loaf. Then round, and back by the lower road. Will that suit you?"

"Fine. I just want to get my bearings before I get down to work."

"Are you looking for anything in particular?" she said. "I'm curious to know how you intend to go about this."

Frankly, so was I. "Well, of course you are. The obvious thing would be to hire a car and make enquiries in Kalikrati, to see if there's any trace of Nick there. But I like to start with the background, then work outwards."

"Oh."

"No use galloping off up there without knowing the *why* of it."

"No, I suppose not."

"You haven't given me much to go on, Maud."

"Oh, I'm sorry . . . What else do you want to know?"

"All I know is, he spent his spare time on archaeology. Tell me more about that: how much time? Did he spend nights away?"

"Yes, sometimes. Never more than one night."

"Staying where?"

"All sorts of different places. Heraclion sometimes, to visit the museum and make notes and sketches—"

"Are the sketches at the house?"

"Some—I'll show you. Then he liked to stay in villages, round here, and on the east end of the island where most of the buried cities are."

"Doing what?"

"Talking to people, looking at things . . . He's good at chatting people up, getting them to talk."

"He always was. Do village people know much about ancient history?"

"They get their facts mixed up with myth and rumor, but

Nick was very patient, treated it all with respect. So he usually managed to overcome their suspicion."

"Suspicion? What of?"

"Oh, all Cretans suspect foreigners of treasure hunting. We've had the police arrive at the house two or three times, looking for anything we shouldn't have in our possession."

"Such as?"

"They're paranoid about foreigners making off with national treasures. They think they're sitting on a gold mine of ancient works of art—"

"But they are, aren't they?"

"There can't be much left, of real value, that isn't already under lock and key in the museums. No, it's a fantasy! But the problem is, they don't know enough to tell what's important—and therefore valuable—and what isn't. Imagine sending ordinary policemen to search your house for antiquities!"

"What happened?"

"A knock at the door—early evening, it was. Two of them, in uniform, complete with handcuffs and revolvers. Very serious. Acting on information received, going to search the house—"

"What information?"

"Oh, a big phrase for local gossip. Somebody—probably Katerina—had told someone about the big pot we grow herbs in. It's a reproduction—there's a tourist shop near Knossos which sells them, and we bought it in a mad moment . . . Katerina wouldn't *know* that, you see, she's only been out of the village once to have her varicose veins dealt with at the hospital, she's just like a child, no education to speak of. But she notices *everything,* and I remember her looking at that pot just after we bought it . . . So, she tells her neighbor that we've got this old pot—we must be *very rich* to be able to buy it. Didn't mean any harm, I'm sure—just adding her drop to the pool of gossip. The neighbor passes it on, with added detail. Now the pot has a price, and we're in trouble because all foreigners are spies, or treasure hunters."

"Then the police hear about it."

"Then comes the knock on the door. It gave me quite a fright, William—I was on my own, Nick had gone out in the boat, and it's horrible having your house invaded by armed men in uniform . . ."

"They searched it?"

"Yes! They went through drawers, cupboards, *everything*! Didn't make a mess, but I felt *abused,* they put their horrible great hands in my underwear drawer . . ."

"What excuse did they give? The pot's in the courtyard, isn't it?"

"Oh, obviously there'd been, as I said, some stupid rumor about what we were up to. I expect they'd simply been told to search the house and see what they could turn up."

"They had a search warrant?"

"William, this is *Greece*. I didn't even bother to *ask* . . ."

"I see. So what happened then?"

"Finally they arrived at the pot. It was then I realized what had probably happened. I explained where we'd bought it, but it was a waste of time—they took it away."

"Oh *no*! They wouldn't believe it was just an ordinary, commercial product?"

"They would not. No, it had to go and be inspected by an expert. I told you, they're full of suspicion, but they don't know *anything* . . . A week later they brought it back. No apologies—in fact, I think they suspected us of smuggling the 'real' pot away and tricking them with a substitute . . . Look, here's the baker—I won't be a moment."

"I'll come in with you," I said.

. . .

The village, in daylight, was a friendlier farmyard animal than the stone monster of the night before. Apart from a scattering of new, detached houses on the outskirts, the place was un-spoiled—or undeveloped, if you believe in progress. We walked along a cobweb of tiny streets, many of them too narrow or crooked for cars, so narrow that we had to stand aside to let a youth go by on a motor scooter, jolting on the cobbles. Further on, a donkey stood in the shadow of a cypress, wearing a wooden saddle piled high with brushwood, swishing its tail at the flies.

By my side, Maud stalked along in queenly style on her long legs. It was a royal progress in another way, too: she seemed to know most of the people we passed, and saluted them with a wave and a stately inclination of the head.

"*Yia* Kiri' Tassoula!" (a black-clad crone).

"*Yia* Kiri' Maud."

"*Yia!* Andrea! *Yia,* Antoni!" (a pair of handsome old men, fiercely moustached and wearing baggy, dark blue breeches tucked into their tall mountain boots).

"*Yia, yia sas!*"

I recalled the stories Maud had related. No sign of such stupidity, such murderous intolerance in these fine faces. There was pride, certainly . . . But it's impossible to tell what a com-plete foreigner is thinking, feeling. And on this, my first visit to Greece, I was having to learn the signs from scratch.

The key to understanding is in the past. Here, the past is palpable—it's all around me, in landscape, buildings, even ges-tures . . .

"I'm amazed at this place, Maud. It's time-traveling, coming up here."

"That's partly why we came," Maud said. "Won't last for long—the bulldozers are on the march."

"Yes, I saw . . . Partly? What other reason was there?"

"Cheap," she said briefly.

"Ah." I'd been wondering how to break into that subject: this seemed as good an opening as any. "I suppose Guy did the decent thing about money?"

She gave a little snort of surprise. "Why do you ask?"

"Perhaps it's a sore point. If so, I'm sorry. I'm trying to put a picture together, that's all. You and Nick."

"Well," she said, "I suppose I don't mind telling you. Guy's been all right, really. We've always had enough to live on."

We, she'd said. "Enough for both of you?" I said carefully. Nick had many talents, and one or another of his schemes was always about to make his fortune . . . but always tomorrow, never today.

"Out here, yes . . . Well, look, it wasn't costing Guy any more than if I'd stayed in London, and he was prepared for that."

"Oh quite, of course."

"Nick was working on the house, fixing things up. That's as good as earning money, isn't it?"

"I'm not criticizing," I said, "just doing my job. So you had your allowance, but no other income?"

"I *told* you. And anyway, there's no reason why it's got to be the *man* who provides, not any more, is there?"

"Maud. If I'm to find Nick, I have to ask questions. It's kind of essential."

She was silent. Then she said:

"All right. Sorry."

"It's okay, lady. We private eyes have to learn to take it."

"And," she said, "he's doing more than earn his keep since my paintings started selling."

"Oh yes, Kate said. Locally?"

"No. Well, an American dealer saw them here when he was on holiday, liked them, and now all I can produce goes straight to New York! It's fantastic! It feels so good to be appreciated at last."

"That's wonderful! How long have you been painting?"

"Ten years. Not so long, really, but I sold hardly anything before this."

"Not being an artist, I have to guess, but I imagine it's not so much the money, but the appreciation that matters?"

"Oh, I like the money," Maud said happily. "That's the proof, isn't it. If they didn't pay, you'd never know whether to believe them or not."

We came to the little square with the café where I had asked directions the night before. There were a dozen or so customers, some inside playing backgammon, the rest sitting on wooden chairs on the pavement. All were men; there were a few youths in jeans and T-shirts among them, but the majority wore shirts, breeches, and mountain boots. With their thick, dark hair, big moustaches, and air of watchful masculinity, they could have been a group of freedom fighters relaxing between battles.

Maud's pace had quickened slightly. Glancing sideways, I saw that her face had frozen into a half-smile: everything's fine, just fine, it announced.

"What's the matter?" I asked quietly.

"Nothing, nothing . . ."

"We don't stop here, I take it?"

"No, we do *not!*"

"Because it's men only?"

"Yes . . ."

"Could you, as a mere woman, sit *outside,* if you wanted to?"

"Look, William, just wait and I'll explain."

Safely past, she said:

"The Sheep Shaggers' Arms, that's what Nick calls it."

"Ha!" It sounded like Nick. "They get a rough crowd in there?"

"It's the headquarters of the Gyparis clan," Maud said. "Every *kafeneíon* has its regulars—and they don't mix."

"What would happen if someone from another clan felt like having a jar in there?"

"They'd be frozen out. Or someone would pick an argument, and there'd be a fight."

I thought about it. "It's a club. *Members Only* . . . enforced with knives."

"William, if you're trying to compare them with the Young Farmers' Association—"

"No, what I mean is, it's not the *idea,* it's the *style* that repels. Especially if you're female."

"That's true."

"Who are they, these Gyparis?"

"Shepherds. And a more arrogant bunch of male chauvinist pigs you'll never come across, believe me."

"Is that such a big thing, to be a shepherd?"

"They think so."

"I thought they looked rather dashing, in a piratical sort of way."

"You're supposed to," Maud said. "There's a long tradition behind them. This island was occupied for so long, you see: by mainland Greeks, Crusaders, Venetians, Turks. The mountain people were always the center of resistance—even the Germans with all their resources couldn't smoke them out."

"The Lords of—what are the mountains called?"

"The Lefka Ori, the White Mountains."

"Perfect! *The Lords of the Lefka Ori, independent and free . . .*"

"To me, they're a perfect pain in the arse," Maud said with feeling. "The war was over forty years ago, and it's high time they stopped sitting about polishing their egos and did something useful."

"Can't be much fun for wives, having a hero about the house."

"No. Normal men are enough trouble."

I felt her hand slip under my arm, and glanced sideways again. This time she was smiling.

"I'm glad you came," she said.

"Oh, that's *better!*" I said. "I was worried about you back there: you looked like someone with stage fright."

"Did it really show that much?"

"I'm afraid it did. Brave but unconvincing."

She made a wry face. "Nick does the public relations," she said. "I've always relied on him for that—it doesn't come naturally to me. And since he disappeared, I've had to work harder to keep my end up—the village isn't kind to single women. The men stare, and their wives think I'm an evil temptress."

"Should take the heat out of that, my turning up," I suggested.

"Oh yes, it should. I'm enjoying showing you off."

"I hope I'm satisfactory."

"Yes, it's good you're tall."

I basked. Maud added:

"And though you've put on weight, it quite suits you, really."

Hmm.

"This," Maud said, "is the rival *kafeneíon*. These natives are friendly."

"There's one waving at you," I pointed out.

"That's Spyro. He speaks English."

"*Hi!*"

"That's not English, that's American," I said.

"He's come back from Canada," Maud said, lowering her voice.

"What was he doing there?"

"Something that made a lot of money."

"Legal?"

"Probably not. But he's civilized."

"Proof?"

Her smile flashed. "Got a French wife."

"Ah. I can't argue with that. . . . She doesn't *look* French."

"That's not her."

"*What!* Sitting in public with a girl not his wife! Let's not get too close to him—I'm allergic to shotgun pellets."

"William, it's *all right*. That's Eléni, she's an Athenian. She's coming to me for English conversation."

I looked more attentively, and liked what I saw. No, I'd put it stronger than that . . . much stronger. About twenty-eight: black eyes, black hair, skin of purest alabaster, a long, perceptive nose . . . the sort of profile that makes a rubbery-featured Anglo-Saxon painfully aware of his mongrel ancestry. Eléni, *Eléni* . . . Can't fault the name, either.

Maud was busy with introductions.

"This is William, an old friend who's staying with me for a few days."

"Hello," I said.

"Hi!" said the man called Spyro, springing up to shoot a plump hand in my direction. Eléni murmured something and smiled lazily.

"Please!" Spyro said, "take a seat. What you like? Coffee, drink, ice cream maybe? Whatever you want. My pleasure!"

"Coffee, I think," Maud said.

"Very good. And you, sir?"

"Coffee would be fine," I said. "Thank you."

"Coffee!—very good." He waved at the proprietor, who came out of the bar without haste, wiping his hands on his apron, and stood before us frowning as Spyro ordered coffee with the expansive gestures of a man who likes his patronage to be noticed and appreciated. That done, Spyro threw himself back in his chair, and smiled at each of us in turn, a small, plump man a little over forty, brown scalp beginning to show through his black hair, his round face creased by what seemed a perpetual anxiousness to please, that impression reinforced by bulging, dark-rimmed eyes which swiveled constantly from face to face, checking responses. "What news of my good friend Nicholas?"

he asked Maud. "No, wait!—I think you look better already. So, the news is good, right?"

"I'm afraid there's no news at all," Maud said.

"No news, no news, Jesus, what can that guy be doing? But listen, no news is good news—right?"

Maud smiled politely. Stonewalled, Spyro switched to me: "So, what you think of Crete? Nice place, huh?"

"Fascinating," I said. "A complete break for me."

"Where you from?"

"London."

"Oh, London, sure . . . What you do here?"

"William is helping me," Maud said rather repressively.

"Helping you? Ah!—okay, I get it. Inquiry agent, right?"

"I'm a wine merchant," I said. Spyro gave a loud laugh, then suppressed it by clapping his hand over his mouth. Then he leaned forward confidentially:

"Excuse me! But that's no good, no one gonna buy that. I tell you what: better be a tourist. You unnerstand me?" His face was towards me, but his eyes were elsewhere, first on Maud, then Eléni, then the next table, then the street, then back to Maud . . . It was unnerving, speaking to this blind face.

"But I *am* a wine merchant," I said.

The eyes were suddenly on me again. There was disappointment in them. "A wine merchant. Okay, okay, if you say so. But I want you to know something: I am a man you can trust, right? Whatever it is, all the way. I have many, many friends tell you that." His eyes shifted focus minutely, seeking my precise range. Why did I matter? It was too much!—I had to look away. Luckily, at that moment, the coffee came.

Tiny cups of muddy black semi-liquid, glasses of water, thimbles of fiery *rakí,* a plate of nuts and sesame seeds . . . after this first time, it was routine.

Spyro had turned away to talk to—or interrogate—Maud. I murmured to Eléni:

"I'm afraid I've upset Spyro. Perhaps you can persuade him that I'm simply what I say I am?"

"Oh no," she said. "For Spyro, nothing can be as it seems. He so much loves complication, I do not have the heart to do it." Her voice was soft, amused.

"We live on dreams," I said.

"We live on dreams, exactly. We must not be unkind to poor Spyro, and tell him the truth."

She smiled again, a slanting smile, half for me, the rest for herself . . .

That was the moment I arrived in Greece.

No, not a thunderbolt. Once past forty, realism rules—you've seen it all before, near enough. All the same . . .

More of a tingle up the spine. Vibrations . . . images of bloody sand and golden helmets, beauty trailed by tragedy, from sunlight to shadow. Her face is *legendary* . . .

Tell me that in Greece, they're everywhere—riding pillion on the motorbike, hanging out the washing, at the supermarket checkout . . . Well, that must be so. All the same . . .

I sense mystery, depths to be explored.

Dangerous depths. Work for unmarried volunteers.

O definitely.

Unless, of course, a man has acquired that friendly but essentially detached attitude that comes with maturity . . .

And also needs information in a worthy cause.

Well . . .

That's all right, then.

"English conversation? Seems to me you're practically word perfect already."

"Maud has helped me very much," she said.

"And when you're not perfecting your English?"

"I work at Rethymnon University, in the library."

"Ah. I didn't know there was a university there, to be honest."

"It is very small, and my work is very dull," she said dismissively.

"I'm sure it isn't . . . This is my first time in Crete—in Greece, even—and I'm shocked to find how little I know. There's a gap of about two thousand years in my education, between Socrates taking the hemlock, and package tours."

"This is *very* bad," she said with her half smile.

"I know. I'm at home in France, but here I feel a complete alien."

"You don't like that?"

"No. I like to understand what I see, particularly the people. And Maud's description of village life . . . well. It sounds somewhat medieval still, to put it mildly. I'm repelled but fascinated—can it *really* be true that a man might shoot his own daughter if he thinks she's dishonored the family, for instance?"

"Oh no. Such a thing is quite unusual, nowadays," Eléni said, shaking her head.

"*Unusual?* You mean it still happens sometimes?"

Maud, who had been listening to a muttered, conspiratorial Spyro monologue but monitoring our conversation with one ear, leaned across the table. "He's talking about the Gyparis family, Eléni."

"The Gyparis!" Eléni murmured. "Oh well, yes. That is quite possible, I think."

"But," I said, "the police . . ."

"Oh, he will go to prison, five years perhaps. But he will keep *respect*—that is what matters to him."

"You make it sound as though it's already happened," I said. "As though it was *unavoidable* . . ."

"Well, perhaps it will not . . ."

"But why can't they lock him up *now,* and make sure?"

Eléni sighed. "Who will report him? To cooperate with the authorities is an act of treason, of disloyalty to the village. This is a tradition from the many, many years of Turkish oppression. The people here have their own traditions, and the police do not like to interfere. This can make more trouble than it is worth. There is not room in our prisons for whole villages, you know."

"They'd all join in?"

"It has happened," Maud said. "Only six or seven years ago, a village a few miles from here took up arms when the police raided them to try to stop sheep stealing and constant feuding with other villages. Eventually the whole village had to be forcibly evacuated and then bulldozed. That's what interference can lead to."

"Good God."

"It is worse, I think, in big cities," Eléni said mildly. "There, you can be robbed by a stranger, killed for what you may have in your pocket. Here——"

"——you have the consolation of knowing the man whose hand is on the knife," I said. "And it will be for some notion of justice, not for money."

"Exactly!" she said, as if her point was proved.

I felt I needed the *rakí.*

Across the table, Spyro caught my eye, snatched up his glass, and held it out. We clinked, and drank. "To my new friend the wine merchant," he said. "Okay, so I believe you—for the moment. *Yiásou!*"

"*Salut!*" I said.

"Oh, *salut,* very good. My wife says this."

"So does mine."

"She is French?"

"Yes. From Bordeaux."

"Ah!—this is very, *very* good! She is here?"

"No, she had to stay behind, in London, to mind the shop."

"I am very sorry. But listen, you have to meet my wife, she will be so very pleased. Will you come?"

"I'd be delighted," I said, and meant it. "But perhaps not today, I've got some work I must get on with, and——"

"Not today, no. But this evening, okay? Everybody come! I take everybody in my car, we go to Rethymnon to a very good restaurant and you will be my guests, I will take care of everything . . . What you say?"

I glanced at Maud. She looked resigned.

A hand touched my sleeve. "You cannot refuse," Eléni said in her soft voice.

Mortal insult? Or friendly exhortation? Either way, we went. "That's extremely kind of you," I said.

*No people under the Sun are more familiar than the
Greeks; wherever we went, they would come
and join company.*

"What about this afternoon?" Maud asked, pushing the
wooden bowl of feta cheese salad in my direction again.

I declined it, and reached for my glass. Local wine, Maud had
said, and I could believe it. What we call in the trade a simple
country wine, unsophisticated but honest . . . Cloudy plonk
wrung from grapes that should have been replanted a century or
so ago, in fact. Nothing superannuated about its kick, though.

"Thought I'd take some time to make notes, get my ideas in
order," I said. Yes, a siesta was essential, especially as we had an
evening with Spyros coming up. "And I want to see the paintings," I added.

"Oh, really?" Maud said, pleased.

"Of course! You're evidently going to be famous, and I'm well placed to write the definitive monograph."

"I don't remember that you were all that keen on art," Maud said.

"Personal recollections of the artist, though . . ."

"Oh *no,* William . . ."

"What she thinks and feels about Life and Work . . ."

"I'd *hate* it . . ."

She was taking it seriously. I said:

"Would you?"

"Well, of *course* . . ."

"All part of the game, though. Isn't it?"

"What?"

"Getting known. Promotion. Public relations."

"Not to me, William, no. I really hate all that."

She was in earnest. It rang bells. She'd always been a private person—too private. That's what I'd found frustrating, what broke us up. I couldn't live with it. I'd assumed that Nick had found the key, but had he? "I suppose I'll have to let Nick write it," I said lightly.

"Nick?" she said, puzzled.

"He must know you better than anyone else."

"Oh, I see." She frowned.

"You did say, earlier, when we were walking round the village, that Nick was the public relations half of your household," I reminded her.

"Did I? Oh yes, so I did. I meant in our dealings with the village."

"But he also sells your paintings for you."

"That's business."

"Don't people want to know about you, the artist?"

"What is there to know?" Maud said defensively.

She could easily have said, *I prefer to let my work speak for itself,* something like that. But she hadn't.

I looked up to find her watching me. "You haven't changed," she said. "I remember whole evenings talking round and round like this, getting nowhere."

"I'm sorry. Boring of me," I said ruefully. So much for my youthful passion—not only misguided, but *boring* . . .

"Oh, I didn't mind, not really. But one thing about Nick, he's too full of his own ideas to bother me about mine."

Hmmm.

File it.

Maud painted upstairs, in a little, light room off the sitting room. But her completed paintings were hung in one of the rambling cellars on which the house was built. We had passed other mysterious doors before arriving at one which had recently been painted (the ubiquitous bright blue which seemed to pull the sky down into the house) and fitted with a new lock. Maud turned the key, opened the door, and switched on the lights.

"Gosh!" I exclaimed. Some more penetrating comment would have to be made in due course, but I'd needed to buy time. In fact, I was immediately impressed.

The cellar was vaulted, white painted, windowless, and equipped with a row of spotlights which dramatized the paintings crowded on the facing wall. So here they were, Maud's children . . .

They were big, and bright. They contained hints of mountains, villages, harbors, all blurred and distorted . . . As they'd appear—an unfriendly critic might say—to a desperately drunken tourist.

But then, but then . . .

There was a strength, a power, behind the blurred and distorted surface. The shapes, maybe, or the light . . . well, I could only guess, not being a painter myself. But there was some

indefinable quality there which caught the attention, and then
drew you in. The more I looked, the surer I became.

I felt that sense of mingled pride and annoyance which you
get when someone you thought you knew well suddenly does
something remarkable. Pride because they're part of your life,
you chose them. Annoyance because they've hidden this from
you, cheated you. Why hadn't I known she had this talent? Was
it Nick who'd released it? Or had it been as she said, a few
minutes ago, that he simply left her alone to get on with her own
ideas, and that's all she'd ever needed?

What else? Well, there were no people in these paintings:
they were pure abstractions. No people. I would have guessed
that of Maud.

But not that she was capable of painting with such force, no.

But wait! How much was I influenced by knowing that she'd
been taken up by a New York dealer?

Well, knowing that must have made me look more closely to
try to see what quality of technique or angle of perception had
appealed to him, sure. But having looked, I could see for myself.

"What do you think?" Maud said. "You can tell me
frankly—I won't be upset."

"Maud, it's very simple, thank God. I have to congratulate
you!"

"Really?"

"Absolutely! For what my opinion's worth."

"It's worth a lot to me," she said, taking my arm. "Oh
William, I'm so pleased."

I looked down at her face and, as in the old days, saw the
moon sliding out from behind the clouds. That smile . . . Oh
wow. And I'd thought it was all over. Well, it *was* all over, of
course it was. Nice to be reminded, though. I said:

"I wish I'd known this was what you wanted to do."

"I didn't know it myself, then."

"So this is what you needed. The space, the light . . . How long did it take you to get your ideas together?"

"Not long. But I didn't get much encouragement. The local galleries weren't interested. They wanted scenes you can recognize—that's what tourists buy. Nick said that's what I should do, but I couldn't, I just couldn't."

"So you stuck to your guns. And then he made this New York contact."

"Yes. That was such a big boost, I couldn't believe it at first. But then the money came through. You can believe that."

"I'm sure. How did he make the contact?"

"Do you know, I haven't the faintest idea. Nick's like that, he always comes up with the right contact when he needs it."

"He always did."

"So I never asked. Perhaps I should have."

"Oh, I don't know. He likes to be mysterious."

"Yes, he does."

We walked to the door, and turned for a last look at the paintings. Then Maud switched off the light.

As she was locking the door, I said:

"Where do these other doors go?"

"Well, that's your bedroom, of course. Then there's a cellar full of junk, garden tools and so on, and another where we keep food stores. It's got an old rainwater cistern in it. Shall I show you?"

"Are they locked?"

"No."

"Do you mind if I poke about by myself?"

"Not at all. What are you looking for?"

"I don't know. Ideas. Anything that might suggest a line to Nick. I've still got very little to go on, haven't I."

"Yes, I'm sorry. Help yourself. I'll go and clear the lunch things away."

"Right, thanks. Then I'll be in my room for a bit."

"Well, if that's what you want. I'll be on the terrace if you need anything. Don't forget Spyro's coming to pick us up later."

"What time?"

"About seven. You've plenty of time. For whatever it is you're going to do."

She crossed the open part of the courtyard, and I watched her climbing the stone steps to the terrace. Alone, I turned to the first of the cellar doors.

There's a dim light from a tiny square of window with a single rusted but still serviceable iron bar against intruders. I take in an earth floor, flaking white walls, a high ceiling beamed with tree trunks, the bark still on them where it isn't peeling away in dusty strips. Between the beams, the roughly plastered ceiling on brushwood has fallen away in places, revealing a space above: through it I can see the underside of the boarded floor to what must be Maud's living room. There's music coming through the cracks—she washes up to Monteverdi. The earth floor is worn as smooth as concrete, and is shiny with wear—must be centuries old.

Now for the dominant central feature. It's like a giant white-washed beehive with, at the top, a crude planked lid. There are steps cut into the sloping sides—I climb, lift the lid. Echoing, cavernous depths carved out of solid rock—good God, it must go down twenty feet or more, widening as it goes. You'd break your neck falling in there . . . What the hell is it? Oh yes, of course—the rainwater cistern, empty now there's water piped from town.

I replace the lid, climb down again. There's a rope ladder lying coiled against one wall—looks rotten, wouldn't trust it myself. Did partisans hide down there during the war? They'd

have been crazy—far too obvious, and no cover from the Nazi
trooper opening the lid, Schmeisser at the ready . . .

What else? A crowd of empty bottles and glass jars. Above
them, a wooden shelf with full jars—homemade jam by the look
of it. Sundry cardboard boxes, some empty and stacked, some
containing kitchen bits and pieces surplus to requirements, tan-
gles of string, a rusty pair of scissors, a light bulb (100 watt, clear
glass—and you can *see* the filament's gone, why not just throw
it away?), one wooden spoon (cracked), a red plastic flashlight
(not working), and a pair of rubber gloves stained with what
might be creosote . . . Look, why am I doing all this? What do
I expect to find? Well, I *told* you—I don't bloody well *know*, but
I've got to start somewhere, haven't I? Nick was here, I know
that, and there may be some kind of trace . . . Well, all right,
that'll do. Try next door.

Ah. This is more like it. No window, but there's a light, and
it came on over what is obviously Nick's workbench, rough but
solid, with a vice and sundry tools scattered about—chisels,
pliers, saws, a hammer, tins of assorted nails and screws, a
brightly illustrated box of weedkiller. He's been making something, recently, by the fresh looking sawdust lying on the floor.
Well, I think it's fresh—still pale yellow, and smells of pine.
There are some planks leaning against the wall nearby, thin,
unplaned, such as you use for making crates and boxes—ah
yes!—Maud's paintings, for shipment to the U.S. of A. Behind
the door, a black wetsuit with yellow taped seams on a hanger.
Elsewhere, sundry garden tools, including spades, a fork, an axe,
etc. Next to them, a coil of plastic hose, a stack of useful lengths
of wood, and a mahogany bedhead. Every workshop has one,
don't ask me why. Well of course I *do* know, really—going to
make a wonderful cupboard one day, isn't it. Workshops are
touching, fascinating places, full of misplaced optimism, failed

dreams . . . Okay, okay—it's time to move on. A last look round, then, and—

I suppose, if he'd wanted to hide that rifle, he wouldn't have stacked it among the garden tools? On the other hand, I didn't see it until I really concentrated, so you could say it was quite a clever place to put it.

"He told me he'd got rid of it," Maud said.

We were on the terrace, keeping an ear open for Spyro's car. The evenings were best for me—cooler, with indigo shadows creeping up the mountains. The vulture was still afloat over there.

"Did he say he *had,* or that he *would?*"

"That he *had,* I think. Well, I'm not sure, actually. The point was, the things scare me to death, and I wanted it out of the house."

"Where did he get it?"

"It was here. Nick found it when he took down some of that loose ceiling in the cellar."

"Aren't you rather lucky the police didn't notice it?"

"Well, Nick said he didn't think they'd be very concerned about it. It's very old, just a souvenir, isn't it? I don't even know if it works."

"It's a Mannlicher-Schoenauer, with the Greek Royal Arms engraved on it."

"Maybe. I told you, I hate guns."

"That means it's Greek Army issue, not a sporting rifle. And it would work all right, if you had any ammunition."

"Well, what a good thing we haven't."

"Nick didn't find any?"

"No, he would have said."

"Of course . . . Where did you say he found it, exactly?"

"On one of the beams under the sitting room. I wasn't there

myself, but that's where the ceiling was loose and threatening to come down on our heads . . . Look, here's Spyro."

From the height of the terrace, the roof of a large white car was just visible over the courtyard wall. A moment later a two-tone klaxon sounded an imperious blast in the street outside.

"I wish he wouldn't *do* that," Maud said irritably. "Well, we'd better go before he does it again."

We went down the steps to the courtyard. "I didn't think you were too keen when he invited us," I said.

"Well, I hope I'm wrong."

Too late to ask her what she meant. The courtyard door burst open, and Spyro was upon us. "Hi, good evening!" he cried. "Everything okay? You expect me, right?"

"We were ready," Maud said.

"Good, good! You go in back, talk with my wife. You sir, Mr. Warner, in front—plenty of room for you there. Okay?"

"Please call me William," I said.

"William, yes, of course. Very good. Oh, excuse me—you have not met my wife. Here she is. Jeanine, here is Mr. Warner . . . William."

I leaned into the car and reached back to shake the hand that was held out to me. She had the same familiar, impeccable gloss which Claudine maintains even after years of living in scruffy old England. But unlike Claudine, she was blonde, blonde, blonde. White teeth glittered in a smile.

"*Ravis de faire votre connaissance, madame,*" I said, giving it the full operatic treatment. The teeth glittered more widely. Spyro looked happy. Well, at least some of us seemed set to make the party go.

Spyro drove as he talked, expansively, with many gestures. Talking stimulated him, so he speeded up. When not talking, he

slowed down and played compulsively with the minor controls.
We had the radio on, off, on again, louder first in one ear, then
in the other. We tried the air conditioning at every position
from min. to max. We had the roof open, shut, half open, shut
again. After each adjustment he polled us: Better? Yes? No?
After a while, nobody responded: it hadn't made any difference,
anyway. I began to understand Maud's lack of enthusiasm for
this outing, but once we reached the restaurant, things should
improve. They surely wouldn't agree to alter the heating or the
music more than once or twice.

We reached Rethymnon, and picked up Eléni at her flat in a
little street below the Venetian castle. Then we drove to the
restaurant, which was on the waterfront. Spyro halted the car in
a no-parking area across from the entrance, stepped out, and we
were all ushered into the restaurant. It looked crowded, but a
waiter came up, and Spyro addressed him with confidence. The
waiter left, looking doubtful.

"He says, no table," Spyro explained to me, "but I tell him
my name, and he goes to arrange. For me, there is always a table
here. It is very good restaurant—the best."

"It certainly seems to be popular."

"Right! Very good, very popular."

"But if they can't find room for us—"

"They will find room. Look—those people there. They can
move. They have not yet their food."

"Move? Where to?"

"Oh, what do I care? Plenty other restaurants here. Not so
good, but you will see—I think they will move those people.
For me, they will."

We waited in a huddle for a minute or so. The manager came,
dark suited, politely firm. I listened, and watched. No need to
understand the language—Spyro's gestures said it all. Disbelief,
reiteration, astonishment, protestation, expostulation, and fi-

nally, insult. We left, and got back into the car. You have to hand it to Spyro—he recovered quickly.

"Okay. He treat me like that, we go someplace else. Is not so damn good, anyhow. You want the roof open?"

"No," said Maud.

"Okay," Spyro said, opening it.

We ended up in a hotel on the outskirts. The restaurant was big, practically a ballroom, with a dance floor in the middle. There was a small band playing Gershwin with uncertain syncopation. The place was more international than Greek, which disappointed me—I was looking forward to *bouzoúkis* and throaty folksingers.

"Better, eh?" Spyro said. "Nice place. I think they take good care of us here."

"It's great."

"I tell them to bring champagne. You like champagne?"

"I certainly do."

"Okay. Very soon, they bring it." He began busily checking the other tables, seeing who was there. I turned to his wife, and got started on the conversation that had been waiting for us since Spyro had announced that I also had a French wife. She was not French-Canadian, but from Lille, a graduate in business studies, and had been working for a French firm in Montreal when she met Spyro.

"So what was he doing there?" I asked.

"Many things," she said, smiling. "You cannot say of Spyro he does this or he does that."

"Business?"

"Oh yes, of course. He likes to make money. That is why he leaves Crete."

"More opportunity there. So why did he come back?"

"This is his home. He always mean to come back."

"And you?"

"Oh, ça va, ça va . . . And now, that is enough about me. You are staying in the village?"

"With Maud, yes. I expect Spyro told you."

"Yes."

"What else did he say about me?"

"What else?"

"Yes."

She considered. "You are looking for Nick, I think."

"That's right. You know him, I suppose?"

"Not so very well. Spyro knows him much better."

"He didn't tell me that."

"You know, I am glad. He talks too much, my husband."

"You think so?"

"Always too much, yes."

"Oh. Why do you mind?"

"In business, it is a bad habit. So, your wife is French?"

"She's from Bordeaux. I'm a wine merchant, you see."

"Ah, Bordeaux . . . That is where you met her?"

"Yes. Her family have been in wine for generations. Offices on the Quai des Chartrons, all that."

"Oh . . . you are really a wine merchant?"

"Yes, of course. Why not?"

"Spyro told me . . . well, it does not matter."

"Do you miss France?"

"What would you think?"

"I would think yes. But, of course—"

"You are right. And your wife?"

"Well, we go back quite often. On business, and for holidays."

"Yes. And of course, to live in London is . . ."

"Well, no. Not at all like here."

"You have not been to Crete before?"

"Never. And never to anywhere remotely like Moustaki."

"Ah."

She looked away from me, across the table to where Spyro was being expansive with champagne, which had just been delivered to the table in a silver ice bucket. Foaming glasses were poured, handed out. We each accepted one. Spyro caught my eye.

"To my new friend!" he called. *"Stin iyiá sou!"*

"Good health, Spyro—and thank you for all this."

"It is my very great pleasure!"

We drank. Menus were passed round. At my side, Jeanine said quietly:

"William."

"Yes?"

"Can I be very frank, very indiscreet?"

"Certainly. What about?"

"I think that you will do no good here."

"What?"

"I am sorry. But I think so."

"I'd like to talk to Spyro sometime soon, all the same."

She had black eyes. Shining, impenetrable black. She said:

"It will do no good. I think so, and now I have talked with you I am sure. So—"

"You think I'll be out of my depth? That this is a job for a professional? Etcetera."

"Perhaps. I am sorry."

"Or is Spyro at risk in some way?"

"Please! I think we must change the subject."

"Jeanine—I *have* to talk to Spyro. Maud is an old friend, and I must do what I can for her."

She shrugged. I said:

"I'll try to keep off . . . whatever it is that you're worried about."

Spyro was calling across the table again. "Hey, William! What

you planning with my wife, eh? It look like you two getting on
maybe too damn good!''

"We're in perfect harmony."

"Is that right? How do you like the champagne?"

"Everything is just fine," I said. Food had arrived: red mullet,
sea urchin salad . . . I occupied myself extracting the orange roe
from spiky shells full of black goo.

Jeanine had turned to talk to Maud. Well, so now I'd been
warned off. You could call that progress, in a way. Something
to get my teeth into. I'd have to—

"Hel-lo," said a soft voice on my other side.

"Oh, Eléni! I'm so sorry, I was miles away."

"I think, perhaps, you prefer blondes," she said.

"Of course not. Dark and mysterious is unbeatable."

"Oh ho. But thank you."

"It was the conversation. Spyro still thinks I'm a professional
inquiry agent, apparently."

"Yes, I think so."

"I convinced Jeanine that I'm not. What about you?"

"You are here to look for Nick, right?"

"Right. But why does it matter if I'm just myself or a professional?"

She looked me up and down in her lazy way. "I think perhaps
you are not professional. Or you would know this."

"Look, Eléni, would you mind explaining what—"

"Unless, of course, you like to be the wolf in sheepskin. Yes,
maybe that is what you are."

"Oh, for Christ's sake! Are all Greeks as complicated as this?"

"What is complicated? Is really very simple: just remember,
nothing is as it seems. Then you cannot go wrong."

"Trust nobody."

"Nobody."

"Not even you?"

"Why should you trust me?"

"Because I want to."

"Then perhaps it will be worth the risk." Again that sleepy smile. I said:

"Someone has to explain to me how things work around here."

"Mmm. I can lend you a book."

"A *book!*"

"Then, if you want, I can introduce you to the man who wrote it."

"Is he Greek?"

"No. He is an American anthropologist, working at the university here."

"You really think a book can help me?"

"Maybe. Why not read it and see. It is called *Macho Man: Field Studies of the Mediterranean Male.*"

"I think you're pulling my leg."

"I have a copy at my flat. You can come tomorrow—I shall be in all afternoon. Or the evening, if you prefer."

She was smiling, but her tone was serious. Jesus Christ! do I fall for this? Why did she say that—*nothing is as it seems*? What does she *really* want? What are *any,* or *all* of them, up to?

Only one way to find out. Anyway, I need to hire a car, buy an accurate, large scale map. "I'll be there," I said.

"Okay."

Across the table, Spyro was twisted in his chair, staring at a large party on the other side of the dance floor from us. He seemed to be finding them irresistibly fascinating.

"Do you know those people?"

"Oh yes," Eléni said. "Everyone does. The one at the end of the table, he is Mr. Big in politics just now. I think he will win in the elections next spring."

Spyro had launched on a series of pantomime greetings, like a tennis player winding up to serve. "Poor Spyro," I murmured. "Not much response there."

"No. Is too soon."

"Too soon for what?"

"To be forgiven. Last election, Spyro vote for someone else, not Papadakis."

"And Papadakis knows this?"

"Of course!" Eléni said, glancing at me with dry amusement. "If you vote for someone and do not tell them, that is a vote wasted, is it not?"

"But you vote for a party, a principle . . ."

"Oh yes, yes, that as well. But first, you make an alliance: I give you this vote, you do that for me."

"Oh, is that how it works. Well, you should know, Eléni—you invented democracy."

"Po, po, po," she derided. "In England it is just the same, though you like to think it is not."

"No, you're wrong!—it's more party, less personal." I checked myself: it wasn't me, this indignant patriot. "Well, most of the time . . . Let's get back to Spyro. So now he thinks Papadakis is the coming man, so he's going to vote for him. What does he want in return—do you know?"

"Spyro is building a hotel on the seafront not far from here. He would like to open with a big event—the Papadakis election dinner, perhaps. Or . . . well, who knows—Spyro has many ideas which will profit from Papadakis's support."

"Meanwhile," I said, "he's not doing too well, winning it." Spyro had left our table, crossed the floor, and was now leaning over Papadakis, both hands going like Bernstein conducting opera. But response was minimal; Papadakis was playing hard to get, and after a failed crescendo, Spyro retreated, putting on a bravely confident smile as he neared our table. "Excuse me—I have to talk to my very good friend Papadakis," he explained. "Later, I introduce you, William. He can help you, perhaps."

"Me? In what way?"

"Oh, Papadakis, he know everybody. Great guy."

"I see."

"Now, I think we have more champagne."

It came. A bottle was simultaneously delivered to Papadakis's table. It earned a polite wave, no more, but Spyro was encouraged—he beamed with satisfaction. He was still beaming at the end of the meal when the bill was brought. I watched as he signed with a flourish, not once, but twice. *Two bills? Surely he couldn't . . . ?*

But he had. As the news of this munificent gesture reached him, Papadakis rose, and strode to our table. Teeth were bared, hands emphatically shaken. Other diners watched as the alliance was given its public affirmation.

"So, Spyro wins, at a price," I murmured to Eléni. "I hope it'll turn out to be a good investment."

"Who knows?" she said, shrugging. "So, you will come tomorrow?"

"It's very kind of you."

"Oh no, it is a pleasure."

She smiled her lazy smile again. I could easily believe she liked me, but I knew more about Greeks now than when we sat down to dinner.

RETIMO is the third Place of the Country:
it extends along the Haven,
and has Walls fitter to inclofe a Park for Deer,
than to keep out an Enemy. The Malmfey Wine of
Retimo was in great efteem
when the Venetians held the Ifland.

I was going to have to fix the goddamn bed. Two nights
running the artistic driftwood planks had parted: the second
night, I'd dreamed of a deep-sea monster whose jaws were
working for a better grip on my buttocks, before waking to find
that reality was not so different.

Some of the other discomforts of Maud's primitive life-style
were surprisingly easy to adjust to. The tap in the courtyard, for
instance: I'd shuddered at the thought of cold water on my skin
first thing in the morning, but the water was so fresh, so different
from the acrid laboratory product that issues from London taps
that I found myself splashing freely, and actually enjoying the
sensation.

But the bed was impossible: the slipping planks would have
to be dealt with. I shaved, dressed, and went into the workshop
to search for nails and a hammer. The worst handyman in the
world has that minimum—almost any size nail would do.
Where would Nick have put them?

I straightened up from groping under the workbench, and
stared round the cellar. The rifle stood where I'd replaced it
among its comrade spades and forks, weapons all in time of need.
More dangerous than an empty rifle, in fact . . .

Ah yes. That reminds me . . .

The collapsed ceiling where Maud had said the rifle had been
hidden was in the neighboring cellar, the one dominated by the
ancient rainwater cistern. Well, why not?—might be nails in
there after all. Feeling slightly guilty, perhaps because I could
hear Maud's sensible shoes rapping the upper side of the floor-
boards only an inch away, I climbed the steps cut in the sloping
side of the rock cistern, reached up into the hole, and felt along
the beam. Tiny avalanches of plaster dust and wormwood
poured glittering into the light from the barred window. My
fingers touched something soft . . . *repulsive!* Jesus!—*a dead rat!*
No—they dry up, turn into witches' handbags. This is too soft.
I reached in again, caught a fold, and pulled, causing a major dust
fall, much of which went up my sleeve. Just as Maud's footsteps
returned, the urge to sneeze became irresistible. Well, why
worry? I'm *supposed* to be investigating . . .

"Perfectly all right," Maud said. "I hope you found what you
were looking for, and didn't get so dusty for nothing."

I unwrapped the little piece of greasy sacking. Maud glanced
and recoiled. "Oh God."

"Six point five millimeter," I said. "The same as the gun."

"Ugh," she said, wrinkling her nose as if the little brass and
nickel objects stank.

"A little corroded, but probably still okay."

"Oh dear."

"Maybe Nick didn't find them—they were pushed out of sight along the beam." Or maybe he did, but left them there.

"I don't know what to say."

"Nor do I. Just thought you ought to know. I went looking for nails and a hammer. No success. Do you know where Nick keeps them?"

"Oh, you were in the wrong cellar—his workshop stuff is in the other one."

"That's where I started. No sign of them."

"Really? I'm sure that's where he keeps them . . . What do you need them for?"

"The planks in my bed keep sliding apart. Easily fixed, once we locate the hammer and half a dozen nails. You're sure there *is* a hammer?"

"Yes, of course."

"That's what I thought. Well, it'll turn up."

"William, I'm so sorry! Are you *terribly* uncomfortable? To be honest, I was a bit nervous how you'd take this place, considering your usual, well . . ."

"If it weren't for the feeling that I'm proving useless at what I came for, I'd be enjoying it all enormously. A little running adjustment to the bed is all that's needed for perfection."

"You don't mean that?"

"Yes, it's only one or two planks that need—"

"No!—I mean about feeling useless. Do you?"

"Yes, I'm afraid so."

"Oh . . ."

"Look, Maud, let's be frank. As you know, I've never been to Greece before, and it's all much more strange than I thought. Last night, for instance, I looked round Spyro's table and it suddenly struck me that I hadn't the least idea who any of those people really *were,* or what they were really *thinking*. I might have just landed from another planet: I'm missing all those little signs behind what's said, the intonations, accents, choice of words, which you need to file and sort and put labels on people. In short, I'm doubting my usefulness, and I thought I ought to tell you so."

Maud's hand on the coffeepot handle was quivering slightly. She began to lift the pot, then changed her mind and put it down. "You've only been here one day," she said, quite sharply. "And I thought I could rely on you."

"I'm not proposing to give up," I said, "just letting off steam. Are you sure there's nothing more I ought to know?"

"About Nick?"

"Yes, of course."

"What could there be?"

I sighed. "Don't go all Greek and opaque on me, Maud. Just *think!*"

"I *have* thought. Don't you believe that?"

"Think some more."

"I don't understand . . ."

I pushed my cup across the table. "It's like this. You ask me here to look for Nick, who's disappeared. Of course I'm delighted to see you again, do what I can. So I arrive. What do I find?"

She was pouring the coffee, carefully. "Well, what?"

"I don't quite know how to put it . . . an atmosphere of less than perfect panic, perhaps. No idea where Nick is, you say. But you think he's somewhere safe, don't you?"

"Why do you—"

"Otherwise you'd be more upset. You're more annoyed than worried by his disappearance. *You're* not Greek—with you, I *can* read the signs."

"I don't know what you're getting at," she said irritably, "beyond the fact that I'm annoyed with him. And why shouldn't I be?"

"Now you're annoyed with me as well. But I can't think why you should be so calm about this, unless you know something I don't."

"I think you've forgotten it was me that asked you to come," she said. "And I'm sorry if I don't fit into your idea of how a deserted woman should behave, very sorry indeed."

"Deserted."

"Yes. What's wrong with that?"

"Dear Maud . . . *he could have had an accident* . . ."

"You suggested that the first evening," she said. "And I told you that he'd been seen on the road to the mountains."

"Are you really so sure that that old woman couldn't have been mistaken? About the driver, at least, even if she was right about it being your car?"

"Yes."

"But that was ten, now eleven, days ago. If she was right that it was him, and if he hasn't had an accident, what can he be doing up there?"

"I rather thought," she said, "that you were going to try and find out."

I decided to ignore the sharpness in her voice. Maybe it was my fault, anyway, for trying to bully more information out of her. "So that's it? There's nothing else you can tell me?"

"William, I'm sorry. No, there isn't."

"Could any of these other people, Spyro and his wife, or Eléni, or anybody else in the village, be involved with Nick in any way? Spyro knows him well, his wife told me. What about that?"

Maud looked doubtful. "I shouldn't think so . . ."

"Maud—don't you *know*?"

"I don't see much of Spyro," she said. "I don't actually like him very much, you may have noticed."

"But—"

"Nick socializes. I don't—I've got my painting. What I know

of the people here is almost entirely through what he's told me.
I never was very social, you may remember. It bores me, to be
honest."

It was true. I did remember. Maud in company had listened
politely, smiled, stayed outside discussion. Some people can get
away with that, and she had. Her silence had usually been taken
to indicate an inner certainty, so that when she did make a
remark, it attracted respectful attention. But she'd simply been
bored . . . I said:

"All right. Maud, I'm sorry. You're more of a recluse than I
realized."

"I suppose I am. I did think of hiring a car and going up there
myself, but . . . well, I'm afraid I couldn't face it."

"Is it that rough?"

"It doesn't help to be a woman on your own. Then there's
the language: I'm not good at making myself understood."

"You left it to Nick."

"Yes. His grammar's appalling, but he can communicate. I
used to correct him, but he got furious—he said that as all I
could manage was a perfectly grammatical silence, I was in no
position to criticize. Which put me in my place . . . I'll come
with you, though."

I'd thought about this. "No thanks. I think I'd rather go
alone."

"Oh, but—"

"It's all right, really it is. I'll manage. And in fact I'd feel more
free—who knows what I may decide to do?"

"Well, if that's what you want," she said with an obvious
relief that gave me a twinge of apprehension up the spine. What
was she afraid of? "I don't suppose I'd be much use—and as a
matter of fact, I *am* just finishing a painting . . ."

Most people would feel they *had* to come, however little help
they might be. But not Maud. No matter—it suited me not to
have an audience while I found my feet, or tried to. "Don't

worry," I said, "I've got a phrase book, and Eléni is lending me some anthropological textbook that she thinks will turn me into an instant Greek. I shall be all right."

I'd thought it was thin, and it didn't sound any better out loud, but there it was. I was going. "Is there a pair of binoculars about the house that I could borrow?"

"Nick's got a pair," Maud said, getting up. "I'll get them for you."

There was a once-a-day bus service into Rethymnon from the next village, but I first had to get myself there. A young farm-hand at the wheel of a big red Mitsubishi pickup gave me a lift, and a foretaste of the problems ahead.

"*Yermanikoss?*"

"Sorry, I've no idea what you—"

"*Yermanikoss? Ne?*"

"No, sorry . . . er, *signómi* . . ."

"*Yermanikoss* . . . Deutschland?"

"Oh I see. No, I'm English, England . . . from *London*."

"Ah, *Inglis! Kalá, kalá* . . . *Tsortsill!*"

"What?"

"*Tsortsill, Tsortsill!*"

"Tsortsill? You can't mean Churchill?"

"*Ne, ne! Tsortsill!*"

"Yes. Well, I'm afraid he's dead, rather a long time ago. We've got Mrs. Thatcher now . . ."

"*Ne! Tatcher, Tatcher!*"

It was a relief to sit in silence on the bus, even though depression was coming over me in waves. Whatever I'd pictured myself doing, it wasn't standing by the side of the road thumbing lifts, it wasn't this solitary jolting in a dusty bus surrounded by black-clad crones clutching shopping baskets, and it certainly wasn't driving in a hired rattletrap into remote mountain villages to interview hostile and uncomprehending peasants, and where the hired rattletrap would inevitably drop its exhaust pipe, crack its sump, cough up its big end miles from any garage or hotel. To feel secure, to make progress, a man needs to have good equipment about him, or at least, *I* do. Reliable car, maps, binoculars, shoes, weaponry if called for . . .

Binoculars, yes. That might mean something. Maud was sure she knew where Nick kept his pair, but they weren't there . . .

File it. (Next to the other one and a half facts which are all I've managed to collect so far.)

"Hel-lo."

"Hello, Eléni. I'm sorry, I'm later than I meant to be, it's nearly three. It took an age to fix the car hire."

"You remembered the way, then."

"Easy enough, just opposite the Venetian fort. What a nice house! Is it all yours?"

"Yes, all mine," she said in the voice which was like a sigh. "All mine . . . come upstairs: the living room is there. Would you like some coffee, or something else? Beer, wine . . ."

"Coffee, if you're going to have some your yourself. As for wine, I wanted to ask you: what wine do you drink? I just had lunch down in the harbor, and there was nothing I've ever heard of except retsina."

"I don't know . . . I will show you. Did you have a good lunch?"

"Yes, thanks. It was quite crowded: I sat with some English people, and watched the boats come and go. They explained to me why so many fishermen have missing fingers, or hands."

"Oh yes. They are so stupid to fish with dynamite."

"I guess they like the boom—more dramatic."

That was what Dottie had suggested—or perhaps it was Maggs. They were as distinct from the T-shirted tourists as

Wedgwood china on a picnic: a pair of retired schoolmistresses on a painting holiday, deliberately eccentric with their disintegrating straw hats and pendulous burdens of beads. They showed me some of their sketches: neat little watercolors, conventional but skillfully done and, unlike Maud's work, fully peopled (with Greeks, not tourists). They came every year, had done for the last seventeen years . . . No, of *course* things were not what they were! Take the hotel, for instance—

Eléni was leading the way into her sitting room. It was wide, and cool, with a high ceiling. A balcony overlooked the street and a rectangle of grass and trees, very like a London square, at the foot of the russet stone cliff which grew into the fort. No, not really like London: not with this brilliant sunlight. I looked up, and could see tiny figures perambulating behind the gun ports. As I watched them appear and disappear like ducks in a shooting gallery, I became aware of a faint, sickly perfume, activating memory cells . . .

"Here is some wine," Eléni said. "You want to try?"

"Perhaps I will, instead of coffee. Thanks."

LATO dry white from Michalakis Brothers, Heraclion. Refreshing, slight retsina effect. Here's the price label: 350 drachmas—under two quid. Mmm.

"So, how are you getting on, Mr. Wine Merchant?" Eléni asked.

"This wine, delicious. My search for Nick, disastrous. I don't know what I thought I was doing, offering to take it on."

"She is your girlfriend, I guess."

"A long time ago, Eléni."

"Oh ho ho."

"Oh ho yourself. The flames have died, almost to vanishing point."

"I am so sorry."

"Oh, it's okay. There's still a pleasurable afterglow. When she smiles, for instance."

"I will play you a song about it," she said, walking—drifting rather—to a bookcase. She searched along a row of tape cassettes and chose one. "Listen. It is Manos Xatzilakis who sings. I like it very much."

"Tell me about it."

"It is about love. It is very sad."

"Oh."

"All Greek songs are about love, and they are all sad."

"Ah."

"Listen."

I lay back in my chair, closed my eyes, and listened. When it was over, Eléni said:

"If you like it, I will give you the tape. I can get another."

I opened my eyes. "You're very kind."

"Oh no."

"You're going to lend me a book as well."

"Yes, it is here."

I got up, walked over to the sofa, and took the book from her.

"Why are you so kind to me, Eléni?"

"I am a Very . . . Kind . . . Person," she said with her lazy smile.

"Mmm. I mean, I'm sure you are."

"Yes, I am."

"But also, you're high."

The lazy smile widened. She nodded slowly, once, twice, and again.

"Yes, I am also high. Would you like one?"

"A joint?"

"Sure. I have plenty."

How long was it? Must be fifteen years . . . And *who* was it? *Nick* . . .

I thought: politic to accept, keep the subject open.

"Okay. Thanks."

I looked at the book, trying not to inhale. *Macho Man: Field*

Studies of the Mediterranean Male. So she hadn't been pulling my leg. But hell, what can you get from a *book*?

"Who is this Emmanuel Hershey?"

"You will like him," she said.

"He's a friend of yours?"

"A friend, yes."

"I'll take good care of it. Listen, Eléni, I'm going up into the mountains tomorrow. I've hired a jeep, and I'm going to see if I can find Nick's car, for a start. There can't be many places up there where it might be—it's not a cross-country machine, he'd have had to keep to well-surfaced tracks. Only one problem—I can't find a halfway-decent map. All I could buy was this tourist thing." I showed it to her.

She looked at it and shrugged. "Is this so bad?"

"It's too small-scale, no detail. The mountains are just blurs, with only the main roads marked. There must be something better available, but where would I buy it?"

"You cannot."

"Oh, but surely—"

"Only the military have better maps than this. And I do not advise you to ask them."

"That's ridiculous! Well, I'm sorry, but it's paranoid!"

"Perhaps. But it is so. I think you would be arrested."

"Oh, for God's sake!"

"Well, I think so. Also, there are many places where photographs are forbidden. You will see the signs."

"Up in the mountains? Why?"

"Not in the White Mountains, where you are going. But on the Akrotiri, certainly. Because of the rockets."

"What rockets?"

"It is a big NATO base, west of here, on the north shore."

"Wait." I opened up the map and found it: almost an island, ten kilometers across, joined to the port of Hania by a narrow neck of land. The Akrotiri . . .

"There's nothing on the map about a restricted area."

"No. You can drive to the airfield, which is also there. But if you try to drive further, you will be stopped. And if you try to take photographs, you will be in big trouble, believe me."

"I see. Well, I'm glad you warned me. Though, in fact, I haven't got a camera, so I'd be all right."

"No camera! Oh, that is *very* suspicious—genuine tourists all have cameras. They will think you have hidden it, and search your car . . ." I caught her expression: she was teasing me again. Difficult, with Eléni, to tell when she was being serious, when not.

On the map, the Akrotiri was exactly north of the White Mountains. I estimated the distance: about thirty kilometers, say twenty miles. Might be able to see the base from the mountains. Another useless fact. I looked forward to the time when I could stop collecting facts at random and start concentrating on a definite line of enquiry. If that happy day ever arrived. A NATO base . . . Oh, *forget* it.

The happy fag was smoldering neglected in the ashtray. Not to be thought unappreciative, I persuaded a last gasp out of it, and then stubbed out the remains. Eléni was watching from the sofa, so I inhaled as shallowly as possible and forced smoke from my nose. In spite of precautions, I felt my concentration had slipped. With effort, I said:

"That really is a concidence, you know."

"What is?"

"Last time I had one of those—a long time ago—it was Nick who gave it to me."

I waited. There was no measurable reaction. "Oh yes?" she said, as lazily as ever.

"Yes. Does he still smoke, do you know?"

"I don't know. Many people do, here. They always have."

"Ah yes, I was forgetting. To me, Crete seems so small, so out of the way. If you know what I mean."

"Oh, we are quite civilized," she said, knowing exactly what I meant. "We have all the usual vices."

"Aha. But the supply . . ."

"I don't get them from Nick."

"Well, it wouldn't have surprised me if you did."

"No, I don't."

"Supply no problem, though?"

"You want me to get you some?"

"No, I don't think so, thanks. Just curious."

She said, critically: "I think, you know, you *will* get in trouble before you go home."

"Too many questions? It's what I'm here for Eléni."

"Oh yes, I suppose so. Well, when it happens, you can call on me, and I will try to come to your rescue. Okay?"

"If it happens—and if you mean it?"

"Oh, I mean it. Shall I play another record?"

"Tell me more about Crete and drugs, first."

"I don't know much more. But when you are in the mountains, if you see some men in a blue jeep doing nothing, they will be police looking for stolen sheep, or smugglers."

"Smugglers? Right up there?"

"To get from the south coast, where the smugglers come in, to the north coast where the towns are, you have to cross the mountains. The south coast is so steep, there is no road in many places. That is why it is good for smugglers. Also, Egypt is only three hundred kilometers away—two days in a caïque, much less in a motor yacht."

"Drugs come in through Egypt?"

"Drugs, and many other things. Cigarette papers."

"*Cigarette papers!* Why?"

"We have a very high tax on them here, so it is very profitable to bring them in. In fact, we have a very high tax on many things. So smugglers can get rich, if they don't get caught."

I sighed. *Smuggling,* now! To add to all the other possibilities that were already buzzing round my head like hornets in a plum tree. Sometime soon I was going to have to write all this down and try to get some order into it. Eléni said:

"Okay?"

"Thank you, Eléni, yes."

"Some music now?"

"Yes, why not."

A thought had occurred to me, startling, innovative. Nick might be doing something *legal* . . .

Oh God. As if I hadn't got enough to think about already.

*Though Candia is a rich Country, yet the beft Land in it
is cultivated but by Halves; nay, two Thirds of this
Kingdom is nothing but Mountains, bald, dry,
unpleafant, cut fteep down, and fitter for Goats than
human Creatures.*

At nine the next morning, I carried my gear to the little
square where I'd parked the hired Suzuki Santana 4WD over-
night, dumped it on the backseat, climbed in, and drove off,
watched by a row of gloweringly male Gyparis occupying the
shade outside the *kafeneíon*. I could understand why they made
Maud uncomfortable: my back was burning from the intensity
of their stares. This, in spite of my having sat up late, swatting
aside clouds of moths and mosquitoes, to study *Macho Man*.
"The one who passes who must greet those already present," I'd
learned, and done it, too!—a polite wave and *Kali méra*!" Response—nil. So what was wrong? Most likely they simply de-
spised me, an outsider from rich but decadent Western Europe.

Yes, I had a hard time ahead if I wanted to win acceptance from these shepherds. *Macho Man* was full of discouraging facts. "One who is good at being a man must: know how to wield a knife, dance acrobatically, sing elegantly, eat meat conspicuously, steal sheep cleverly . . ." There was a lot of vital information about stealing sheep, not a subject I'd encountered much in Church Street, Kensington. You don't just grab a stray mutton on a dark night, oh no—Macho Man does it with style, with *poetry* . . . His strategy must include surprise, ingenuity, shock, the seizing of chance advantages . . . Then what?

Then he boils and eats the evidence, not avoiding the pound or so of hard belly fat . . .

These thoughts, or the jolting of the jeep, made the acid in my stomach start to seethe before I was a mile off the hard road and up the track into the mountains. Behind, a trail of white dust drifted sideways and sank slowly into the valley. Above, a thin heat-haze of cloud was spread across the sky like steam, dissolving into pale blue towards the horizon. Ahead, the stony track, rutted and covered with loose shale, wound up a series of hairpin bends to the cleft which swallowed it. Beyond, according to the map, was the small black dot in the midst of square miles of mountainous nowhere, labeled Kalikrati. I felt sure of only one thing, that it would certainly be the most remote spot that I'd ever been to. And, hopefully, back.

The Suzuki had been a pleasant surprise, though. It looked nearly new, not at all the rattletrap I'd been resigned to hiring. Even if they hadn't bothered about servicing, it ought to last this trip: I'd insisted on oil levels being checked while I watched, and bought a ten gallon jerry can of spare petrol. There were basic tools for changing a wheel under the bonnet, and the spare tire was pumped up. The only snag was that it was a condition of hire not to drive it off tarmacadam roads. I'd hesitated when I

read that, but signed all the same. Someone, suffering a similar
crisis of conscience perhaps, had stuck a tin St. Christopher
medallion on the center of the steering wheel. Faith would have
to take over where insurance companies left off.

It was a rocky, lunar landscape. The bare upper slopes I could
see in the distance shimmered in the heat—more a pale gray
than white, but "the White Mountains" was no more than a
slight exaggeration. Lower, at the level I was climbing through,
there was some patchy, spiky, inhospitable vegetation: broom,
thistle, lavender, sage—the scent of herbs floated in through the
open windows of the jeep. Goats bounded away as I drove near,
stopping to gaze down at me from the security of a rocky
outcrop. Others peered from the shade of stunted carob trees,
arrested in mid-munch, leaves hanging from their mouths.
Thirty yards off the track a shepherd rose to his feet from behind
a clump of sage, stared, and then waved—ah!—so not all the
natives are hostile! I waved back, and he then held up something
in a lordly gesture of invitation: it might have been a bunch of
grapes, but he was too far away to be sure. I made a return
gesture, signifying (I hoped) gratitude, and regret at not being
able to stop on this occasion, and he sank out of sight again.
Perhaps I *should* have stopped, asked if he'd seen Nick's car on
this track ten days ago . . . well, how would I communicate that?
In the village, it should be easier, there might be someone with
a smattering of English. I'd been at the phrase book again, in the
intervals of mugging up on *Macho Man,* but it wasn't much help
unless you'd had your handbag stolen or, curiously, *wanted to
marry someone* . . . well, it must happen, but I couldn't see myself
working through "I Would Like Very Much To Talk To You
But I Do Not Speak Your Language," then on to "You Have
Beautiful Eyes And A Nice Body," and ultimately to "As I
Really Love You I Want You To Be My Wife." I would be
certain to lose my place in the book, and alarm the girl with
"Please, Quicky, An Ambulance—My Fried Is Wounded . . ."

Well, it was the best I could find at the airport bookstall, but the more I studied it, the lower my confidence sank. One of these days I'd like to meet the nerveless paragons who wrote it and learn how they managed to stay so courteous and unflappable while having their pockets picked, their bills added up wrongly, and their hotel rooms set on fire. I'd be interested to see the girls they married, too.

Shale squeaked and scattered under the knobbly tires as I began the climb to the cleft. The track had been recently and roughly bulldozed out of the hillside, a series of zigzags connected by hairpin bends which were so steep I needed first gear to get round. The penalty of careless driving, of a foot slipping off the brake pedal or a bungled gearshift, yawned at my elbow—a long, battering roll before the final crunch several hundred feet below. There wasn't a tree, not even a shrub, to break the descent—nothing but slippery shale all the way down . . . Well, it wasn't *really* dangerous, not if you concentrated. So I told myself, denying the impulse to get to the top as quickly as possible. Just take it steady, it's as simple as that. Think about something, anything else. All right, then . . .

Before the track was made, I supposed, only donkeys and men on foot could have climbed up here. Kalikrati must really have been out on a limb, deprived of all supplies except what would go on the back of a donkey. And that couldn't have been long ago, by the raw newness of the track—five years, ten at the most. And I'd thought Maud's village was remote . . .

We reached the top, the jeep and I, passed through the cleft, and stopped for a moment to get our breath back. Yes, I get anthropomorphic about machines, especially cars: they're either going to be friends or enemies, and you learn which very early on in the relationship. This jeep was all right, we were going to get on.

I sat and looked through the dusty windscreen at what lay ahead. It was extraordinary, and not at all the bleak, inhospitable valley I'd expected. I got out of the car for a better look, shading my eyes against the sun's dazzle. On all sides, the mountains rose up higher, and I was probably no more than halfway to the top, counting from sea level. But in the center was a vast area of gently rolling landscape, rough pasture interspersed with groves of little trees, wild fig, stunted maple. Something about the brilliant, almost vertical light, the shape of the land, and the spacing of the dark-shadowed groves, put a word into my head—*biblical*. As if to confirm it, a flock of goats accompanied by a shepherd flowed out from behind a grove in the middle distance. Too far for salutation this time. But it was perfectly picturesque, a scene Maggs and Dotty would have loved to record.

I turned to look back down the valley. Far below, a tiny cloud of white dust was rolling along the track towards the first of the hairpin bends. A spark from the sun flashed off a windscreen. So I wasn't alone. Two cars on a track like this was practically a traffic jam.

Come on! There's work to be done.

I got back into the jeep, started up, and rolled forward along the track. It was, if anything, even rougher than before, but at least you couldn't fall off it. After that hideous climb, this was mere relaxation. I felt cheerful, almost confident. Partly it was because I now had an ally, at last. Good old jeep.

I yanked on the hand brake, and sat staring, my brief surge of confidence leaking out through my boots. I'd just rounded a bend in the track, and there was Kalikrati, in plain view. So, I'd almost arrived. If that sounds like good news, it wasn't.

It's a ruin!

I told Eléni, I told Maud, I told myself: *This map is no bloody good!* I just had a feeling about it, the tourist garbage round the borders, the vagueness of detail. Now I'm being proved right, though for once I'd rather not be. Kalikrati, the black dot, is just that—a complete *ruin*.

Now why didn't Maud *ask* someone, before sending me up here on this futile expedition? All right, so she's shy, nervous about talking to people, and all that. But she should have made the effort, shouldn't she?

What had the old woman said? That she'd seen Nick drive past, heading up the valley. It was Maud who'd said there was this village here. She'd also said she knew of no reason for Nick to come up here. But as there's no other track—I've seen that for myself now—he must have come this way, and I was going to try to find out if anyone in Kalikrati had seen his pickup. Now that plan's down the drain. It's a ruin.

So now where do I go, what do I do? Back to one of those shepherds, perhaps, and try to—

Wait! *Is that smoke from that chimney?*

It could be, could be . . .

Better drive the last quarter mile, then, and check it out.

I couldn't make it out. Even from a few hundred yards away the village still looked a ruin. But somebody had a fire going—I could smell wood smoke, and could see a feather of smoke rising from a distant chimney. I reached the outskirts of the place, driving slowly and looking first to one side and then the other in search of an explanation. There'd been some terrible catastrophe, that was clear. These buildings hadn't just been neglected—they'd been *burned*. The evidence of fire still showed: there were sooty streaks on the jagged piles of stone which rose above the weeds and scrubby bushes, and which were all that remained of the walls. Some of these piles still had a skeleton of blackened timber bound to them with vines and brambles where roofs had collapsed. It would be a dismal existence, living next to all this.

But somebody did. As I drove further in, signs of clearing and then of rebuilding began to appear. It was, or had been, a larger place than I'd at first supposed. Concealed from the approach track by the ruined outskirts, several of the houses in the center were in quite habitable condition. They were small, square, single story, with flat roofs of beaten earth and tiny barred windows. I passed the house with the smoking chimney, and there was a face looking out: wrinkled, ancient, wrapped in a black headscarf. A little further on, I came to an open space surrounded on three sides by restored houses; crude sheds built of unpainted concrete blocks piled up without mortar and cor- rugated tin roofs; wired-in runs where chickens as thin as feather dusters scratched in the dust. On the far side, built on a mound with a view of the mountains beyond, was a single, larger house standing in a narrow pool of deep purple shadow, the beams of its flat roof projecting from stone walls of fortress solidity. The glaring light, the dust, and the impression of limitless horizon beyond gave this place the air of a trading post in a John Wayne movie. It only lacked the hitching rail.

Whose was it? The village mayor's house, perhaps. It could be the headquarters of the local brigandry. Or just the post office . . . except that there were no visible cables leading to it.

My gaze fell on a signboard, hung vertically and painted black, with straggling white letters which read:

C

O

F

E

E

B

A

R

Well yes, an anticlimax. All the same, it was just what I needed. Thank you, St. Christopher, and keep up the good work.

"*To prásino,*" I said adventurously. "The green one" it means, and Heineken is what you get, all other beers being in brown bottles. As usual when you succeed with a colloquialism in a foreign language, nobody looked at all impressed.

The greeting had gone all right, too. Grave nods in return from the two youths and one old man sitting on benches against the wall, and a brief flash of gold teeth from the burly, middle-aged, red-check-shirted proprietor. I leaned on the bar, drank some Heineken, and considered my next move. I didn't have to consider long.

"*Yermanikoss?*" the proprietor asked.

Ah! I've had this conversation before, with the farmhand who gave me a lift to the bus stop . . .

"*Ochi, ochi . . . Inglis.*"

"Ah, *Inglis! Kalá, kalá!*"

This time, the gold teeth were much more welcoming. A good thing in these parts, it seems, to be English . . .

The proprietor pointed to the old man. "Speek *Inglis!*"

"Really? Does he?"

"*Ne, ne!* He speek you!"

I looked at the old man. Could it be true? He was dressed as if for a walk-on part in light opera, in full traditional gear: a black silk shirt, embroidered waistcoat, baggy dark blue trousers tucked into tall, polished black boots. His eyes under the fringed black turban returned my inspection, without any sign of resentment. On the contrary, the mouth under the big hooked nose and large white moustache was friendly, humorous. I said:

"Is it true? Do you speak English?"

"*Ne*. I speak."

"Ah." I took my glass, and went to sit on the bench beside him. I held out my hand, and he shook it: for an elderly man, he had a very firm grip. I said:

"Have you been to England, then?"

He smiled, and shook his head. "Inglis come *here*," he said.

"An Englishman?" *Nick, perhaps? So expert at making contacts, no matter who or where* . . .

"*Inglis, ne*. Many."

"Many." Not so good: it was only one I was after. "Who were they, all these Inglis?"

"Tsortsill send them."

Oh yes, of course. We were talking about the *war*. We were talking about fifty years ago, when he would have been a young man. Interesting, but useless.

Except that he did speak some English. I said:

"What did they do here, the English?"

He thought, then said:

"Hide. Send messages."

"Spied on the Germans?"

"*Ne, ne*."

I was still struggling to accept that this negative sounding word meant the opposite, meant *yes*. So the British maintained a radio post up here, sending details of troop movements and defenses to London, or Cairo . . . As Eléni had said, you could see a long way from these mountains, right down to the harbor at Hania, and Suda Bay, on the north coast. And you'd be fairly safe: the Germans could never keep control of this wilderness, and you'd see a patrol coming miles off . . . I said:

"They sent messages. What else?"

"Tsortsill send guns, money. We make fires, go find."

Parachute drops. Tommy guns. And . . .

"Paper money?"

"No paper. Gold money."

Oh *Jesus!* Here we go *again.* I can just imagine Nick up here, looking for the missing drop of gold sovereigns. Oh yes, that's *just* what would turn him on. For me, it's bad news: the list gets longer, and longer. *Will they ever end, the possibilities?*

"You remember those times very well, I expect."

"*Ne.* Very well."

"Did you find all the parachute drops?"

"All?"

"Or did some equipment, money, get lost?"

"*Ne.* Sometime night dark. Sometime snow fall. So . . ." He shrugged. We couldn't find the drop . . .

Just as I'd feared. Well, let's get on with it.

"Perhaps you can help me. I'm looking for my friend. Has another *Inglis* been up here recently, do you know?"

He took time to think about it. I swallowed some Heineken, and mentally crossed my fingers. This was crunch point. If the answer was no, I was left with accosting shepherds at random.

He was shaking his head. *Damn!*

"You might have seen his car," I said. "A white pickup truck, a Hyundai?"

"White?"

"White, like . . . like the wall. That color." Pointing.

More head shaking. But had he understood? I should have brought a photo of the pickup as well as of Nick: I'd meant to ask Maud if she had one, but stupidly forgot, then decided it didn't matter. Well, might as well get out the one of Nick. I got out my wallet, found it, passed it over.

He looked, carefully. "*Inglis.*"

"Yes, Inglis." He went on looking. "His name is Nick," I said hopefully. "I suppose you might say, Nikolaos."

"*Nikolaos, ne.*"

"You know him?"

"*Ne.*"

"But you haven't seen him recently?"

"Not seen."

"Oh. Well, I'll have to—"

"Not for one week, two . . ."

"You saw him *then*? A week or so ago?"

"*Ne*. White . . ."

"White car?"

"*Ne*."

"Oh, terrific! That's wonderful"

He smiled deprecatingly. Did he mean it? Or had I misunderstood? *Oh, please God, I hadn't.*

"Has he been here before—Nikolaos?"

"*Ne*. Many time."

"In here?"

"*Ne*. We drink."

Then the landlord might also . . . I almost snatched the photograph back, leaped up, and showed it to red-checked shirt.

"Ah, Nikolaos," the landlord said. The gold teeth glittered.

"Drinks!" I said happily. "*Raki!*" I made a gesture to include everybody, including the two youths who had sat silently on the bench, watching with interest but incomprehension. Oh yes, drinks all round—and hang the expense!

Well, I hadn't lost my head exactly: the round cost the equivalent of a pound, including the little dishes of nuts and seeds that come without asking. When the landlord had served us all from a battered tin tray, glasses were clinked, and we all knocked back the tots of colorless spirit. (Tasteless too, to be honest, but that isn't the point, is it. Then I went to sit on the bench next to the old man again, to continue this laborious but promising conversation.

It must have been a time of high drama for him, as a twenty-five-year-old who had never seen the outside world. It had been in May 1941 that the men in gray uniforms came tumbling out

of the sky with their equipment, to overwhelm the hastily as-
sembled English and Australian defenders, with their Greek
irregular supporters. The German parachutists were picked off
in hundreds before they even touched the ground but, after
fierce hand-to-hand fighting, succeeded in capturing the airfield
at Maleme in the northwest of the island, and in reinforcing their
foothold in Hania. That done, they launched assaults along the
north coast, and eventually the Allied forces had no option but
to save what troops they could, and evacuated over the mountains to Hora Sfakion on the south coast, from where they were
taken off by ship through a hail of dive bombing. A handful of
Greek-speaking British officers and men were left behind in the
White Mountains to maintain an observation post, and to keep
up contact with the Cretan irregulars, with the aim of recaptur-
ing the island at a future date. I looked up the facts later: at the
time of talking to him, I had to extrapolate from his few words
of English reinforced with gestures. The gestures were vivid,
though, as was his memory still.

"Pam, pam, *pam!*"

"They came to the village, then?"

"*Ne!*"

"Why did they come so far?"

"Look for *Inglis*."

"They wanted to find the radio?"

"*Ne*. But we stop them. We shoot—pam, pam, *pam!*" He
grinned, white teeth beneath the white moustache.

"How many?"

"Many. Tirty, tirty-one."

"What happened then?"

"One too quick. He run. We run after."

"The only survivor . . . did you catch him?"

"Run after, is blood, here, here, here . . ."

"You trailed him . . ."

"*Ne.*"

"So you caught up with him?"

"Too quick. We do not find."

"He escaped!"

"*Ne.*"

"And then?"

He shrugged, made a wide circling movement with both hands, ending in a downward gesture that plainly said: *All over . . .*

"They came again, more of them," I filled in. I could picture it, the half-tracks loaded with helmeted troops; the motorcycle machine gunners, an armored car perhaps. Crushing force . . . no chance of resistance this time.

"Catastrophe," I said slowly. I should have known, there are still villages like that in France, left to remind people what Nazism did.

Here, though, the ruins weren't a memorial. Most probably, there simply hadn't been enough villagers left to rebuild them.

"I'm sorry." I put my hand on his arm to try to help the inadequate word along. What must he have felt, when the ambush he'd taken part in had led to this appalling reprisal, the slaughter of friends, family, women, children?

He shrugged again. Then, surprisingly, he gave a snort of amusement. "Tirty-one," he said, looking at me. "Tirty-one!" Then a short phrase in Greek, repeated several times, with relish . . .

I remembered it later, and Eléni told me what it meant:

"Like rabbits . . ."

The Inhabitants of Candia are naturally tall proper men, vigorous, robuſt; they love shooting with the Bow, an Exerciſe they have been distinguiſh'd for in all Ages. The Cretan Bowmen, commanded by Stratocles, were a great Help in the Retreat of the Ten Thousand.

An hour later, I was on the road again, wishing that the old man had not insisted on another round of *rakí,* and that I had more than a canvas hood between the sun and my head. This sun was something else! The haze was thinning, doing less to diffuse its power, and now it burned with a new and unexpected ferocity: I hadn't anticipated such heat, or such glare, and was now regretting I hadn't a hat to protect my head and shade my eyes. But discomforts apart, I was well satisfied. Nick had come this way more than a week ago. He hadn't been seen to return. He could have gone over the mountains, but the track further along was very bad—the bulldozer was still at work, improving it. I knew his Hyundai pickup didn't have four-wheel drive, and so thought this unlikely—in any case, why drive *over* when he could have driven *round,* on ordinary roads? Much further in distance but, given the crawl that was all a car could achieve on these tracks, probably no longer in time. It seemed obvious that he must have been on his way to some destination in the mountains.

But where? Opinion in the *kafeneíon* was vague. How could one tell what Nikolaos, an *Inglis* and a foreigner, wanted in the mountains? He was not hunting—he had no gun. He did not bring anything to sell. He simply arrived, was friendly, talked, laughed, bought drinks—and then drove away.

One of the two youths said something that provoked indignant cries of disagreement, as if what he'd said was a grave insult. He has suggested, the old man explained, that perhaps Nikolaos works for the Government! Ask him, I requested, why he thinks this. The answer, when it came, seemed to be that the youth had no reason, just a general suspicion of strangers. I remembered Maud saying that in these mountains, any cooperation with authority was seen as an act of the most villainous treachery. The old man was contemptuous: I watched as he dismissed the suggestion with growls and emphatic gestures. From these and from the boy's reaction I could imagine what was being said: the boy was young, he had no experience, he did not know that the *Inglis* had always come as friends and comrades, never as spies.

I was left with the impression, so far as I understood what was said, that Nick had come through the village several times at least—because they seemed to know him quite well—and that each time he drove on, stayed perhaps two or three days, and then returned the same way. This last time, however, he hadn't been seen to return. Of course, the track *was* being improved: perhaps he *had* gone on, right across the mountains, after all.

If not, where?

There'd been a lot of head shaking and shrugs before the name of Arcadés began to sound in the conversation . . .

Arcadés . . . Where or what is that? I asked.

Oh, it is nothing the old man said. Nobody lives there, only the goats . . .

But where?

To the south, off the track.

Why is it empty? The Germans again?

No, not the Germans.

Who, then?

I astinomía . . .

No, it didn't mean anything to me. I got out the phrase book, asked the old man to repeat the word. Then I found it.

The police.

I'd thought that Kalikrati was remote but, well, that was before I'd heard of Arcadés. Kalikrati's small black dot on the map was recognition that it existed, at least, but Arcadés didn't figure at all. I had to steer by the hand flapping and pointing that had accompanied my send-off outside the *kafeneíon*. *Somewhere to the south, off the track* . . . They were high on goodwill, but low in precision. I had two things in my favor: the jerry can of spare petrol, and the knowledge that the south coast, where the mountains ended in a steep drop to the sea, was only ten miles away. If I found myself getting wet, I'd know I'd gone too far.

The track wound along the edge of rough pasture, and began to climb again, into an area of scrub: here, the ground was broken by small cliffs of grizzled limestone, frozen waves of rock, where goats lined up to watch me pass by. The mountains marched alongside, seeming to move with me. The bulldozer had obviously been this way, opening up the narrow places and shoving the loose stones into makeshift embankments. It was early afternoon and the last of the heat haze had cleared, letting the sun through at full strength: I could see the heat coiling off the rocks, and feel my left elbow burning where it was outside the shade of the hood.

Somewhere to the south . . . I hadn't seen any signs of a turning so far, and I'd been looking hard. It would be overgrown . . . or perhaps not, if it was still used by shepherds and their flocks. Now the track led downhill again . . . By the sun, I was heading roughly west, and I needed to turn south. That's something: with a sun like this you hardly need a compass. Try crossing foggy Dartmoor without one, and you can find yourself going round and round in small circles . . .

That way, perhaps?

I stopped the jeep and sat, engine running, studying the side track. If this led to an abandoned village, it was more used than seemed natural. Of course, it could be animals that had kept it open. I switched off, climbed out, and went to take a closer look. There were goat droppings, but no tracks on the stony surface. I went a few yards further. There, in a patch of dust, were . . . well, what I'd like is to be able to say: *I observe that a vehicle has passed this point recently: note these tire tracks, tread pattern Michelin XLR. Good God, Holmes! Yes, my dear Watson, driven by a fair-haired Englishman with pale eyes behind his glasses and inscrutable intentions . . . You never cease to astound me, Holmes!* Oh yes, I'd like that, but what I can actually see is a sort of smudge which might or might not have been made by a car of some sort.

So?

Well, I don't know.

Drive the jeep through the dust patch and compare the tracks?

Ah. Good idea . . . there!

The result?

Guess what.

Well, come on, then—compare them! Let's have your deductions!

The jeep track is clearly a jeep track. The other is still a smudge . . . which might or might not have been made by a car of some sort.

Oh. Well, sorry . . .
Let's get on, shall we.
You're going to try this track?
Just hold tight—and shut up.
Look, I was only trying to help . . .

The new track was unsure of itself. It began hopefully, ran for perhaps half a mile through the scrub, past vestiges of stone wall, through groves of carob and holm oak. Then it emerged into a clearing where it suffered an identity crisis, gave up, and turned into a wavering and fainthearted footpath. I followed the thin line of this across the clearing, and on the far side found my way blocked by a rough barrier of thorn bushes. I got out to inspect it and found that, though there was a path on the far side of the barrier, it was too narrow to drive up. So this was it—the end of the road.

I looked round the clearing. It was a peaceful place, walled in by crumbling gray cliffs. There was a low square stone structure near the center, which I'd already passed: I left the jeep, and walked back to look at it, mainly to stretch my legs after the jolting drive. It was an ancient well, but still apparently in use judging by the newness of the rope attached to the rusty but serviceable bucket. So, what next?

I walked back to the jeep, got in, and drove slowly round the perimeter of the clearing, looking for another exit. There was nothing obvious, but there was a place where, if you were careful, you could edge between two stunted oaks, and into a carob grove surrounded by brambles. It was quite hard to find and made a kind of natural, leafy garage. Nick's Hyundai was in it.

Under the neglected, dusty surface, the path was well paved with rounded stones, quite painful to walk on, but no doubt a hard-wearing surface for donkeys' hooves. After a ten-minute walk, the path turned back on itself and began a steep climb: the paving stones here were so smooth and shiny with wear you could have mistaken the path for a stream bed. More than that—it was like a stone waterfall.

I climbed on. There were low stone walls on either side of the path, with small oaks, holly, and more carobs growing on them, turning the path into a shady green tunnel. The sun sparkled though the gaps. I came to an overhanging boulder with a slow trickle of water dripping into a muddy pool from a rock channel: I stopped, tasted it, and drank a cupped handful. Then on, and up. By now I was regretting the weight of the well-filled *sakoúli,* the woolen Cretan haversack woven with a bright red and black design, that Maud had loaned me to carry my supplies in. But I hadn't wanted to leave it in the jeep, and anyway, I didn't know how long I'd be away from the jeep or how far I was going. It was heavy, though, and getting heavier as the climb got steeper.

A path as well made as this must once have led to a flourishing village. It gave off a strong sense of the people and animals who must have passed every day, the morning descent to the pasture, the evening climb to supper and the fireside. Generations must have labored to build a path like this. Now, there were gaps in the paving, and the walls were crumbling.

I came to the first signs of building: a tiny, ruined shrine, too small to be called a church. The roof was fallen in, but a solitary painted saint was still visible where the plastered walls had not yet collapsed. Somebody had been here recently: there was a jam jar full of wilting wildflowers in front of him.

Now the path began to level off, and other buildings appeared through a wilderness of trees. Nearer still, and I could see the pattern of the place: the houses grouped to one side, with another church facing them, somewhat apart, at the end of an overgrown avenue of cypresses. I stood for a moment, and listened. It was so quiet that the sound of insects was disturbing, seemed for a moment to compare with the roar of traffic at home in London.

Where is he?

Something inhibited me from calling out. I never like shouting into a void, find it ridiculously embarrassing. *Is anyone there?* You hear your own voice echoing back at you, cracked and false. How can you confidently address *nobody*? Well, I know it's stupid, but there it is. Anyway, if Nick is here, I'd like to know what he's up to, catch sight of him before the mask goes on and the smooth misinformation comes sliding out. I've come a long way for this, and now I'm here, I want the truth, no less. *The truth*—and *I* shall decide what to do with it, afterwards.

An abandoned village is a melancholy thing. There were no signs of violence, of fire and deliberate destruction, of sudden catastrophe, no, none of that. There was just the crumbling, collapsing, growing over of natural decay. It was a slow death, strung out over many years. I remembered Maud talking about a village in the mountains that had been closed down about ten years ago by the police because of interfamily feuding: if this was it, the decline must have started long before that. There were plane trees twenty, thirty feet high with their roots, like nests of snakes, embedded in the fallen stonework. It had been a village of small enclosures, and the boundary walls had been breached by generations of goats, leaving a series of well-trodden openings. What had been a central lane—High Street, Arcadés—was still identifiable by the density of ruins which lined it, but riotous fig, pomegranate, and walnut trees now filled it where knots of people had gone before. The roofs were of the traditional Cretan type with a thick layer of beaten earth over wooden beams, needing regular patching and plastering over to keep the rain out: here, nearly all the earth had been completely washed away, leaving only piles of mud, a central stone arch, and some rotting beams to show where they had been.

I walked along the central lane, ducking under the invading trees and climbing over the piles of stone that had spilled into it. I hadn't noticed the goats at first, but they were here, as everywhere in this land, and as soon as I'd learned what to look for I began to see them, dozens of them, watching warily from behind cover. I rounded a corner where the walls were still standing and came face to face with one: we were both startled, but the goat reacted first, making a hasty getaway with a rattle of small hooves.

Where are you, Nick?

Where would I be, if I wanted to hide out in this place? A sheltering roof was the basic need. There were three or four buildings which hadn't yet lost their roofs. All were dilapidated, appeared on the point of collapse, might still keep the rain out—just.

I began to check them out, one by one, pulling open the crude planked doors and peering into gloomy interiors. The first was still used as a store: rolls of wire netting, a pile of sacks fit for use, a giant earthenware jar . . . Somebody still comes here, then, to see to the goats, harvest the carob beans. Not Nick, though.

The second was more ruined than it had looked from outside: there was already a large hole in the roof, a corresponding pile of mud on the dusty, rubbish-strewn floor.

I tried the next—and couldn't resist a crow of triumph.

It doesn't have to be Nick, of course—the blankets in the bed alcove, the cheap aluminum saucepan with the dregs of vegetable soup in it, and the neat pile of firewood by the huge, blackened hearth might all belong to a shepherd.

Except that it would be a sophisticated shepherd whose tastes include tins of smoked oysters, asparagus tips, and cream of celery soup . . .

I sat on the bed and waited.

After half an hour, I'd run out of thoughts, and was in need of something to relieve boredom. I got up and, suppressing the same feeling of guilt I'd had when searching Nick's cellar in Moustaki, went through the place carefully, replacing exactly as I'd found it everything I disturbed.

There wasn't much. There was his bedding, the cooking equipment and food supplies, and the stuff in his suitcase, which included several pairs of clean and dirty socks, shirts, and under-pants, one pair of Levi trainers, one pair of jeans, some packets of plain white candles of Greek manufacture, and a heavy brown paper packet which raised hopes of something interesting but contained ordinary oval 2-inch nails, which by their brightness had been bought recently. Plus a book: *The End of Atlantis* by J. V. Luce, published by Thames & Hudson, 1969, and a paperback copy of *The Towers of Trebizond* by Rose Macaulay, published by Fontana Books, 1967.

I don't know what a professional sleuth would have done at this point. Me, I sat down again and opened *The Towers of Trebizond.*

"Oh *Christ!*" Nick said. "I don't *believe* this!"

"Hello, Nick," I said. "It's been a long time, as they say."

He loomed in the doorway, blocking the light. It must have been about seven in the evening. I hadn't quite finished the book.

"What the hell are you doing here?" he said.

"That's not much of a welcome," I said. "Aren't you pleased to see me? Must be a lonely life here, all on your own."

He came through the doorway and stood in the middle of the

room, looking down at me. Just as I remembered: *pale eyes behind
his glasses.* Looked tired, but fit. He said:

"How did you get here?"

"Hired a jeep. Drove."

"But *why*, for Christ's sake?"

"Maud's worried about you."

"Oh *Christ* . . ."

"You disappeared without a word."

"Yes, but . . . doesn't she *trust* me?"

"For a week, she did. Then she got worried. Normal, I'd
say."

"But why *you*?"

"She couldn't think of anyone else."

"That figures," he said drily.

"I arrived on Saturday night, spent Sunday getting my bearings, hired the car on Monday, and here I am."

"Bloody marvelous."

Silence, while he stared down at me and I stayed seated on the
bed, keeping my place in the book with my thumb. "Very
entertaining," I said, displaying it. "Your bedside reading, I
suppose?"

"So you drove here," he said. "But how did you know where
to drive *to*?"

"A village woman told Maud she'd seen you on the road to
Kalikrati about ten days ago. So I drove up to Kalikrati, and
talked to the chaps in the *kafeneíon*. They know you, of course,
and they'd seen you go up, but not back. So I drove on, checking out the possible places, found your car, came on up. Maud
could have done it herself, but was scared for some reason.
Personally, I thought the chaps at Kalikrati were not at all scary.
And they like the English, it seems. Very happy to help—"

"The chaps, the chaps . . . Oh *Christ*, William. Why couldn't
you bloody well have stayed in London where you belong?

What do you think you are, some kind of fucking white knight? Maud's nothing to do with you anymore, hasn't been for years."

"No she isn't, not in the sense you mean. But she was worried, so I came to see if I could help. After she'd asked me, that is. If you'd kept in touch with her, there wouldn't have been a problem, would there."

He was silent. Then he said:

"You don't know what you're talking about."

"I don't know what you're doing here, that's true. Are you going to tell me?"

"No."

"Why not?"

"I said no."

"What am I going to tell Maud, then?"

"Tell her you've seen me, that I'm perfectly all right, and that there's no need to worry. Tell her to relax, keep calm, get on with her painting."

"Just like that?"

"Just like that."

"Won't she want some sort of explanation?"

"She can't have one. Not yet. She's got to trust me. I'll be down to talk to her before too long."

"When?"

"I don't know, William. Not yet. Your coming up here hasn't helped, you know."

He was as maddeningly mysterious as ever. Never a straight answer, nothing ever his fault . . . "Listen, Nick," I said angrily, "if my coming here is an inconvenience, it's *your* fault, nobody else's. What the hell did you think Maud was going to feel, to *do,* when you suddenly pissed off without warning? Can you really not *see* that?"

He didn't answer. He'd moved across the room, and was

stooping to see out of a little square unglazed opening, put there
for some long-forgotten purpose, ventilation, draught for the
fire, cats . . . I said:

"Well, come on! You *must* see that—"

"Shh!"

"Come off it, Nick! It's time you—"

"*For Christ's sake!*" he hissed urgently, "*Keep quiet, will you!*"

"What is it?"

He flapped his hand behind his back, keeping me back. I
ignored this. If there was something out there, I was going to see
it for myself, not let him spin me some invention to get himself
off the hook.

"Get *back!*" he hissed again.

"Let me see."

"Oh Christ. Help yourself, then."

I looked through the tiny opening. It faced across a small
enclosure, on the far side of which I recognized the ruined
shrine I'd passed on the path up. Coming up the path now were
two men, young, black haired, identically dressed in black shirts
and jeans. Both had shotguns slung over the right shoulders.
Their pace was steady, purposeful. As I watched, one unslung his
gun, broke it open to check the breech, snapped it shut again,
all without slackening pace. He did it with the easy movements
of one who knows what guns are for . . .

I turned away from the opening. Nick already had his belong-
ings in his suitcase, and was strapping it up. I said:

"Who are they?"

"You wouldn't know them, and it doesn't matter. What
does, is that—"

"Are they the Gyparis brothers?"

He was startled into looking up. "Oh. Been around, haven't
you."

"Is this all about their sister?"

He finished strapping the case, stood up straight. "They're a bunch of homicidal idiots, and they're after the wrong man. Otherwise yes, it is."

"Did you—?"

"No, no, of *course* I didn't. I've met her, but that's all . . . look, if we stand here chatting, we're both going to get our heads blown off. Better split up, that's safest."

"*Both? Why me?*" I croaked.

For the first time since we'd met, he smiled. "You led them here, didn't you? So you must be on my side, against them . . . Take care, William. And remember—these guys mean business. Hope you can remember your field craft."

"What shall I tell Maud?" I hissed.

But he'd slipped out of the door and gone, vanished, evaporated. That was Nick.

What a shit!

I could put it more strongly, later I *would,* but just now it was *sauve qui peut!* as the French, selfish realists all, put it. They love principle, theories, and this one is a great help and consolation as you're trampling the women and children on the way to the lifeboats. *Save yourself if you can . . .* and to hell with the rest. Nick may not have been born French, but he had all the . . .

Oh Christ, I'm *yammering.* Well, I'm scared, that's why. What am I going to do, where am I going to . . .

There's a back door, I saw it while I was searching the place. Through here . . .

It's closed. Bolt rusted solid, too. Can't kick it open, too much noise. What then? Try levering bolt open with piece of wood. No. No. *Yes!*

The door opens, jams again on some obstruction outside . . . but the opening's already just wide enough to squeeze through. Ah! *Freedom!* Well, comparative. Better to be in the open with a chance of dodging them than in there, waiting.

Move away now, aim for the path, get down it and to the jeep while they're busy searching the village . . .

Movement. *Drop!*

Did he see me?

Find cover to raise head, take a look. That clump of bramble is the place. I'm going to have to crawl there, using elbows, on belly like snake. Field craft, it's called. We were given a manual, exercises. *Nah then you lot, idle trash the lot of you, let's see you do it properly this time, on your fucking stomach I said, not on your fucking hands and knees like a lot of nancy boys asking for it, right then, let's see yer, see yer MOVE!!!*

Yes, I was quite proud of that. Twenty yards crawl, and invisible all the way, I'm sure of it. If he saw me before I dropped, he'll be headed over there, not to where I am now.

Raise head slowly, look through bramble.

He's still there, so hadn't seen me. Crawl wasted. Too bad, but now I know I can still do it. So, what *is* he doing? And where's the other one?

Aha. I get it. This one isn't moving, has posted himself where he can watch this side of the village, and the path. His brother will be working round the other side, acting as beater. Nick and I are in between, the meat in the sandwich. Unless Nick managed to get out the far side before Brother Two got round there and outside him.

They're not stupid, these Gyparis brothers. At least, at doing *this* they're not. Animal instincts, animal cunning. With shotguns instead of teeth and claws.

Let's review what I know about shotguns. They will almost certainly be hunting us with twelve-bore double-barreled guns, each barrel loaded with a fat cartridge containing approximately three hundred small pellets. The pellets start to scatter on leaving the barrel, and at thirty-five yards will form a cloud of flying lead approximately thirty inches in diameter. At that range each pellet will be an inch or so from its neighbor, and if you held up your hand (should you be so careless) you could expect to collect maybe ten or a dozen pellets in it. At twice the range, because of the continuing spread of the pellets, you'd only collect two or three.

Conclusions as follows. First, if I'm not seen, I won't be shot at. Second, if I can't avoid being seen, I should try to make sure it's at long range, say a hundred yards or more.

Any other conclusions?

Yes. Don't get mixed up in this sort of thing in the first place.

*Through a Paffage full of Precipices, we entred, the 2nd of
June, into the Valley of Mirabeau, fhut in with other
Mountains, the Valley being difpos'd in manner of an
Ampitheatre, from whence it ftretches out as
far as the Sea.*

The shadows were lengthening and fading. I watched with
keen interest and appreciation. Oh, they were beautiful shadows. Not only because they brought relief from the heat of the
day, but because they meant that soon I would be wrapped in
the relative safety of darkness.

I'd crawled further away from the houses which would certainly be searched, and had gone to ground among the gnarled
roots of an ancient olive tree. If I raised my head far enough, I
could see Brother One fifty yards away: he was keeping his
position with the patience of a true predator, waiting for the
quarry to be flushed out of the ruined village towards him. I was
only twenty yards from the path, but there was no way I could

get to it without breaking cover, and he'd have time to blast off with both barrels before I could get over the wall and away. A useless move in any case: he was younger, fitter, and faster, and would have caught up with me with a reloaded gun before I had time to get round the first bend.

I couldn't hear or see anything of Brother Two, but I was sure he'd be working his way back here through the village, poking the shotgun through each gaping window and crumbling doorway, finger tight on the trigger. The house which Nick had camped in was on this side of the village: it would be one of the last he came to. Meanwhile, the light was definitely going.

He'd find Nick's abandoned food and bedding, of course. What would he do then? If he'd caught sight of Nick himself as he made off, he'd know it wasn't worth waiting: the bird had flown and wouldn't be back. If he'd seen Nick, though, he would surely have been unable to resist taking a shot at him, no matter how far off he was, both in the hope of a lucky hit and to alert his brother that the quarry was located. So, no shot, no sighting—that was most probable.

But in that case, when he found the food and bedding, he wouldn't know that Nick was forewarned, and he might decide to lie in wait for the unsuspecting target to return. That'd be bad news for me: they'd be watching both sides of the cottage, and I might find it hard to slip away unseen, even when it was dark.

What stage was the moon at? I couldn't remember. It would be too bad if a fat-bellied moon rose just as friendly night was due to come to my rescue, but it could happen . . .

Better try to put a little more distance between me and Brother One before Brother Two arrives at Nick's late residence.

I wriggle back from the olive tree, planning to get behind the next in line. This was an olive orchard . . . still is, I suppose, if anyone could be bothered to harvest them.

Crete is a prickly place, it must be said. Especially on the elbows. I'm becoming an expert on the different sorts of stab inflicted by bramble, spiny broom, prickly pear, and a particularly vicious type of small bush with spikes arranged in a sort of octagonal chain-mail pattern. But at least the ground is *dry* . . .

It's getting cold, now, temperature dropping fast as the sun goes down.

Oh Christ, I'm going to *sneeze* . . . Can I make it sound like a goat coughing? I'll have to try . . . Pinch nose with hand tight over mouth, and . . . *ugh!*

Did he hear that?

If he did, he's ignored it. Not surprising—it was hardly human . . .

What am I *doing* here?

Half an hour later, I watched Two's shotgun barrel emerge from the back door of the house, followed by the man, or youth, himself. He paused, and I kept very still as his stare swept slowly across the olive orchard. Then he shrugged, and shouted angrily to his brother, who shouted back. It had to be: "*The bastards got away.*" I hoped it was. I hoped they'd give up now, and go home. I was scratched, bruised, stiff, cold, scared, and longing for all this to be over. I wanted out. I wanted to pad down the path, climb into the jeep, and begin the weary drive back down to Moustaki, where there was most of a liter of duty-free whiskey and, surely, after today's blazing sun, the roof tank would have heated up and I could have a hot bath. I'd have to decide what to tell Maud, what to do next . . . but that seemed easy, trivial, after what I'd just been through. No, what I was *still* going through . . . They hadn't gone, yet. Two had joined One, and they were standing on the path, talking over their plans. Mine would have to wait a while longer . . .

Oh no, it's all right—they're off. Down the path they go, and in a minute I can stand up, stretch, dust myself off, and . . .

And *what*?

Steady, *steady,* let's just think this through.

They've given up, here, terrific.

But that doesn't mean they've given up altogether, does it. Remember the purposeful way they came steaming up the path? They must have known we were here, or somewhere nearby. Why? Because they'd seen Nick's Hyundai, my jeep, at the bottom of the hill. So what will they, what would *I,* do next? Obvious, isn't it?

If I go down that path and try to reach the jeep, I'll be doing just what they hope and expect—they will, of course, be waiting. So, good-bye whiskey and hot bath. I'll have to make myself as comfortable as I can up here.

But where?

Not in the house Nick was using, obviously, in case they come back. I daren't even take the blankets because that might set off another search if they come back. And it's getting colder by the minute.

Where, then?

Oh yes. *There . . .*

You could call it sanctuary, and you wouldn't be far wrong. Though, with all due respect, it isn't God, but four walls and a sound roof I really need.

It wasn't the ruined shrine, but the church I had in mind. I slipped round the long way, back through the village, avoiding the path just in case the Gyparis brothers changed their minds and came back up to watch the house. Then I walked up the cypress avenue, past a rusty iron gate which was off its hinges and leaning against a stone wall, and entered the churchyard.

The church faced me, its whitewashed façade glowing in the half-light. It was tiny. There was a single oak-boarded door in the center, and the edge of the red-tiled, barrel-vaulted roof made a protective semicircle above it. I walked up and tried the door. It opened.

Had Two been in here? The church hadn't been visible from my hiding place, so I didn't know. Was it too risky—should I stay in the open, find a tree to curl up under?

No, it should be safe enough. Either he'd checked it out, and it was cleared, or he'd had a reason for ignoring it. In any case, he knew now where Nick had been camping. No reason to come here again.

I went in. It was only the second Greek church I'd been in: the other had been with Maud, in Moustaki, on our Sunday tour of the village. Here, in the semidarkness, I could see the outlines of the same jumble of practical equipment and religious paraphernalia: a hillock of candle grease on a side altar before a framed picture of the patron saint, a fretted brass oil lamp hanging on brass chains (similar to the one in Nick's loo), strings of foil medallions each stamped with a symbol—an eye, a foot, a leg—to remind the Saint of the afflicted part needing his attention. On the floor in a corner a collection of Coca-Cola and squash bottles contained blue paraffin for the oil lamp, next to them a mop, and a tin of floor wax. The place was still visited then, if only on the Saint's day. I sniffed: the air was musty; the smell of moldering plaster mingled with incense and floor polish in an unappealing combination . . . Perhaps I would be better outside, after all.

Out in the churchyard, the light seemed brighter than it had been, either by contrast, or because there was a moon on the way up. There was a stone-built wellhead to one side, next to the only standing gravestone: I began to stroll over there, and stubbed my toe. Looking down, I saw the stone lid of a grave concealed in the grass. It was askew, the grave half open. I had to bend, look inside. It was shallow . . . and empty. The standing gravestone, at the head of a shiny new slab, bore a photograph in a chromium frame: either he'd died young or, more likely, this was him in his glorious youth, all black hair, staring eyes, and the inevitable fierce, bushy moustache. A Macho Man, a *pallikári,* born here, probably, before the village was closed down, now home again. Well, that's enough of moonlit grave inspection: let's see if there's any water in the well. Ease the lid back, and—

Christ!

Not a well, no. After a session in one of the shallow graves, everyone goes in here, jumbled up. The whiteness of the bones is startling, even in this level of light, or because of it. I beg your pardon, I'll replace the lid . . . There.

Perhaps I'll sleep in the church, after all. It feels somewhat overpopulated out here.

I was woken by a narrow, dusty shaft of sunlight coming in through the little arched window to the east. Yawning, I sat up, stretched, got to my feet, stretched again. I could feel worse, I suppose—but not much. Maud's bed was a Hilton of luxury compared to the narrow bench I'd balanced on, wrapped in the only covering I could find, the red velvet curtains from the *iconostásis.* I told myself it didn't matter, but I found myself hurrying to put them back, sliding the brass rings onto the rail, hooking it up across the opening again. There were painted saints on the walls: their eyes noted the restoration, their raised hands approved it.

I was hungry, too. Fishing in the *sakoúli,* I pulled out the last of my provisions, a packet of salted almonds, and began to crunch them gratefully. They'd make me thirsty, but there was water not far down the path.

Down the path . . .

Could I risk it? Would the brothers have given up?

Why should they, while the jeep was still there?

Damn, damn, *damn . . .*

I moved to the door of the church, and carefully produced a crack just wide enough to see out. I stared . . . and then shut it again, quickly. There was someone in the cypress avenue which led to the church.

Look again, while there's still time . . .

A woman, black dress, black head scarf. Coming this way . . .

I decided to brazen it out. After all, the place was unlocked, anyone could come in, even an English tourist . . . They *like* the English, don't they?

On the other hand, dirty, unshaven, with scratched hands and a fugitive air . . . I'd rather not be seen, anyway. Suppose she was startled, cried out, screamed even—and the brothers were near enough to hear? No, I'd rather not be seen.

There's no other door, no other way to get out without being seen . . .

Behind the *iconostásis* then. And hope she doesn't need to come in there. Yes! Didn't Maud say (scornfully) that women were never allowed in there, or even to peep beyond the curtain? And *Macho Man: "Men are like the noble sheep; women like the lustful goat, shameful, devil-influenced . . ."*

I shot through the curtains, pulled them tight, took up position behind the wooden screen. Ikons were hung on the carved, polished, public side—hence, of course, the name. From the hidden, forbidden side I was on, the thing was plain, a simple screen of rough oak boards, poorly jointed, closing off the east end of the church. There were cracks between the boards. I moved well to one side, to avoid blocking the light from the window behind, which would have given me away.

The door at the far end of the church opened, and the woman came in. I could see quite clearly when I put one eye to a crack. She was elderly, her face under the black head scarf deeply lined but, although bent, she moved with energy, like a crab foraging for prey. She got the mop, dabbed it in the tin of polish, set to work on the stone floor slabs.

I had time to review the situation while she mopped slowly down the length of the church towards me. How does a reasonably intelligent, moderately resourceful six-foot-two Englishman get himself bottled up in the forbidden end of a tiny church in an abandoned village miles from anywhere, waiting for an elderly Greek peasant woman to finish mopping the floor before he can creep out and get on with his life?

Put like that, the answer's only too obvious. And the recommendation, too: *This has got to stop* . . .

Right *now*!

Well . . .

As soon as she's finished mopping, anyway . . .

She was putting a small bunch of wildflowers on the *pallikári's* grave and had her back turned as I slipped quietly out of the church. I waited a moment, and then coughed. She looked round, frowning, straightened up as far as her bent back would allow. I smiled, and inclined my head politely.

"*Kali méra!*"

She said nothing, but inclined her head in return, watching me with more suspicion than alarm. A tough old bird.

"*Inglis,*" I said, putting my hand on my chest.

She inclined her head again. That was all.

"Well, it's a lovely day. I must be getting along now," I said, giving up on the Greek. I started down the path to the gateway, slinging the *sakoúli* onto my back.

She watched me go, and then suddenly began to scuttle across the grass to intercept me, flapping her hands. I halted. She came up to me, took me by the sleeve, and let fly with a rattling torrent of Greek in a high, thin voice. It came to an end. I said:

"I'm sorry if I startled or upset you. But I must go now. Good-bye."

First, she pulled me back, quite roughly. Then she scuttled in front of me and set off for the gateway at high speed. I let her go, mystified. She turned at the gateway and beckoned, impatiently.

"I'm to follow, am I?"

She beckoned again. I hesitated, then complied. We set off in convoy down the cypress avenue. She was surprisingly quick—I don't normally walk much faster myself.

I kept looking round for any sign of the brothers, but there was none. However, if she started to lead me in the direction of the path, I would have to refuse. It was too soon to risk going down the path to the jeep, I'd decided. I might try a sweep round, though, and approach from an unexpected direction. Meanwhile, I felt inclined to go along and see what all this was about—there might be other people up here today, witnesses to inhibit youths with murder on their minds.

We came to the end of the cypress avenue, and the old woman swerved off to the left, into a small field. There were two donkeys waiting there, and a pile of filled sacks . . . Ah, so that's it. Well, I don't mind at all, glad to help. I've got time to waste, in fact.

I loaded the sacks for her—they were heavy, full of carob beans—and roped them in place. The donkeys had wooden saddles with ledges to support the load, and although it wasn't a professional job, the sacks were secure enough. When it was done, I stood back smiling, waiting to fend off gratitude and wave good-bye.

No, nothing like that. She frowned and twittered over my amateur knots, and then seized the leading donkey's halter and set off across the field, beckoning insistently.

Oh well. All right. I followed.

We came to a path. Started down it. Kept going. No other people about. I looked for the sun. We were headed south, towards the coast. Did I want to go towards the coast? Well, I certainly didn't want to go back north towards the shotguns, not yet.

Just as far as it suits me, then. No further.

The mountains were closing in. After we'd been going at a fair pace for twenty minutes, it seemed as though the narrow path we were on must be coming to a dead end. Possibly the old woman's cottage was there, at the end of the path. But what a place to live, especially if she was on her own! The end of the path, the end of the world . . . The cliffs on either side were now too steep for vegetation, sheer walls of gray limestone, channeled by winter rain and miniature waterfalls which left yellow and black streaks on the pale surface. Looking up, I could see the sharp edge of the top of the cliff outlined against the steely sky, with small bushes breaking the silhouette like Indians watching the pass. Underfoot, the trodden earth had given way to jagged white stones which caught the foot at awkward angles, and occasionally clattered one against another with a surprisingly loud report which echoed off the cliffs from side to side, adding to the sense of impending ambush.

She couldn't live here, I decided. The place was now too narrow, too bleak . . . , Where, then?

The answer lay round the next corner, contained in a startling glimpse of distant blue, like a chink in almost-drawn stone curtains, and far, far below. The sea . . .

I hadn't realized we were so close. The stupid map, of course, had had nothing to tell about all this, but had taken refuge in the misty gray cloud effect that meant "*Well, er, mountains hereabouts.*" How far was the sea, in fact? The glimpse of blue had vanished again, but as the stone curtains drew apart a second time I made an effort at accurate estimation: about four miles, perhaps five, as the crow flies.

I wouldn't have minded being a crow, right now. The path

had taken a steep downward dive, and we were having to scramble down steps adapted less to human requirements than to the shape of boulders lying in the way. The old woman led, her short legs seemingly adapted to this kind of terrain: the donkeys followed, their hooves pattering quickly from one tottering stone to the next. And I brought up the rear, glad that my clumsy, stumbling progress was taking place unobserved. The pace hadn't slackened. Also, the sun was now high enough in the sky to send burning shafts into the gorge, arrows of heat which I was glad to get through and into the chilly shadow of the next outcrop.

Of course there was no turning back, now. I was on a mystery tour, and had to go on, see where it led. In addition, the idea was forming that where there is a coastline, there are usually hotels offering drinks, dining rooms, menus *á la carte,* gleaming bathrooms with clean towels and packet soap, and beds with sheets and little bedside lights to read by. Well, it's no good pretending: I'm addicted to that sort of thing. I can take a certain amount of danger, but I like it interspersed with hot baths, on the lines of Lord Cadogan, who came ashore from his luxury yacht to take part in the Charge of the Light Brigade. A shit, but I know how he felt.

An hour later my legs felt like jelly. The path was leveling out, though. We tracked across a treacherous rockfall of loose stones, with a gushing torrent of clear, icy-looking water in the bottom of the gorge to our left, and then, ahead, the sea appeared again, much nearer and not nearly so far below. A clatter of stones from behind startled me, and I looked round. *Jesus!*—I'd thought we were going quite fast, but we were practically stationary compared to the figure approaching. He was catching up quickly, and next time I looked round I could see his face: a young man,

big black moustache, unshaven, but wearing clean blue jeans and
a big, red-checked lumberjack's jacket. In spite of a bulky backpack he was moving with a springy trot that hardly let his
thick-soled trainers touch the ground. I stood aside to let him
pass, and got a nod of thanks. So that's how shepherds do it, I
thought, feeling old and tired.

The worst was over, though. Ten minutes more, and we
emerged from the bottom of the gorge into farmland. I could see
a wide stretch of coastline now, at the far side of a flat plain a
mile or so wide. On the far side, outlined by the blue of the sea,
there was a large, square building with battlemented walls shimmering in the heat haze: an old fort, perhaps. In Spain I remembered with a surge of hope that they often turn old castles into
superb hotels . . . Well, we'll see.

The view of the coast was cut off as we passed through a gate
into an olive grove—and compared to where we'd come from
it seemed incredibly soft and civilized. Even the goats looked
friendly. There was a village ahead, nicely situated a few hundred feet above the plain. And—good God!—I can hear traffic,
there must be a tarmac road!

The old woman scuttled on faster, and started beckoning
again. The home stretch . . .

It was a tiny cottage, badly in need of repair. She led the way
through a gate at the side into an equally tiny and filthy yard no
bigger than a room. Animal faces bobbed and ducked in wire
cages on every hand: rabbits, chickens, even a small plump
puppy, his paws balanced uncomfortably on the netting floor,
greeting his jailor with a feverish tail wagging. The old woman
dragged open a shed door, led the donkeys in. I followed and
unloaded them. In one corner was a stained concrete tank, waist
high, a rusty pipe protruding from one side. I looked in. Good
Lord, how frightfully amusing! It's half full of *grapes,* ready for
winemaking! Well, I am a wine merchant, but nowadays it's all

stainless steel tanks and plastic hosing, chromatographic analysis and *macération carbonique*. I've never seen anything this basic before!

The old woman is beckoning yet again. Must be about lunchtime—I expect she's inviting me to . . .

No, that's not it.

The *tank*? What about it?

Something needs looking at. Pipe blocked, perhaps?

She can't want me to get *in* there? "I'm afraid I . . ."

She *does*.

Well really! I don't think I . . .

On the other hand . . .

No good just rolling up the trouser legs, the juice will splash higher than that. Take trousers off, then, and—

Ugh.

9

*Add to this, the French Deſerters who, after their
Commander M. de St. Paul was kill'd with a
Cannon-ſhot, being fed with nothing but Biſcuit-duſt full
of Mouſe and Rat-dung, went over to the Enemy in a Fit
of Deſpair, which brave Men are often driven to by want
of Neceſſaries.*

I have to report that treading grapes is nothing like the romantic, creative process eulogized by travel writers. Feet and ankles ache with being dragged through the sticky sludge, grape stalks scratch and catch between toes and, above all, it's *cold*. The old woman appeared every few minutes to drive me on with shrill, querulous instructions, and empty the galvanized bucket of purple produce which stood under the outlet pipe. After an hour or so, she brought me a hunk of yellow bread, some goat cheese, and a plastic bottle of, I suppose, last year's vintage. Whose feet had flavored this? I wondered briefly, but drank some all the same. It had the same fiery, port-like taste and syrupy consistency as the Moustaki village wine. The grapes in a hot climate tend to shrivel and concentrate, of course . . . Well, back to the treadmill.

At just after five I reckoned the treading was done, to my satisfaction anyway. Ignoring the cries, complaints, and sleeve pluckings, I washed my legs with cold water from a tap, got my trousers, socks, and shoes back on, and firmly said good-bye. She pursued me a hundred yards down the road, but then gave up. I was on my own again, at last.

It was an easy walk down to the plain and across it to the coast. The fort loomed larger and larger. In an hour, I passed beyond its pink, castellated walls and arrived at a small, rock-sheltered harbor: half a dozen fishing boats were anchored in it. Beyond, oily calm and peaceful, was the Libyan sea.

There was a single newly built, two-story hotel, with a restaurant terrace shaded by bamboo matting, overlooking the harbor. I sat down, the only customer. A youth in jeans sauntered up, and I ordered "the green one." He brought it. I drank, sighed, had another. Then I went into the bar and booked a room.

The youth showed me up, handed me the key. I shut the door, threw the *sakoúli* on the bed, and went to open the sliding window onto the narrow balcony. There was a clear view of the harbor. I left the window open, looked round the room, opened the door into the shower, and inspected that. Should I have one now, or . . .

Later, later.

I joined the *sakoúli* on the bed, and fell asleep at once.

When I woke, it was almost dark. There was a circuitous whining of mosquitoes. I got up and shut the sliding window, and then pulled off my clothes, got under the shower, and scrubbed the purple staining, or most of it, off my legs. Then I shaved, and slid luxuriously into the clean shirt and socks I'd saved in the hope of an occasion like this: the trousers would have to do. Oh wow, it felt good! Humming happily, I went down to the restaurant.

The joint wasn't exactly popping, but three other tables were occupied. One had a group of fishermen huddled round it, shouting stories and roaring with laughter: I knew how to tell fishermen now, by the missing fingers. At the second table, an ash-blond, sun-burned couple sat opposite each other, not saying much, but exuding contentment. The third table had a solitary occupant, an unsmiling, tough-looking character in his late thirties, who looked away as soon as he caught my eye. There was a black leather jacket looped across the back of his chair.

In the harbor, the sea was still oily calm, streaked with orange and gold from the last moments of the sunset. A fishing boat appeared from behind rocks, diesel put-putting, bow wave following it in through the harbor entrance to set all the other boats rocking. It was about thirty-five feet on the waterline, heavily built in brightly painted wood, equipped with a comfortable wheelhouse and a full set of the masts, aerials, scanners that go with modern communications. A caïque, in short. There were two others like it already in the harbor, among the smaller boats.

Food came. I soon found I'd made a mistake with the octopus, which was cold and greasy. I killed the taste with retsina, and started on the souvlaki, which was nicely charred and not bad at all. Something other than retsina was called for: the youth brought a bottle of Castello Minos, bright red, light but with plenty of fruit . . . Maybe my luck was in again.

After supper, I went to look for a telephone. There was one in the hotel, and the proprietor was helpful—somehow, I hadn't expected it to be easy, I felt so far away. It seemed a miracle to be talking to Claudine, but she couldn't know that.

After we'd got over the usual greetings and assurances, she said:

"So, have you found Nick, *chérie?*"

"Yes, but lost him again. Listen, I want to get a message to Maud. Will you do it?"

"But of course."

"She hasn't got a phone, but there's a French woman who lives in the village: I'm sure she'd agree to go round with a message. Here it is, and the number . . . are you ready?"

"I'm ready."

I'd have to keep it short, omit the uncertainties and, of course, the shotguns—Nick hadn't asked for help, didn't want it. I said:

"Tell her two things: one, I've seen Nick and he's all right, she's not to worry. Two, I'm at a place called Frangocastello on the south coast, and I don't expect I'll be able to get back for a day or two, but not to worry about me either. Okay?"

"D'accord. So, you are at the seaside. In a superb hotel, j'imagine."

"Of course!" Best to play along with her.

"Of course. Well, I am very happy to hear it, because we agree you need a little holiday. Take care, enjoy yourself, and I will give the message. Good-bye, chérie."

I put the phone down feeling a little sore, but it wasn't the moment to relate the hideous hardships I'd endured. Anyway, that was all over now. I'd found Nick, and could enjoy myself with a clear conscience until I reckoned it was time to recover the jeep, drive back to Maud's, and decide what next, if anything. Quite probably I'd done all I could, now, and might as well pack up and go home. All in good time, though.

The evening was too perfect to ignore, so I went for a stroll along a path behind the shoreline, and got as far as the castle. It was abandoned, a huge, hollow shell. From the top of the sand dunes beside it, I looked down to the beach. I could hear music: a guitar, and singing. Strolling further, the source came into view: a camp fire, surrounded by a group of hippies sleeping rough. I caught some of the words: the singer, at least, was

German. So, probably, had been the blond couple at the next table. The war was over down here, then.

Yawning, I went back to my room, plugged in the antimosquito gadget thoughtfully—or ominously—provided, got into bed, and read a chapter of *Macho Man*. There was a remark on wine making, interesting in the light of what I'd been doing today: women aren't *allowed* to tread the wine, absolutely not, in case their goatish devilry pollutes it!

Of course, that means Macho Man has to do it himself . . .

Could he be, well, just a little bit *dim*?

No better sound to wake to than the gentle lapping of waves on a shore.

I lay for a while listening to it, and to the voices from the restaurant below. A caïque's diesel spluttered, roared, and then settled down to a steady thrum. A sea gull called. Claudine was right: I *was* on holiday now. I could go back to sleep again . . .

But, well, there's nothing much I want to do, here, and I'd better not leave the jeep too long. If I leave mid-morning, taking food, I should be back there by mid-afternoon. That will put me in a position to approach it under cover of dusk, or lie up near it, watching for the brothers, until morning . . .

No, wait! I don't have to go through all that! I could report it *stolen*! Yes, of course. That would also get me off the hook for having driven it off the tarmac road . . .

But, hold on, it's not that easy. How did I get *here*?

Try this. Went touring—that's what the jeep's for. Stopped to admire coastal scenery. Returned to car—*gone*! Walked to hotel . . .

But didn't report it until next day. Hmmm.

Won't do, will it? Nor does it explain why I arrived looking so scruffy and filthy.

There's a way, of course there is. It'll come to me while I have breakfast.

I walked to the window and pulled back the curtain. There'd been a change since last evening: a sizable motor yacht had arrived and was anchored just inside the harbor, a flashy white swan among the multicolored duck-like caïques. A smart white dingy with a large outboard was pulled up on the beach. I found myself regretting this invasion: it spoiled the old-fashioned, workmanlike air of the place. But there it is: build a hotel in a place as unspoiled as this, and money will come. Give it five years, and it'll look just like everywhere else.

I showered, shaved, dressed, packed the *sakoúli,* and took it down to breakfast with me. The table I'd had last night was free, next to some people I hadn't—

"Hel-lo."

I stared. "Eléni!"

"Yes, it is me." She was shading her eyes. Below the shade, her slow smile.

"Well . . . what a surprise!"

"A nice one, I hope."

"Well, of *course* . . ."

"You are very kind to say so. Please, why don't you sit with us. This is my uncle Stavros. And this is Nikos, our very able seaman. I like very much that phrase, 'able seaman'. I will tell them to bring more coffee, another cup."

"That's very kind, thank you. If you're sure."

"I am delighted to meet you, Mr. Warner," her uncle said, putting out his hand. "Eléni has told me about you." Behind him, Nikos, who had stood up politely, sat down again.

She just *would* have an uncle like this, I thought, as he released me from his firm, smooth grip. Late fifties, a big, brown, bald head with a neat gray fringe, an imperial nose, dark brown, intelligent eyes, wide mouth with pronounced, curving lips

. . . a big man. With the yacht to prove it. Had to be his, of course. I wasn't going to be so naïve as to ask, oh no.

"So she has, has she?"

"Oh yes. I know what you are."

"Hmm. And what am I, according to Eléni?" I smiled, but my mind was whirring like a pocket calculator.

"A wine merchant?" he said, also smiling. "Am I right?"

"Absolutely."

"I have an excellent memory. It is a great advantage."

"I'm sure." So good, he'd remembered my name as well as my occupation—she hadn't included it in the introduction.

"And how do you find Crete, Mr. Warner?" the uncle said.

"Fascinating, Mr. . . ."

"I should be pleased if you would accept to call me Stavros."

"Honored. And I'm William . . . I find it fascinating. The scenery, the customs. The people."

"I am so glad. And is this your first visit?"

You know it is . . . "Yes."

"Ah. So you are enjoying your holiday—you are on holiday, I suppose?"

Crunch point—the opportunity to confide, or not. I said:

"At the moment, yes." *Confidence deferred.*

"Ah."

"And you?"

"The same. A beautiful morning, is it not?"

"Lovely."

A pause for coffee. I glanced round the terrace. Two other tables were occupied, but there were no fishermen, no blond couple, nobody I'd seen last night. Nobody, but at the far side, a black leather jacket hung across the back of an empty chair.

Eléni leaned across to me and said:

"I have, I think, a very good idea. You will be here this evening?"

"Could be," I said.

"Then we would like to invite you to dinner. Will you come?"

"Sounds a very good idea indeed," I said. *What did they have in mind? Oh, it's obvious—loosen him up with drinks, then on with the questions . . . I could handle it. Besides, people like this live on lobster—and I could handle some of that, too . . .* "Thank you very much, both of you."

"Shall we say at eight?"

"Perfect. In time for the sunset."

She smiled. "Yes, for the sunset. Nikos will be at the beach to bring you."

"I'll be there," I said. "And thank you again."

"It will be a great pleasure," Uncle Stavros said with grave sincerity in his deep voice.

There was no difficulty in taking the room for an extra night. I went up to dump the bag, and sat on the bed collecting my thoughts. Through the window, I could see Eléni and her uncle being motored back out to the yacht by Nikos in the dinghy. There was only one caïque left on its mooring. If the others were out fishing, they were doing it somewhere out of sight.

If only Maud had been able to find Nick's binoculars, this would have been the perfect observation post. Perfect! I'd have been able to watch every detail of everything that went on in the harbor, all the comings and goings, even the expressions on people's faces. I'd have been able to see the easy greeting that showed familiarity; the quick sideways glance or the avoidance of eye contact that hinted at tension; the indifference that proved no connection at all. Without binoculars, all I could see was the movement, mannequin figures passing and re-passing like clockwork toys.

What was I looking for, anyway? Nick was up to something,

I knew that much, though not what it was. Maybe he *had* got the girl, Maria, pregnant, and was up in Arcadés hiding from her brothers, hoping to slip down here and get a boat out to . . . Libya? Egypt? Morocco even—a caïque could get that far with extra fuel. Then he could get a plane back to the UK, or cross to Spain and set up there. Would he send for Maud, or did he intend to drop her? They were both such cool customers, it was hard to imagine what they really thought or felt about each other. But *Jesus!* To let himself be driven out of Crete by these crazy shepherds! It was incredible! Nick, of all people, the great fixer and con man, always so clever at avoiding domestic entanglements, getting himself into such a mess over a girl! It was possible, just, but it wasn't *him,* it wasn't in character. Maud suited him as well as any woman could, made (as far as I could tell) few emotional demands on him, left him free to wheel and deal and chase after the gold at the end of the rainbow to his heart's content. Gold, yes! Forget Churchill's parachuted sovereigns, I don't mean *real* gold, but money, the green stuff, spondulicks. That had always been what turned Nick on, not for itself, but as the proof of his ingenuity, his ability to score against odds and usually against authority. Well yes, that's the criminal mentality, but Nick was different in that it was against his personal code to hurt people, at least in a way that they would recognize as damage. That was why he'd been a failure, of course—he hadn't the ruthlessness, the indifference of the genuine criminal.

So much for Nick. What about Eléni, and her uncle? And Spyro—does he fit in somewhere? And the man in the black leather jacket . . . Oh no! I must keep a grip on myself, I'm starting to imagine things. Not all frozen-faced characters in leather jackets are up to no good: many or most just like to *look* as if they are. *Don't mess with me, man . . .* And he may have spots, a squeaky voice, and an inferiority complex that the thickest, blackest leather jacket can't conceal . . .

Eléni and her uncle, then. What do I know? They're transparently inquisitive about my affairs—what do they think I'm up to that could possibly interest them? Plus, she smokes pot, and he's obviously rich . . . doesn't add up to a row of beans, does it! I hope this evening to learn as much about them as they do about me—it's an odd little fencing match we're into. Oh, and one more thing—how did they know I was here? Coincidence? No way!

And Spyros? Well, he could easily be peddling drugs, gold, girls, bicycle tires, cigarette papers, any and everything else you care to mention. He's the type—but it's not my business, and his wife made *that* quite clear. He's trouble I could do without. So let's simplify, and forget Spyros, if he'll let me.

Why not, in fact, *forget the whole thing?*

Yes! *Why not?*

I'm under no obligation, I'm not being paid, I could go home *right now* . . .

Well, not quite true. Some people could, and would, but I'm not sure I'm one of them. How would it feel, saying good-bye to Maud without having completed my self-imposed mission to restore Nick to her, or at least giving her the reason why he *wasn't* coming back so that she could get used to the idea, start to rebuild her life? How would it feel to be walking onto the plane, turning my back on all this, acknowledging that I was never going to know what it was all about?

Tough, that's what. Nobody does this sort of thing for the money, anyway, of course they don't. Basically, they do it because they want to know *who,* and/or *why* . . .

You could say I'm hooked that way. But that's not the only reason I'm staying on, of course not . . .

No, it isn't. You haven't mentioned Eléni with the slow-burn smile. Nor the lobster supper. Plus, people like this are bound to have the Chablis to go with it, nicely chilled of course, and probably Premier Cru . . .

Oh God, that's just trivial! Listen, you don't understand my motivation at all if you think that I . . . What it is, quite simply, is that I want to help Maud, get Nick out of trouble. Do my bit to make the world a better place, in short. The rest is just—

Will it be grilled or in a salad, do you suppose? Or even, God willing, thermidor . . .

Not listening. Over and out.

The heat was building up. It was a flat-roofed hotel, cheaply built, and by mid-morning the room was getting uncomfortably stuffy. I decided to continue my study of harbor activity from close-up, went out into the corridor, locked the door, and down the outside stair to the restaurant. The blond couple had reappeared and were having a late breakfast, looking more pleased with life than ever, but otherwise it was empty. The black leather jacket had gone from the back of the chair. I decided to have a beer under the bamboo shading before braving the heat, and sat, sipping it and watching the harbor. Uncle Stavros's yacht lay silent at anchor, reflected sunlight sparkling off the white hull. There was still only a single caïque on the moorings, with a muffled noise of metallic hammering coming from inside. One of the smaller boats had someone sitting in it, mending or folding a net. Nothing else moved, except for a lone sea gull patroling the beach.

I finished the beer, and strolled along the shore towards the fort. The German hippies were in the same place, some sunbathing in the dunes near the ashes of last night's fire, others sitting at the edge of the sea, or swimming lazily in the shallows. There were a few small boats moored in a small cove near the fort which I hadn't noticed last night.

There was nothing remarkable about any of this, but I kept looking all the same. It passed the time, and gave me the feeling of doing something useful. Of course, it could well be illusory.

• Maybe Eléni and her uncle *had* arrived here by chance. Maybe the discovery that Nick was hiding out in a village only four hours' walk from the sea, from this harbor, was a chance fact, and meant nothing. Maybe, maybe.

Meanwhile, having strolled up and down a couple of times and noted everything there was to note, boredom was setting in. Yesterday had been rough, but had had its moments of mild drama and interest. Today was, well, like being on holiday. Or worse, without even a wife and children to share the boredom. I went back to the now familiar restaurant for an early lunch.

Leather Jacket was there. I had him in profile: he looked straight to his front, avoided my eye, and became fascinated by the menu, half a dozen items handwritten in a printed folder. I decided on fried squid; feta cheese salad came with it automatically. And retsina, which I was getting to like with fried things.

Time passed. I nibbled salad, sipped the chilled retsina. Then . . .

Was it my imagination, or had Leather Jacket started, and then frozen in mid-munch? His profile pointed towards the far side of the harbor, where two motorcycles and a pickup truck were parked on the grass. There was a man standing there, with something familiar about him . . .

It's the jacket, *the jacket*. What delayed identification is that he's not wearing it, but carrying it slung over his shoulder. There can't be all that many, can there? Not in that style and color. Red-checked, lumberjack-type, with zip front . . . it could well be the same one. And he still has the backpack, slung over one shoulder now.

He's walking past the restaurant terrace, not with the spring-heeled speed that I envied when he passed us in the gorge yesterday, but slowly, as if killing time. And yes, Leather Jacket's profile is swiveling . . .

The Courier. Let's call him that. Imagination, perhaps, but it's just feasible, and as a working hypothesis, it'll do.

Leather Jacket is parking his knife and fork, leaving some food uneaten on the plate. He's taking a last swallow from a glass which he's putting down again, half empty. And he's getting to his feet, nothing hasty, all very deliberate.

That's life, isn't it. Chase about in the hot sun, and you get nowhere. Sit quietly in the shade, sipping chilled retsina, and it all happens, right there in front of you.

Leather Jacket is sloping off after the Courier. Well, it's as good as an invitation. What else can I do, but slope after Leather Jacket . . .

I was inside the fort. It had no roof, only a row of empty sockets where the beams had been, but the wall facing south over the sea provided a deep slab of shade on the inside. There were gun ports at ground level with a good field of fire over the foreshore. From the one I'd chosen, I could see Leather Jacket failing to impersonate an idle holidaymaker on the dunes to my left, and the Courier wandering aimlessly beside the cove to my right. There was a third actor coming on stage: a caïque about half a mile out, heading this way at speed.

We waited. The caïque grew rapidly in size and colorfulness, until it slowed, dropped anchor, and then . . .

Sat there.

Ten minutes went by.

A figure moved out of the shade of the wheelhouse, did something nautical with nets and ropes, and went in again. The Courier sat down, spread out his jacket, lay on it.

Ten more minutes. My spirits sank.

Leather Jacket appeared, surprisingly close—my attention must have wandered. I shrank back from the embrasure, leaving him only a cheek and an eye to notice if he looked my way. He passed the fort, seemed to be heading back to the hotel. *It's a trick, of course!* He's going to double back, catch the Courier unawares! Very neat, very professional . . .

Except that the Courier has risen from his couch on the dunes, and is also making for the hotel. The roles are reversed, the hunter now the hunted. Leather Jacket is going to have to confront the Courier and declare himself, or keep going, away from the cove. Me, I'm fine thanks. I'm just going to hang on here, quite comfortable in the shade, and watch the caïque. I'm feeling hopeful because, when the Courier left, he wasn't carrying the backpack.

It was a full hour before the caïque spawned a rubber dinghy, which motored ashore, and was pulled up the beach near where the Courier had been relaxing. There were two men in it. They didn't see me, but I saw one of them collect the backpack from the dunes while the other lit a cigarette and kept watch. Then they both went back to the caïque.

Casual, but competent, I thought. Leather Jacket would have to improve his tactics if he wanted to move up in his profession. Or perhaps he'd seen all he wanted, and arrests would follow another time, in another place.

Meanwhile, what was in this backpack, that had come down the gorge, if not from Arcadés, certainly from that direction? It was definitely going out, not coming in. That didn't rule out drugs, though—it could be payment for past or, more likely, future—shipment. If not that, then what?

I looked at my watch. It was only two, and I had nothing else to do. Might as well stay on watch. I worked a fallen stone nearer the embrasure, where I could sit on it and still see out. It was cool, leaning against the stonework in the shade. If I'd brought *Macho Man* to read, it would have been perfect.

I'd been resigned to a long stay, but not more than ten minutes passed before the two men reappeared from the wheelhouse of the caïque, dropped into the dinghy, and came ashore again. I waited while they pulled the dinghy up the beach, and then walked off in the direction of the harbor and the hotel. Then I was out of the shelter of the fort, into the heat, making for the place where the dinghy was drawn up.

Sand flowed into my shoes, and I paused to pull them off and stuff my socks into them. The sand was painfully hot for bare feet. The air was stifling. Sweat trickled in my armpits . . .

What more natural, then, than to go for a swim?

The water was lukewarm, unpleasantly so, and very salty. I'm not a fast swimmer, but I didn't want to cut a splash and draw attention to myself, anyway. I slid along quietly, alternating from breast- to backstroke, aiming for the seaward side of the caïque. Five minutes got me there.

The hull was a painted cliff, the gunwale well out of reach. But towards the stern, a short length of rope ladder was trailing in the water, for access to the dinghy. I caught hold, hauled myself up.

My head came above the gunwale, and met a reek of fish and diesel oil rising from the open cockpit. I was prepared to come face to face with another crew member, and had the speech ready: "Hello! *Inglis!* Can I come aboard?" Any old rubbish, as long as I kept it cheerful. But there was no one there. I called— not too loud. No reply.

So, keeping low to avoid being seen from the shore, I rolled over the gunwale and was aboard.

The cockpit was deep enough so that, as long as I crouched, I couldn't be seen. I began to search for the backpack. I knew, of course, that it was probably in the wheelhouse, but I'd tried the door and it was locked. So I thought I'd check the cockpit out first, pulling out coils of rope, empty fishboxes, to look behind them, and going through the lockers.

No joy. *Sod it!* I was going to have to get into the wheelhouse, or accept failure and retreat . . .

A soft thud on the side of the boat startled me. Oh *Christ!*
They can't be back this soon, can they? I should have kept a look
out, was going to, but had left it too late . . . Just have to brazen
it out—

A face appeared above the gunwale. Young, sunburned, with
a wispy golden beard and thin line of hair on the upper lip,
hardly a moustache. Blue eyes stared at me.

"*Scheisse . . .*"

He was as startled as I was. Then we both laughed. I said:

"*Willkommen!*"

"*Ja? . . . Aber . . . nicht Deutsch?*"

"English."

"*Ah so!* Engleesh!" He slipped in over the gunwale. What is
it about Germans that they're so keen on nudity? My parts were
decently obscured by Marks & Spencer underpants, soggy, but
civilized . . . I said:

"Speak English?"

"*Ja.* I speak."

"Good. What do you want?"

He shrugged, looked foxy. "I ask same question."

"Okay." There was only one way to tackle this—join forces.
"I think there are drugs on board."

"*Ja.* I think so."

"So, what shall we do?"

He considered, looked me up and down. I could imagine
what he was thinking: *He's not police, so what is he?* I said:

"Now's our chance—they may not be long."

He seemed to make up his mind. "Okay. We look, half for
you, half for me."

"Okay. I've already looked here, so they must be in the
wheelhouse, there. But it's locked."

He grinned. "No problem."

"Better not break it."

"No, no. No problem."

He looked round the cockpit, found a piece of wire . . . I moved to the side, and peered cautiously over the gunwale towards the shore. All clear.

It wasn't so easy. He muttered and cursed. Then he lost patience, seized a heavy galvanized shackle and broke the corner out of the glass in the wheelhouse door, put his hand through, and opened the door. *Oh, that's it! I'm an accomplice in burglary now! I hadn't meant to go this far . . .*

But we were in. The backpack was in the first locker we opened. Here was solid evidence . . .

There were two large tins in it. He pulled one out, wrenched the top off, swore.

"What is it?"

He showed it to me. Gray granules—not drugs, judging by his disappointment. What then?

"Boom," he said.

"What?"

"*Boom!* To kill feesh . . ."

"Oh, dynamite . . . *dynamite?*" I took a step back.

"*Ja, ja. Für Bomben. Sehen sie . . .*" He pointed to a shelf, where a stack of tobacco tins was stored. I lifted one down cautiously. There was what must be the fuse sticking out of one end. It looked harmless, ordinary, but . . . On impulse, I helped myself to a couple.

He was still looking for something. I said:

"There aren't any drugs. So what are you after?"

He didn't reply. I said:

"I'm going."

"Bye-bye," he said, without interrupting his search.

It was money, probably, and I didn't want to be involved in that. I slipped the two bombs into my underpants, and made for the shore.

*There were hardly 200 Men in the Town fit to bear
Arms, and the greateſt part were Renegadoes: that is to
ſay, Fellows without either Faith or Fidelity; who always
ſide with the ſtrongeſt, and ſeek for nothing but Plunder.*

Would I like to be rich? I wondered, as the dinghy sped out
to the yacht across the calm water of the harbor, the wake
catching the gold of the evening sky, and setting the smaller
boats rocking uncomfortably. Not that I ever will be—if I had
that kind of talent I'd have made it by now, perhaps twice
over—but how would it feel? It's a cliché, but the rich people
I've met haven't seemed wonderfully content with their lot:
more often, they've been short-tempered, worried, mostly
about what other rich people think of them. It's a competitive
business.

But I like the perks. Delightful to get the VIP treatment once
in a while: to be handed into the boat by Nikos, made to sit in

comfort while he gets his feet wet pushing us off, leaps in, deals with the oily outboard. He doesn't mind: he smiles, enjoys displaying his competence like a nursemaid with children.

Eléni was leaning over the rail with a smile of welcome as we came alongside. No scrambling with a rope ladder: there was a chrome and teak ladder slung, waiting. I ran up it lightly: the only lack was the shrilling of a bosun's pipe to acknowledge that visiting brass was aboard. I got a kiss on the cheek from Eléni instead.

"Come!" she said. "My uncle is in the saloon. We will have a drink there, while Nikos lays the table."

We were on the afterdeck: the bare table stood under a blue awning. "We're going to eat here?"

"Oh yes. Then you will have your sunset. But perhaps it will be too cold?"

"Not for me," I said, smiling. "Remember where I come from."

"Well, you must tell me if it is. Come, this way."

Oh yes, the full treatment! Or—horrid thought!—do I appear to her as *an older person,* needing to be protected from chills, placed away from draughts . . . Can't be more than fifteen years between us? And you often see Greek girls with the more mature type of man . . .

That's a thought! *Is Stavros really her uncle?* Ha! I'm not going to take that for granted, oh no. She herself said, as if it was a warning: Remember—*nothing is as it seems* . . .

"Ah, good evening, Mr. Warner!"

The uncle, or the sugar daddy, himself. "Good evening," I said. "And 'William,' please. 'Mr. Warner' sounds like someone I hardly know."

"I'm so sorry! Of course! Do forgive me." Again the firm, smooth handshake.

I took in the paneled, carpeted saloon. Books, pictures, glass-fronted cabinets of personal treasures, even what appeared to be a real coal fireplace. Reflections from the water made golden highlights on the ceiling. I said:

"With a room like this, I should never want to go out. And if you should get bored with the view, you can tell Nikos to change it."

Stavros chuckled. "I like what you say. It is always pleasant to have one's possessions admired, is it not? From childhood, it is so. What do you hear most, when children are playing? *'Mine! mine!, it is mine!'* It is best not to be ashamed of one's childishness, but to be honest and admit it. So, I am pleased you like my movable room."

"I think it's beautiful," I said. *And was Eléni one of his possessions? If enviability was the test, she easily qualified.*

"Now," Stavros said, "I have a very serious question to ask of you. May I?"

My pulse quickened. So we were through with fencing, and going to be frank, were we? All right by me—provided it was going to be a fair exchange. I looked at the broad smile, the brown intelligent eyes fixed on my face. I said:

"Of course."

"It is this. Do you like champagne?"

Oh, it's that tired old joke! To which I always make the same tired old reply . . . "I usually manage to force it down," I said.

"Good." He moved to a bell push at the side of one of the cabinets, and pressed it. "I should be most interested to have your professional opinion of it. Perhaps you will be able to impress us by telling us what it is."

"You're not going to spring a blind tasting on me, are you?" I said, perhaps rather too sharply. "People are always doing that, and I'm afraid I always refuse."

"William—I am very sorry," Eléni said, coming forward. "We did not mean to upset you."

"*I* didn't mean to be so blunt, Eléni, but . . . Well, I'd better explain. Even some quite knowledgeable people don't seem to realize just how sensitive wine is to temperature, movement, and serving. There's absolutely no point in giving me a glass of, for instance, white burgundy straight from the fridge, with all the taste frozen out of it, and then asking me to identify it as Le Montrachet. I'm sure you wouldn't waste good wine like that, but people who ought to know better sometimes do, and it leads to nothing but embarrassment all round. So I always refuse to play. Sorry."

"But William—you must taste wine sometimes in this way?" Eléni said.

"Oh yes, of course. Blind tastings are very useful, professionally organized, given the right conditions . . . Look, I'm sorry, I overreacted, automatically. Of course I'll give you my opinion, for what it's worth. Champagne's not so tricky, anyway. Forgive me."

"Thank you," Stavros said gravely. "And of course there is nothing to forgive. A professional does not like to be consulted on a social occasion—I should have remembered this. A surgeon prefers to discuss your appendix in his consulting room, not over the dining table. I understand perfectly how you feel. Now, here is the subject of our discussion. Let us simply drink it and enjoy it."

"No," I said, "I'll do my stuff."

The door at the far end of the saloon had opened, and Nikos came in, having replaced his sailor's T-shirt for a waiter's white jacket, and bearing a silver tray with three tall glasses on it. He distributed them, and went out. I said:

"Does Nikos do everything on this boat?"

"We have two more crew," Stavros said, "but they are ashore now. We have no need of them in harbor. Nikos can do all that is necessary, and he is an excellent cook—at least, I hope that you will think so."

"Sure I will," I said. "Well now—the mystery champagne."

He was watching me as I inspected, swirled, nosed, tasted,

considered, and finally swallowed. Oh ho. Sometimes the luck
is with you—he'd given me my own special favorite! I wasn't
going to make it look too easy though . . .

"Excellent!" I said. "Now then. French, of course—the
Spanish can't match that depth of flavor. One of the great
traditional houses. Not Krug—too bold for that. Nor Veuve
Clicquot, though La Grande Dame is somewhere near. Greek
shipowners are supposed to live on Dom Pérignon, aren't they?
No, I'm teasing you, it hasn't got the hint of almonds. How
about Bollinger RD? I'd throw in the year, seventy-nine, but
that would be cheating—we all know they keep it on the yeast
for ten years or so and haven't released any later vintage yet, and
that the seventy-six is getting hard to find."

Stavros had his head on one side, and his smile had broadened.
Oh Christ, I thought, *he's tricked me*—he's going to tell me it's
that new brand developed by French experts in India at an
amazing bargain price which I haven't got around to trying . . .

"Thank you," he said. In the background, Eléni had put
down her glass and was giving me a silent, ironical hand clap.

"I could still be just an enthusiastic amateur," I said.

Stavros pretended, mildly, to be shocked. "Now, really, you
must not think I doubted you. Why should I?"

"I'm hoping you're going to tell me that," I said. "But later
will do. Bollinger RD is not to be argued over."

He nodded. "Perhaps we can move to a position of mutual
trust. You *are* a wine merchant—or if not, you should be."

"Thank you."

"But you are not here either on business, or simply on holiday, I understand."

I glanced at Eléni, who made a deprecating gesture. I said:
"I've made no secret of that. I'm looking for a friend."

"Yes, Eléni has told me. And now that I am getting to know
you a little better, it begins to make sense."

"You mean, I seem crazy or naïve enough to take the job on?"

He tut-tutted. "Please! I think it is an admirable thing you are doing."

"It's not quite like that. I'm managing to amuse myself at the same time. Well, that was the intention. See Crete, catch up on old friends, that sort of thing."

"Good, good . . . And why not?"

"It's not turning out quite like that."

"No? How, then?"

Do I tell him? About Nick on the run, the shotgun-toting shepherds, the dynamite delivery . . . I said:

"Things keep happening . . . As an outsider, it's difficult for me to know what's coincidence, and what's linked."

His eyes were intent on my face. "Really! I wish you would tell me what you have seen, to make you think this?"

"I will."

"Ah."

"But first, I would like to know who *you* are, apart from Eléni's uncle."

He went on looking at me for a few moments, then smiled. "I see your glass is empty," he said. He crossed the saloon to the bell push, pressed it. Eléni said, to me:

"You are quite right, you know. Why should you answer all the questions, and ask none? I think we should all speak openly."

"It's a start to have you admit that there's something to speak about," I said wryly.

"Oh yes, I know. Of course you are suspicious of me, I understand it. Also, I am Greek. No one trusts a Greek, unless he is a fool—we say that ourselves."

I sighed. "Eléni, you're doing it *again*!"

"What am I doing?"

"Warning me not to trust anybody. Including yourself."

"It is because I like you," she said.

"Oh, terrific. You like me, and I like you, but nothing is what it seems, and anyway Greeks are not to be trusted. No wonder your songs are sad! Not to say bloody miserable."

"Po, po, po," she said. "Now you are upset again. I think, you know, you are very, very emotional for an Englishman. Let Nikos fill your glass. Then perhaps you will feel better."

I held it steady, and got a refill. I drank some. I didn't feel much better. She maddened me. What was it about her that she had this effect on me? Well, I didn't have to keep on absorbing it, letting her get away with it. "Listen," I said, "listen . . ."

"What is it?" she said mildly.

Stavros was opening one of the glass-fronted cabinets, over by the fireplace. I said quietly:

"I'd like to get one thing straight, before we go on from here. Is he your uncle, or . . . not?"

"Or not," she said.

"Oh." *Sod it!* "Well, thanks. Just wanted to know."

She looked at me curiously. Well, of course. What on earth had I been thinking of, anyway? She wasn't the sort of girl you could have a lighthearted fling with, and then go home and forget it. She said:

"We work together."

"What?"

"Of course, we are good friends as well. But not in the way you are thinking."

"I see." *Good news!* No, of course it wasn't good news, it was bloody awful, *terrible* news.

"You are not upset?" she said, looking into my face. "This will be the third time since you are on board, you know."

"An all-English record," I said, starting to laugh.

"Yes?"

"No. I mean, of course I'm not upset."

"You say this, but you laugh like a crazy man."

"Take no notice."

"Okay. Anyway, here is Stavros. So now we must be serious and all speak the truth. You also."

"I usually do," I said.

"Ah! So not always. There, you see, I *thought* you—"

"Eléni," I said.

"Yes, William?"

"Shut . . . *up*."

Stavros approached, carrying something from the cabinet. He stood it on a side table, stood back to admire it. He said:

"What do you think?"

"Oh no!" I said. "Wine's one thing, but don't ask me to give an opinion on your art collection."

"Please. Just look, tell me what you see."

I sighed. He really was making me work for my supper—it had better be worth it. I looked.

"A statuette, seven or eight inches high, made in painted pottery. She has a cheerful expression, an elaborate hairstyle, a long skirt, and big bare breasts which she's supporting with her hands—and at that size, they'd need it. But I suppose the gesture is meant to be generous, rather than cosmetic. That would make her a goddess rather than a harlot, but by the cheerful expression she could well be both. I like her."

It was the first time I'd heard Eléni laugh, a surprisingly deep, throaty sound. Stavros was wearing his broad smile, accompanying my speech with nods of agreement. He said:

"Exactly! I could not do better myself."

"Oh, I'm sure you could. The date, for instance."

"About two thousand five hundred B.C. Perhaps a little later, but not much."

"Over four thousand years old!" I bent to look more closely.

"Yes." He sounded confident.

"It's hard to believe—she looks so lively, so colorful and uncomplicated. Found on Crete?"

"Yes, she is early Minoan. As you say, she looks pleased with life, and it was indeed a golden age, with beautifully painted palaces, with music, games, and dancing, before the art of war spread from the mainland."

"Oh yes," I said, "I remember now."

"What do you remember?" Eléni asked.

"Something Maud said." What she'd said was that Nick had a book on the period. "So there was an invasion from the mainland which destroyed it all?"

"There are several theories," Stavros said, picking up the goddess and/or harlot, and taking her back to the cabinet. He opened it, and replaced her carefully, locking it afterwards. I said:

"Isn't it rather a risk, keeping her there? She must be almost priceless."

"The price was considerable, I will not tell you how much. As for the risk, I take what precautions I can. When we are at sea, and when I am not on board, she lives in my safe, in a special compartment," he said.

"But if there was an accident—I'm sorry, but if it didn't happen we wouldn't need insurance companies."

"If the ship goes down, she goes with it," he said simply. "It would be a loss to the world, but there are several others in museums, quite similar. So, as I am fortunate enough to be able to afford her . . ."

Mine, mine, she's mine . . . "It isn't a dilemma that's come my way," I said. "Or is ever likely to."

"She was full of life," he said, "the girl whose image this is. I do not think she would be happy in a museum, do you?"

"It's a point of view."

"Which you do not share?"

"Oh, I don't know. I suppose the authorities decide what is a national art treasure, and what is not."

"Yes," he said.

Something in his voice alerted me. I looked into his eyes, and saw what it was. "Oh."

"Quite."

Maud had told me, of course. *All* antiquities are public property, without exception. That's what the police had been looking for when they searched her house. I said:

"I'm honored. But *why?*" A word from me, and he could face arrest, trial, massive fine, or even prison sentence. The goddess was no trifle—they'd throw the book at him. There had to be a price for this demonstration of confidence. It had to be high, high enough to match the risk. And I hadn't asked for it: it had been thrust on me. Suppose I refused? *What then?*

"I believe in trust between friends," he said in a voice which, with its tone of deep, deliberate sincerity, sounded just like Spyro. So they're all at it, the strong as well as the seedy. Forcing obligations on you. *Alliances . . .*

"Indispensable," I said. It didn't sound as sincere as he had, but I'd work on it. How else was I going to find out what he intended?

"I'm so glad." *Oh no! Now he's holding out his hand! Of course I have to shake it.*

Nikos has appeared again, thank God. It must mean supper is ready.

"Nikos says that supper is ready," Eléni translates.

Yes, yes, yes . . . I had understood *that* much. It's the rest which is floating further and further out of reach.

Not lobster, but crab salad, which proved that Nikos had mayonnaise among his other accomplishments—I've seldom had better. Not Chablis, either, but a Greek white wine which was similarly flinty and delicious. I asked to see the bottle.

"Ah ha!" Eléni said.

"Yes, I'm ignorant . . . Santorini Boutari—it's new to me. Cretan?"

"No, but almost," Stavros said. "It is from the volcanic island of Santorini, a few miles to the northeast. You approve?"

"Very much."

"Good. And the crab?"

"Perfect."

"I am very pleased. Tell me—"

Is this it? He's being terribly, terribly casual . . .

"—have you had success in your search for your friend?"

Yes, this could be it . . .

"Up to a point," I said.

"You know where he is?"

"Not at present. But I've turned up a few clues . . . Do you know him?"

"Myself, no. But Eléni does, of course. And his . . . let us say wife, though I understand they are not in fact married."

"No. So, you are interested in Nick. Will you tell me why?"

"You have known him a long time?"

"A very long time. Maud was a friend of mine. Then we split up, and both got married to other people. Maud's marriage came to an end, and she then took up with Nick. They seem to suit each other. She's now a successful painter, and he is in effect her manager, but has other interests."

"Ah yes, so I have heard."

"Have you?"

He didn't respond. I said:

"I wish I knew more: it might help me to find him. Will you tell me what you know of him now?"

Stavros delicately wiped his mouth with a white linen napkin. I thought. *Come on! I've done all the talking so far.* He took his time. But then he said:

"I believe he is interested in antiquities?"

"Maud told me that, yes."

"As you have seen, I also am interested."

"You put it mildly," I said, smiling.

"Perhaps I do. In any case, we certainly have an interest in common. I am wondering if you would care to suggest to your friend that, knowing what you now do, a meeting might be mutually beneficial?"

It was oriental. I tried to grope through the mist of innuendo to the meaning beyond, but failed. "To compare notes? Exchange ideas?"

"Possibly," Stavros said, "rather more than that."

"More?" I looked to Eléni for help, but she was gazing at her plate, apparently withdrawn from the conversation.

"I have substantial funds available," Stavros said with a deprecating little shrug.

"I'm sure," I said, groping for a lifeline. "But . . . as I said, I really don't know where he is, at present."

"I'm sure you will find him," Stavros said. "As his friend, you will know best how to do so. And when you succeed—"

"I'll certainly give him your message, yes, of course."

"I would be most grateful. And also, if you would tell me when you have made the contact, however disappointing his reply may be. I am so sorry I cannot give you an address, because I am so much moving about, but Eléni always knows where I am to be found, and you could tell her, if that is not too inconvenient."

"That's easy enough," I said. I drank some wine to give my brain a little time to sort all this out. *Substantial funds available . . .* "Shall I tell Nick that you have something particular in mind?"

"I think not. In this field, it is more a question of what is available."

Let's have the cards on the table . . . "But you have a particular fondness, it seems, for Early Minoan. Or have I misunderstood?"

He looked at me with something like approval. "Excellent! I believe we understand each other very well now."

"I certainly hope so," I said.

A while after, this long carrot-bearded Trickster bid our
Convoy tell us that, to ſerve us, he expos'd himself not
only to the Infamy of the Baſtinade, but likewiſe to the
Forfeiture of all he was worth. This gave us a ſuſpicion
there was a Fellow-feeling between him and the Turk, and
that they jointly contriv'd to worm us out of our Mony:
the Greeks have not quite forgot thoſe ways of their
Forefathers in this Iſland, which Plutarch calls Cretiſm.

I was happy to be back in the gorge after the stuffy heat of
the coastal plain. By the time I'd climbed through the olive
groves and begun to negotiate the rockfall at the entrance to the
gorge proper, the morning sun had swung far enough south to
be on my back, dispelling the chill and gloom of the deepening
chasm. In the *sakoúli* was a packet of tomato and garlic sandwiches which I'd persuaded the hotel to make up, and a bottle
of Castello Minos. There was water in the gorge, if I climbed
down for it. I was feeling rested, well fed, optimistic.

Rested and well fed—that was undeniable. Memories of last
night's supper floated into my mind from time to time: after the
crab, there'd been lamb kebabs, spiced and interleaved with

herbs, grilled by Nikos on a charcoal barbecue at my elbow. The excellent wine had been Minos Palace from Miliarakis of Heraclion, a smooth red aged in oak and similar to Rioja. After that, honey cakes, coffee, and cognac, while the last rays of orange sunlight faded beyond the horizon and the world beyond the afterdeck and its blue awning became an unreal, starlit backcloth. When, eventually, Nikos was summoned to ferry me ashore, Eléni came too, to see me to the door as it were. It gave me a chance I needed. I spoke into her ear, above the throaty purr of the outboard.

"Wonderful evening, Eléni!"

"I hope so."

"Oh yes! I really mean it."

"Then I am very pleased."

"Thank Stavros again for me . . . And tell me something—I started to ask, several times, but he always managed to escape me: what does he do?"

"He is a businessman."

"Just that? He must be a very successful one!"

"Oh yes, he has many, many interests."

"Tell me."

"I will. Sometime."

"What do you do for him?"

"Research."

"What into?"

"Oh William!—so many questions!"

"It's because you work with him, as you said. I want you to tell me he's legitimate, that you're not working for a crook."

"Do you think I would?"

"No. But nothing is as it seems . . ."

"That is true."

"Then . . ."

"Not now. Come and see me, then we can talk. I will be back in Rethymnon on Sunday."

The boat grounded on the beach. Nikos leaped out, helped me with the vault to dry land.

"I will expect you!" Eléni called from her seat in the boat as Nikos pushed off and jumped in. Then the outboard restarted, and we could only wave. I watched the boat speed across the dark water and disappear behind the yacht, then went up the beach to the hotel.

Maddening! That was just one of the increasingly frequent moments when I wished I was a professional, had a badge to flip, the authority to insist on answers. Instead, I had to make do with what people chose to tell me, a mix, most likely, of crumbs of truth, half-truth, and damned lies. Not that I thought Eléni was an outright liar . . . But why not? There was no reason to *think* that—only, perhaps, to *feel* it. How far would a professional trust his instinct in a case like this? And with a girl like her? I could do with a professional's hard-boiled, seen–it–all cynicism too, that's for sure. Instead, I wanted to believe her on the side of the angels, which was like going to work with one hand tied behind my back.

No, let's be fair to myself. I want to believe that, but I'm reserving judgment. Reason tells me she could be Stavros's girlfriend, and that he could be Mr. Big in something horrible. Where did he get the money to buy that Minoan goddess? It must be worth, not just a bomb, but a *thermonuclear* quantity of cash. Four thousand years old! That *costs*! And he *must* be bent, as it's illegal to buy or sell antiquities.

He seems to be doing it for his own private pleasure, however: he freely admitted the kick he got from owning it. Whereas Nick . . .

Ah, yes, Nick. According to Stavros, Nick is dealing in antiquities. Could be true, though I didn't see any. Nick is up to something, and if it's antiquities he could have his stock hidden in the mountains near Arcadés, ready to be taken down the gorge for shipment out. That's one theory.

A second is that he's back into drugs, but on a larger scale than in the old days in London. In this theory, the goods come into Frangocastello by caïque from North Africa, and are taken *up* the gorge to Arcadés. Eléni says drugs are coming into Crete via the south coast, and my comrade in crime, the German hippie, was after what he hoped was a shipment . . .

But if that's what Nick's up to, where did Stavros get the idea that he trades in antiquities? He sounded sure, and Stavros is intelligent, a man who would take care to be well-informed and who can afford it. Take, for instance, his persistence in getting me to promise that I would let him know, through Eléni, when I'd located Nick. There were moments, then, when I felt sure he was about to offer me what is euphemistically described as "expenses" in situations of this sort—but then thought better of it. He was right—I would have refused, of course. For better or worse, Nick was my friend, and payment implied betrayal. A good dinner was all the bribe Stavros could risk . . .

Or was it?

Oh *no!* Not *Eléni?*

I was to contact *her,* not him. I was invited to her flat a second time, the day after tomorrow—*her* suggestion, not mine, on a pretext *she'd* created by refusing to talk now. All very smoothly done, oh yes. Was I meant to understand that she was—why do I hate the idea so much?—*on offer?*

I hate it because I didn't think she was cold-blooded, calculating, mercenary—and that's what it would mean. I hate to think that I could be so wrong about her. I hate it although I know I'm a passerby, that I'm going home soon, that I will never see her again . . .

Pull yourself together, fool. Or get someone to write the opera. Okay?

. . .

Going down, it's the ankles that take the strain. Going up, it's the knees. I wasn't doing too badly, though. Half-past ten, and I was nearing the narrows, where the rock walls close in and where, even from two or three hundred yards' distance, the path looks impossibly blocked. If I hadn't come down this way, I'd have been convinced it was. High above, against the sky, the first of the thorn bush/Indian warriors waited in ambush. It's a filmic cliché, of course—real warriors know not to appear on the skyline, for which the instant penalty is a faceful of hot lead. Yes, odd remnants of my two years' training in the art of killing on behalf of Queen and Country seem to be stuck in my subconscious, and often pop out to surprise me, like skeletons at a Ghost Train. This gorge, for instance: I can't deny I find it menacing. This must be because, in tactical terms, it's a highly dangerous location—but there isn't a war on, so why worry? No matter, it's an automatic assessment, and it's there at the back of my brain whether I want it or not.

No, it's there, and it only takes some little alarm signal, the shadow of a cloud or a bird, a sharp or unexplained sound, to bring it to the surface. A rattle of stones, for instance—

A rattle of stones . . .

Could be a small landslip. The steep cascade of loose shale back there is built of a million small smooth flakes, each one slipping over those below until it arrives at a point of perilous equilibrium. Then something happens to disturb the balance, and off they go again. Rain makes them slippery, wind adds just that touch of external force . . .

Well no, not today. Everything's as dry as a desert, and inside the gorge it's sheltered, silent, the air hardly moving.

Most likely it's an animal, then. A goat . . .

Did we see any when we passed?

No, but they can appear from nowhere.

Some other animal, then.

Yes.

Such as—

Of course, of course, just what I was thinking. The two-legged kind. The Courier, perhaps, on his way back up.

Perhaps. Nervous?

No, no . . . Not nervous, exactly, but . . .

Why not take a look then?

Well, I mean, I'm sure there's nothing to . . . it's really not worth going to a lot of . . . Perhaps I will.

I climbed to a projecting boulder, and eased myself forward over the painfully hot surface. No, I wouldn't be on the skyline—the cliff face was behind. There was a better view down the valley than I would have got by going back down the path, and though I'd lost a little time, I'd kept my distance.

I saw them at once, four figures just my side of the shale landslip. Once again, I wished Maud had been able to find Nick's binoculars, or that I'd brought my own, a miniature Zeiss pair that fit in a shirt breast pocket . . . Well, I hadn't.

Four figures, striding up the track towards me. Not shepherds: they looked too tall, too thin. Too far to see what they were wearing, but there was an impression of paleness about their upper halves—white shirts, or even no shirts at all. One was smaller, could have long hair—a girl, then. So, they're tourists . . .

Tall tourists. Exploring the gorge—and why not.

Or tall tourists *not* exploring the gorge. In other words, a bunch of German hippies . . .

I scrambled off the boulder and set off up the track at the best speed I could manage. I'm not prejudiced against Germans, well, not more than any other Englishman whose father escaped their gas and machine-gun attacks on him at Ypres only to find that, twenty years later, they'd sent the Luftwaffe to his home address to try again. And as for hippies, I feel a nostalgic affection for the original, genuine, love 'n' peace article, now in their balding forties and doing their own thing on the metal market or in multiple retailing . . . No, I mean hippies like the one I'd got into an unintentional partnership with on the caïque, the new breed which goes on holiday with enough money for two weeks and stays for several months. The budget has to be balanced and so it is by means of muggings and burglaries, not hesitating to use pickax handles to break in doors and the heads of guard dogs, and car chains to drag out window grilles. Other countries produce them as well, but the German version is bigger, stronger, and hungrier . . . And there were four of them coming this way.

I wasn't going to outstrip them, I knew that. They were younger and fitter, and would catch up with me before I reached the top of the gorge.

There was no way out of the gorge except by the path.

Only one thing to do, then.

Go to ground . . .

I moved on at the best speed I thought I could sustain, the faster pace already beginning to tell on lungs and leg muscles. Ten minutes, and I turned to look back. I could see a hundred and fifty, two hundred yards down the track, and it was still clear. I set off again, safe for the moment, but aware that time was running out. I had to find my hiding place soon, before they caught sight of me. Within the next five minutes, not more . . .

Ahead, the gorge closed in further, with sides that rose sheer to the sky. I remembered coming down: it was from there that I'd seen the plain and the castle for the first time, far below. The watercourse below the path was squeezed to a narrow torrent spilling over boulders, open to view. It was no place to be caught . . .

Here, then. It has to be here, *now.* Whatever I can find, the best available . . .

I was coming to a rock formation that had resisted erosion while the softer ground to each side was washed away. It stood out from the cliff face, house high, a natural buttress, cutting into the line of the path, which was forced to make a frightening swerve on a ledge high above the stream to get round it. On the way down, even the sure-footed donkeys had balked at it.

But I wasn't out to hold the pass: it wasn't the narrow path, but the buttress that interested me. If I could get up there, out of sight, the hippies should overtake me without knowing it. Even if they realized what had happened later, and turned back, I'd have had some time to decide what to do next: to stay hidden, or make off down the track to safety . . .

If I could get up there . . . that was the question.

The near side was almost vertical: an experienced climber might have got up there, but I couldn't. In any case, all my instincts were screaming, "*Go on, get round it, and out of sight . . .*"

I followed the path round, hardly aware, this time, of the drop from my right elbow to the stream below—I had other things on my mind. On the far side, the buttress was not so steep. It looked climbable. There were ledges to provide footholds—most had clumps of prickly shrubs clinging to them, but once I was up, they'd provide cover.

Go for it!

I began to climb. Ten feet, fifteen, twenty . . . I'd hoped the buttress might have a flat top, but it hadn't. I reached the top, where it joined the cliff face, and raised my head just enough to see over . . .

Jesus! They've caught up fast! A mere hundred yards away now, and going like hounds on a scent.

I looked for the best place to hide. I wouldn't need it until they passed the rock, and not even then unless they looked back . . . but I had to assume they would.

Where?

A chill seemed to start in my stomach and then spread . . .
Come on! There must be *somewhere?*

The rock sloped to the north, the side I'd just climbed up.
There was an excellent view of the path as it wound its way
further up the gorge . . . Excellent, that is, if you aren't on this
bloody rock *for the express purpose of trying to hide from anyone
looking back from that path . . .*

I looked over the top of the buttress again, and hurriedly
pulled my head down. *Fifty yards now . . .*

Far too late to look for anywhere else. *Choose the biggest clump
of shrub,* and lie flat behind it . . .

This is the second time I've had a close-up of Crete, a genuine
worm's-eye view, and frankly, I hope it's the last. The smell of
crushed herb is delightful—but why does the place have to be
so goddamn *prickly?*

They passed, of course. I had an anxious moment as the German
voices echoed off the rocks opposite, sounding so close that I
thought they might have guessed my ploy, and were climbing
the rock to check it out. But then the echoes shifted, and
looking through the spiny shelter of the shrub that was at least
obscuring my outline, I saw the four of them striding up the path
and away. From the back, it was hard to tell if any of them was
the one I'd already come across, but one was certainly a girl, long
blond hair swaying from side to side, ample buttocks quivering
in tight white shorts as she pounded after the men.

I lay still, feeling sweat crawl from my armpits and trickle over
my ribs. I felt relief, then anticlimax, then irritation at myself for
going to such lengths to counter what was almost certainly a
nonexistent threat, caused by the oppressive atmosphere of this
gorge working on an overactive imagination. That girl's buttocks . . . I mean, they were so *normal,* so domestic . . . They

wouldn't have brought her if they were after me with intent to commit robbery with violence . . . Of course not. What they're doing is taking a day off from the beach to walk the gorge, to see what's up there, and the purposeful speed is just that German energy they apply to everything they do. So, I got it wrong. All the same, it's better to take too many precautions than too few. *One* too few is all it takes for a catastrophe to happen.

So I'm safe rather than sorry. And what now? Do I follow them up, or wait here (or in some better place) until they come back and *then* go on, or get down now and head straight back?

I don't know. Think I'll have a swallow of wine and think about it. They're safely out of sight, now.

I sat up, pulled the drawstrings of the *sakoúli* apart, and took out the wine bottle. I pulled out the already half-drawn cork, and drank straight from the bottle: just a single mouthful, to give my stomach something to think about while my nerves finished the process of returning to normal. Although I was on the north side of the rock, the sun was now almost at its midday highest, and it was hot, hot, *hot!* The glare off the rocks further up the path, facing due south, was tremendous . . .

Did something flash, by the path up there? *Yes*—there it is again. A tiny but brilliant flash, like the sun reflected off a camera lens. Or . . .

Binoculars . . .

They haven't gone on. They're smart, and they suspected I might do this. Perhaps they knew when I left, how far ahead I was . . .

No matter. What am I going to do now, because . . .

Here they come!

It was the one I'd already met who opened negotiations—and it was immediately clear that that's what they were. He stood at the bottom of the rock, shading his eyes with his hand, and shouted:

"Hello, Engleesh!"

"Hello," I called back. "So you're not going all the way up today?"

He laughed. "Today, no. Today we like it here."

"It's a nice spot."

He laughed again. The others were grinning. Not the girl, though, who, I now noticed, was the one carrying the binoculars. She scowled, said something in German. The youth nodded, and shouted up:

"She says, we waste time. Throw down the *Rucksack*."

"What?"

"You heard me. Throw it down."

"Of course I won't! Look, you're going to get into trouble if you—"

"Or we will come for it. Then you will be sorry."

"You'd better be on your way. I know who you are, and where to find you. The police will be on you like a—"

"Police! Ha! You will tell the police?"

"Of course!"

"I think you will not. I think you forget where we meet, and what you are doing there. No, that is no good. You must throw down the *Rucksack now*. I advise it. For your health."

He stood, grinning up at me. I would have liked to hurl a rock at his golden-fringed, mocking face—and there were plenty suitable lying ready to hand—but it wouldn't have been wise, not with three of them ready to rush me. Persuasion was the only way I was going to get out of this. They were only youths, I just might succeed. I shouted:

"Not a chance. Go on home, back to the beach. I haven't got anything you'd want, anyway."

He shook his head, still grinning. "We think you have. So, I ask you one more time. Then we will come up. You will be sorry."

Oh *Christ*! Because of what happened on the caïque, he thinks I'm into drugs. Maybe the stuff *does* come in through this gorge, and he thinks I've got a load in the backpack . . . Maybe I'd better take my wallet out, and throw the rest down, so he can see I haven't . . .

"I'll throw the bag down," I shouted. "But you'll be disappointed, unless you like tomato sandwiches."

The girl was scowling and talking again. Her voice was loud, harsh, authoritative . . . *My God, I thought, she's the leader . . .*

The youth shouted: "We think you hide it. So we come up now. Do not try to stop us."

"Wait," I shouted, "I'm going to throw the bag down. Wait till you see what's in it."

He consulted the girl, who nodded. "Okay," he shouted, "but you better be quick. We lose time."

The *sakoúli* was beside me, already open. They couldn't see exactly what I was doing with it behind the prickly bush, but they could see I was doing *something* . . .

"No good to hide it!" he shouted. "So, we come up *now*!"

I wasn't happy about what I was doing, no, not at all. But neither did I want them beating me up to find out where I'd hidden the package I hadn't got, or stealing my wallet with passport, money, credit cards, jeep keys . . . Well, I *was* going to warn them. They'd better believe it!

My other worry was, I didn't know what length of fuse was in it. Must be somewhat haphazard, anyway, judging by the missing fingers I'd seen . . .

I flicked the lighter, breathed deeply, and applied the flame to the end of the fuse. It caught, and started hissing. So I stood up, and shouting "*Bombe!*" half threw, half slid it down the rock, adding "*Achtung!*" as an afterthought.

I heard the tin rattle its way down, and saw the blank faces suddenly switch to comprehension as the youth screamed a warning. He knew, he'd seen me steal the things. Then they scattered, two up the path, the youth who'd done the talking and the girl round the rock to take cover there. They're the brains behind this lot, obviously.

Seven, eight, nine. Nothing. *Nothing.* If it doesn't go off, all I've done is annoy them. Twelve, thirteen, fourteen— *BANG!!!!*

So it worked. An impressive din which echoed up and down the gorge for some time, plus a spray of stone shrapnel—one of the youths who'd run up the path instead of taking cover was apparently hit by a piece because he's sitting down, holding his hand to the back of his head. Nothing worse, thank God. So, that's one down, but two more and the girl still in action. Are they scared? Or mad? That's the question.

There's a conference going on around the fallen warrior. To go home, or come and get me. I have a feeling they're not going to give up—young men don't like to when there's a girl looking on. Of course, she might decide for them . . . but, on the evidence so far—the scowls, the commanding voice—she's more likely to order an advance than a retreat. And I've got one bomb left . . .

If I hadn't shouted a warning, my troubles might now be all over . . . Well, no, forget that. I *had* to, and I'll have to next time . . . Unfortunately, they *know* that, now . . .

Look out, *look out,* here they come. Just two, leaving the injured one sitting, and the girl watching me carefully. The two are collecting stones . . . so that's it, we've slipped back a few millenia and are going to war the old-fashioned way. I've got plenty of stones up here, luckily, and I've got the height, too . . . I reckon I can hold them off . . .

Yes, but for *how long?* They can take turns attacking, but I've got to be on guard *all* the time. I'm going to get tired, careless . . .

Perhaps someone will come before then. Meanwhile, might as well fire off the first stone before they get any closer . . . Mmmm, he felt the wind of that. And here comes the return fire—*Christ!* That was close. *Too* close. I'll hold the faithful *sakoúli* in my left hand to help ward them off . . .

They're gaining ground. I scored a hit, but nothing serious, and he's back in action again already. I'm getting a very uncomfortable feeling this is not going my way . . .

Should I surrender? Goes against the grain, both the idea, and the thought of them getting away with my wallet . . . But they're getting closer all the time, working their way up the ledges, taking hits but coming back. Oh *shit*—I'm going to have to fight them hand to hand . . . And I'll lose, no chance.

And what the hell am I *doing* here, anyway?

Yes! I scored with a kick, and one's gone rolling down again. But the other is on me. We fall, me underneath. Now there's a piece of rock under me, trying to excavate my spine. Plus his hands round my throat. The boy's a madman, and *strong*—I think he's trying to kill me . . .

The trouble is, I'm not as interested in this as he is. I don't want to kill *him*, I just want to prevent him killing *me*. It takes the fire out of what I'm—

What was that?

This is it, I'm afraid. I never expected to go this way, fighting, shot . . . yes, it was a shot. *There's another.* Why didn't they use it before, the gun I mean?

He's taking his hands off my throat, this blond beast with murder in his eyes. An Arab woman told Lawrence of Arabia that his blue eyes gave her the shudders, looked like the sky shining through empty eye sockets . . .

I seem to be free. I shall try to sit up . . . Yes. Nothing broken, apparently. The boy is standing, a sullen expression on his face, but with his hands raised in surrender.

But who to?

Well, well, well . . . So that's who! There are three of them, each armed with a long-barreled .32 Smith & Wesson revolver, not that the details matter. The leader has shifted his to his left hand, the better to help me to my feet with his right.

"Thank you, Nikos," I tell him.

Nobody ever said it more sincerely.

*In every Houſe there's Merry-making; ſome dancing,
others eating and drinking: in ſhort, this Nation, ſo grave,
and which always ſeems to be on one pin, is of a ſudden
quite off the hinges, and run about like ſo many mad
things: happy that theſe Feſtivals return no oftner. Your
Lordship will believe me, without ſwearing, that we were
perfectly ſick of theſe Gambols . . .*

h dear," Maud said, screwing up her face with what looked
more like distaste than alarm. But then she put a hand across the
table towards me, a mark of great emotion in one so reserved.
I put out mine to meet it, and said:

"Don't worry about it. I feel fine now, apart from the
bruises."

"Oh well, I do hope so . . . But you might have been—"

"Well, I wasn't."

"Thanks to this . . . Stavros?"

"Stavros, yes. I never got to know his surname. It was all
terribly friendly."

She frowned. "You can't doubt that, can you? You said Eléni

was on the boat with him. And he did send his men to make sure
you were safe?"

"Eléni was there. And I assumed that the two crewmen on
shore had seen the hippies start off after me and raised the alarm.
Probably they did."

"You're not so sure now?"

"Nothing is as it seems," I said.

"Why do you say that?"

I didn't reply. I was going through it yet again. I'd felt pretty
good, watching the defeated hippies limp off down the gorge,
felt even better when I understood that Nikos and his men had
orders to see me safely to Arcadés. My personal bodyguard, as if
I were a mafia boss. I didn't have to worry about the brothers,
if they were still up there. My three would easily see them off,
no trouble.

We walked in single file, the two new men in front, then me,
then Nikos as rear guard, without unnecessary hurry, but at a
steady pace such as real professionals in any field adopt, to save
their energy for emergencies. All three wore an informal uniform of dark blue T-shirts, dark blue cotton slacks, blue canvas
shoes with thick rubber soles. Nikos carried a canvas bag slung
across his shoulder, and was the only one to sport dark glasses.
Each had his Smith & Wesson stuck into the back of his waist-
band, handy but unobtrusive if we should meet anyone coming
down the path. With that long barrel, it was a marksman's
weapon, and revolvers are more reliable than automatics, which
jam . . . I loved it all: the calm, the equipment, the obvious
competence.

Twenty minutes passed, half an hour. The men exchanged
the occasional comment, or joke, but mostly we marched in
silence. And I'd begun to organize my thoughts.

I *owed* Stavros now. He wouldn't be unhappy about that, oh
no. It was the Greek system Spyros had demonstrated so clearly
in the restaurant: no gift without a purpose. Stavros had a call on

me now. And he'd already told me what he wanted: to know where Nick was . . .

But *why* did he want to know? And what did I think of Stavros now, since he'd sent his private army to protect me? Why did he *need* a private army? For that's what they were: not a casual posse of crewmen armed with anything that came to hand, but disciplined professionals: I enjoyed the competence, yes, but what it told me about Stavros wasn't encouraging. Men who hire bodyguards aren't usually on the side of the angels, are they.

More time went by, and more thoughts. Was I *really* being protected, or had Stavros *organized* the hippie attack in order to rescue me and gain my confidence . . . Oh no! That can't be right—that youth could have killed me, I saw it in his eyes. No, it was a genuine rescue, no doubt about that.

But it could have been accidental, a lucky chance. Nikos and his men were on the way to overtaking me, and happened on the attack. Because of that, I'd been pleased to go along with them, but suppose there'd been no attack—what were their instructions? Were they to escort me somewhere, whether I wanted it or not? In which case they're not the bodyguard I'd assumed, but an *armed guard,* with me under arrest . . .

Later, after I'd been allowed to direct the way through Arcadés and down the path to the clearing, I felt that that theory could be safely discarded. Nick's Hyundai had gone but, much to my relief, the Suzuki jeep was still there, and apparently untampered with. I hadn't expected the brothers to have had the patience to be watching still, but if they were, they kept out of sight. I got in, put the key into the ignition. The engine started easily. Everything seemed to be fine, and my doubts and fears took a backseat. Nikos closed the car door for me, stood back politely, and smiled. Then he stepped forward again and tapped on the window. I opened it, and found the butt end of a Smith & Wesson on offer. Well . . . yes! I took it, followed by a handful

of gold, spare ammo. Very kind, most thoughtful . . . Nikos
stood back again and, with a fine display of salutes and smiles
from both sides, I drove off. It was a pity that, on balance, they
had to be villains . . .

It was nearly six before I felt I could leave Maud to think over
what I'd told her, and go down to my cell for an hour or so
before supper. My bruises were playing up, and I was feeling
stiff, sore, and in need of a nap. I got out of my clothes, and lay
down on the driftwood bed, pulling a sheet over me, more to
keep the flies off than for warmth. I couldn't live in this climate:
it's all right for lounging about in, but as soon as you try to do
anything, you're encapsulated in sweat—horrible! Well, I'd
soon be back in London . . .

How soon? And what more could I do? I'd told Maud everything that had happened, but she hadn't been able to add it up
any better than I could. We had a series of events, a catalogue
of suspicions, but no conclusion. We now knew where Nick
was—or rather, where he had been three days ago, but not what
he was doing. I didn't like to speculate to Maud as I had to
myself, but she herself said, without prompting, that she would
have suspected drugs were at the bottom of it, if she could see
any way in which he could have distributed the stuff. It wasn't
that easy, was it? And surely she would have noticed something—
what was he doing with the money, for instance? They were still
living on her allowance from Guy, though things had been quite
a bit easier since her paintings started to sell. But Nick never had
any money of his own, he was as broke as always.

I waved the flies off my face, but they were back in a moment.
Like my problems . . . I stirred without managing to swat. Maud
seemed to assume I'd be going up to the mountains again, but
I didn't much fancy my chances of finding him a second time,
now that he was alerted. I'd have the brothers on my tail again,

too. I'd debated with myself whether to tell Maud about them, but finally thought she'd better know: it explained why she, and I, had got the cold shoulder from their faction in the village. Maud was indignant, then contemptuous. "She's a *waitress*, William! Well, call me a snob, but she's just a village girl, pretty, but that's all. And frankly, Nick's at the age when he's losing interest in *that* sort of thing, well, so am I, we all are, aren't we. They're quite, quite *mad*, those Gyparis!"

A chilly thought! Not the Gyparis brothers—who could be avoided—but losing interest in all *that* . . . At *our* age? I didn't like to contradict Maud, and it would have sounded smug, but the fact is, Claudine and I . . . no, never mind, it's Nick and Maud we're looking at. Maud never was very keen on all *that*, so perhaps she's quite glad Nick's gone off the boil, or is generalizing from her own experience.

Anyway, I've had quite enough for today. I'll let the bruises wear off this evening, call on Eléni tomorrow, and then see what I think. Meanwhile, until supper, and if the flies will let me, a zizz . . .

It was the German hippies again, but this time they had a machine gun! And I wasn't me, I was my father . . . The sides of the trench were muddy, I couldn't get a foothold. And I knew, any moment now, I'd see the muzzle poke over the edge, aim at my stomach, and then— ratatatatatat . . .

I found myself sitting bolt upright. Silence. Then I heard it again:

Ratatat. Ratatat. Ratatatatatat.

Jesus! That *is* a machine gun!

I swung my legs off the bed, grabbed my clothes, and scrambled into them. The gun fired twice more while I was dressing: short bursts which echoed down the valley. Then I was on my way to the terrace from where I could see into the valley, not forgetting to snatch up the Smith & Wesson from under the bed.

Maud was up there. She was laying the table. Some people resort to simple tasks in times of stress, to steady their nerves. She looked up, did a double take, and stood staring.

"Don't worry," I said, lowering the revolver. "But I'd better find out what's going on. Thought I might be able to see something from up here."

"It's a wedding," she said.

"What?"

"A wedding."

"Oh my God! Clan rivalry broken out, has it?"

"No. They just like the noise."

"The *noise!* You mean, like *fireworks?* Is that all?"

"I think so."

"But Maud—you wouldn't know, but that's a machine gun someone's letting off down there! A *serious* weapon."

"I think I've heard it before," she said, "but I'm sorry if it woke you up. Perhaps you'd like a drink."

"I think I would."

"The whiskey's in the living room, if you'd like to help yourself. And William—I'm afraid we've got Spyro and his wife coming any minute now. She came yesterday with your message from Claudine, and I rather had to ask her."

"I don't mind at all," I said. "But I'm surprised she accepted, though, if she knew I was going to be here."

"I thought you got on quite well the other evening?"

"That wasn't my impression."

"Oh. Well, then she's revised her opinion. She asked us both down there, but I really couldn't face another of Spyro's evenings, so I said it was our turn and asked them up here for a drink before supper. Then they can't stay too long."

· · ·

"Hi! Good evening!" Spyro called up the steps to the terrace. "Hello. Do come up," Maud called over the railing. She turned away, smile switched off and face glum.

He appeared first, Jeanine following. "So William is back! Good, good. This is very, very nice!"

I shook his hand, touched cheeks with Jeanine. A whiff of *Je Revien* slid into my nostrils. I said:

"So Claudine telephoned?"

"Yes, I have a nice little talk with her." *How do French women get their teeth so white?*

"Kind of you to pass on the message. I couldn't think of any other way to—"

"It was no trouble."

"Well, thank you anyway."

Maud was looking hopelessly at a collection of half-empty bottles. I excused myself, and went to the rescue. "What would we all like? There's whiskey, village wine, sundry types of fruit juice . . ." They all had whiskey, *my* whiskey. Maud didn't even *like* it, I knew that, but stood holding the glass apathetically. I made a mental note to get some more in Rethymnon tomorrow.

Spyro herded me towards the side of the terrace overlooking the valley, and waved a proprietorial hand at the sunset. "Nice, eh?"

"Beautiful."

"Yes, beautiful . . . Now tell me, how is my good friend Nick? You saw him, right?"

"Yes, I saw him, briefly. He's okay."

He waited, but I didn't add to it. He said:

"I worry about old Nick, you know. I lie in bed, nights, and I think: what is this trouble he is in? Then I think, I must do something, anything, to help him."

"Nice of you," I said.

"No, no, not nice. This is how I get, you know, when a friend is in trouble." He tilted his face round to see into mine: his large brown eyes scanned north–south, east–west . . .

"I think he's okay," I said.

"You think so?"

"Well, whatever he's doing up there, he wasn't asking for help," I said.

"Oh, Nick, he is like this. But I think he got some trouble, all the same. Listen, when will you see him again?"

"I don't know that I will."

"Oh yes, I am sure you will. Tomorrow maybe?"

"No, certainly not tomorrow."

"What you do tomorrow?"

"I'm going to Rethymnon."

"Aha!" He looked round. Maud and Jeanine were talking, or making social noises. "You see Eléni, right?"

"Probably."

"Aha, yes, very good. Now, that is one helluva nice kid. I think so myself, very much." He winked.

"It's nothing like that," I said.

"Okay, okay. I understand." His face became serious again. "So, you see Nick the day after?"

"Spyro, I really don't know where he is, now."

"Well, you find him once, you find him again. So listen, when you see him, tell him from me: '*Spyro is ready.*' Right? You will do that?"

"Ready for what?"

"Whatever he want. You got that? *Whatever he want, I am ready.*"

I gave up. "Okay."

"Good, *good.* I think we understand very well."

There was a rattle of shots from lower down in the village. I said, as a diversion:

"So that's a wedding going on, is it?"

"A wedding, yes. Some guy that don't know what's coming to him, eh? Aha, aha!"

I chuckled politely.

"You want to see?" Spyro asked.

"See the wedding?"

"Yes, yes. If you want, I take you."

"Well, I was rather thinking of——"

"Lotsa food, drinks, dancing . . . Oh yes—you like it very, very much."

"I wouldn't like to go without being asked."

"What? Oh, no problem. You come with me, everybody know me. I think they will be very pleased."

"And in any case——"

"They are not like you and me, you understand. No, these are poor people, country people. Very poor, very simple. So they will be pleased to see me and my friend from London. Oh yes, I am sure."

I went, partly to please Maud, who after an hour of Spyro was visibly wilting. But also, because I realized that my instinctive passive resistance to Spyro's importunities was a mistake. Instead of clamming up, I should be making friends, dealing in confidences. At Spyro's supper party, Jeanine had been polite, but discouraging: this evening, she was positively friendly, a significant change of attitude. I had something they wanted, so now they were prepared to talk. If I hadn't been so tired, I'd have realized this earlier, but everything was still on offer, nothing had been lost. My only problem was going to be staying awake and alert enough to profit from the exchange.

Jeanine came: Maud firmly opted out, saying she'd seen it all before, and the noise gave her a headache. I thought I should stay to eat the supper she'd already prepared, and join Spyro later, but she said it wasn't anything much, and what she didn't eat herself would keep for tomorrow. So we left her on her own, looking more than content to be so.

Spyro led the way down through the village—not that a guide was needed, the noise was enough. It was almost dark, but in the narrow streets there were pools of warm air where the sun-baked walls were breathing out the heat of the day. At one point there was a soft hooting from above, and I looked up to see a little white owl sitting on a power cable, blinking down at me, unperturbed by the display of Cretan firepower which was shattering the evening a hundred yards further on.

We rounded a last corner and there was the wedding party: a hundred or more villagers milling round long tables, covered with white sheets, laid out in a wide street in front of the church. A barbecue fire was being coaxed to life, sending clouds of smoke drifting down the street. On the steps of the church, three musicians were tuning their lutes, and snatches of tunes, chords, runs were blasting, painfully amplified, from loudspeak-ers. A group of children, jointly supporting a single huge candle dressed up with a long white tulle skirt, proceeded solemnly through the crowd, and back again. A tall, black-skirted, white-bearded *papas* watched them from the church door. Old men sat solitary and motionless, magnificent in tall boots and embroi-dered waistcoats, some with a wife or daughter in attendance. Younger men sat in rows, eyeing the girls and each other. The girls stood in groups, giggling. Mothers fussed, children ran. I said:

"Spyro—are you sure . . ."

"Of course!" he said. "We are welcome. We sit here."

We sat at an outer, empty table. Two tables away, a hand appeared above the heads, flourishing a large automatic pistol. Four or five rounds blasted off into the night. From a distant table, two other pistols replied. Our neighbor fired again, emp-tying his magazine, and lowered the gun for reloading. I caught

a glimpse of his face: there was no particular expression on it.
Perhaps the gun spoke for him, the shots were all he had to say.

"The *papás* retreated into the church when the firing broke
out," I said. "Not fright, but tact, I suppose?"

"Sure," Spyro said, nodding. "He don't like it, but what can
he do? Better to see nothing, hear nothing. That way, no trouble
with the police . . . Hey, wait. I gotta talk to that guy—just a
moment, please."

He got up and dived into the crowd. Between strollers, I saw
a lot of handshaking and gesticulating, then waves in our direction. Then he returned, looking pleased.

"Okay. Like I said, we are very welcome."

"Good."

"You like it here, eh?"

"Very interesting."

"Soon, bride will come. Then we start. You hungry?"

"I'm okay, thanks. No hurry."

"Good, good . . . Listen, I just had wonderful idea!"

"What?"

"I come *with* you, day after tomorrow! We look for Nick
together! How about that?"

I choked back my automatic reply. "You want to do that?"

"Sure, you bet. Why not."

"Perhaps you're right. We should join forces."

"Right! I am very glad you think this."

"Compare notes."

"Exactly! Oh, this is very good."

I thought: *Right, my friend! Let's see what's on your side of the
bargain.* "So, tell me what your interest in Nick is."

I watched his eyes pause in their habitual search pattern,
become still, and concentrate on my face. He said:

"My interest?"

"Yes."

He tried to look puzzled, decided a diversion would be safer,

turned to Jeanine as if for explanation, but she hadn't been able
to follow what we were saying for the festive hubbub all around,
and he was left to play it solo. Turning back to me, he said
reproachfully:

"It's like I told you: Nick is my very good—"

"Apart from his being your friend."

"Apart from . . . Listen, what more can I say?"

"You've got interests in common, I think."

"What you mean? Why you say this?"

It was my turn to perform. I shook my head, sadly, woefully
disappointed. "I thought we were going to work together."

"Right!"

"Then I must be able to speak freely."

"You can! You can!"

Time to offer a nugget. "As you know, I've been to Frangocastello."

"Was Nick there? Is that where you saw him?"

"He wasn't there. But that's where the stuff comes in, of
course. Or is that all over, now?"

"Stuff?"

I looked hard at his face. He was attempting ignorance, but
it was badly overdone. A ham. A small-time blusterer. I had
thought there might be something useful behind the bluster, but
not anymore.

"Spyro, this is going nowhere," I said.

He looked at me, made tentative passes at a number of possible expressions, and finally settled for his favorite, sincerity.
"Okay. I'm gonna really trust you," he said. "Right?"

I decided to play. "Right!" I said. "And Spyro, I really appreciate it, believe me."

He looked round to see if anyone was listening. Because that's
the gesture you make before confiding a secret.

. . .

It was drugs, of course. No, what I mean is, that's what he *said*. And, of course, he was totally innocent himself. He had heard that drugs were coming in by this route, and was afraid that Nick had somehow got involved.

"So listen, you and me, we gotta get up there and save the poor guy."

"Save him?"

"Sure. We gotta find him, and talk him out of it."

"You think we can?"

"I don' know. But we gotta try, right?"

"So you're dead against drugs, yourself?"

He made his eyes pop. "How can you *say* that? Listen, let me tell you something. I hadda friend . . ."

He told me about his friend. Who got the habit, couldn't kick it, oh Jesus how awful. At the funeral, leaning over the grave, he cursed all those involved in the abominable trade. Nick was a nice guy, really nice, one of the best, he just didn't *realize* . . . So we gotta *explain* it to him, William. Right?

It was hard work, I must say, listening to him listening to himself spinning me this fable, convinced he was doing a terrific job. But I had to listen, pretend to believe. Later, I could try to work out what lay between the lines.

Other people were drifting to our table, now, and soon we were full up. I got some curious looks, but Spyro explained who I was, a visitor from England. More conversation which I couldn't understand, and people were smiling and nodding approvingly. I said:

"What are you telling them, Spyro?"

"I tell them you have ten children, all sons, and you think Crete is most beautiful place in all the world, you wish you can stay forever."

"Is that all?"

"It's all they want," he said cheerfully.

I grinned. *Tell them what they want to know.* That was Spyro.
He did it to everyone. He'd just done it to me.

I stay on, to see the bride and groom arrive to applause, and take
their place at the center table, behind a brass candelabra. Girls
come round with trays of small glasses containing sweet, colored
liquor—one sip, then you replace the glass for the next guest.
Then we all get a spoonful of honey and walnut—same spoon
for everyone.

After that, the feast proper. Liter bottles of village wine and
Fanta lemonade bottles of *rakí* are already on the table with the
first course in dishes covered with cling film. Jeanine uncovers
one. Almonds, raisins, olives: *oréktika,* she says—hors d'oeuvres.
Spyro pours red wine into paper cups and passes them round. A
little later, youths bring dishes loaded with enormous chunks of
boiled mutton, all greasy, with the fat still on. Then they come
round again with tomato salad and chunks of roast mutton. The
gunfire has subsided, but now the musicians open up instead,
two *lýras,* a violin, and a singer, all at megawatt volume, making
conversation impossible. Dancing follows, first the bride with
her father, then there's a circle for close family, then women
only, then everybody. *I* could have a go, I think I *would,* but for
nearly being murdered this morning and still feeling the bruises.
As it is, well frankly, I've just about had it. Faces are beginning
to blur. Somewhere out there is a series of crashes like plates
being smashed. Prop the eyes open again. Plates *are* being
smashed. And now the automatics are out again, *bang bang bang
bang bang.* You can see the muzzle flashes, smell the cordite
. . . Oh *Christ!* I must have overdone the raki, I can see a man
carrying a handbag, a *handbag!* In this macho environment! I
point him out to Spyro, who says he's got his stomach in it, his
stomach, yes. Poor guy, got shot by accident, and the hospital

gave him this portable . . . Oh yes, it happen at a wedding, sure.

I get up to go home.

And see, over by the wall, a familiar figure in a leather jacket. Now, how long has he been there?

You know, my Lord, that the Venetians purchas'd this
City in 1204. The Body of the Place is good; the Walls
well fac'd with Stone, and well terrafs'd, defended by a
deep Ditch, and there is but one Gate land-ward.

*T*he best thing about Maud's breakfasts was the Turkish
coffee, strong and black, with a fine bitter flavor once the
sediment had sunk to the bottom. After the second cup, I felt
ready to face the day.

With luck, it wouldn't be too exciting. It was Sunday, but
even without that excuse I needed a day of rest for aching
muscles and overstretched nerves, a day of calm and quiet before
I took off on an attempt to contact Nick again. I'd been here a
week, and this second attempt would probably have to be the
last. If I couldn't find him, or if I found him and lost him again,
time would be up: there'd be nothing left but to admit failure
and go home.

Opposite, at the terrace table, Maud sat patiently, waiting to hear my plans. It was hard to tell what she thought about me, and what I'd done so far. She was curiously detached, politely solicitous about the hazards I'd encountered, but it hadn't oc- curred to her to propose that I drop the search because of them, nor had she come up with any suggestions, helpful or otherwise. She made me feel like a plumber, come to mend the sink: so I'd burned my fingers with the blow lamp? Here's a cup of tea, now get on with the job.

Well, not so very curious—she'd always had that air of de- tachment from us ordinary, vulnerable mortals with our sickly dependence on being loved and wanted. *The lovely Maud—* expecting service and getting it. Some people just have the knack.

But the spell wasn't working, not as it had. The smile had faded. I could opt out. I was cured, in effect.

But there remained the mystery. Another day, two days, and I might have solved it. Now, that *would* be something . . .

Anyway, today I was going to see Eléni. That was something else . . . I said:

"I'm going down to Rethymnon, to follow up a lead."

"I see," Maud said. She hesitated, and then said slowly:

"William, it won't be anything *dangerous,* will it?"

I looked up in surprise. Well! Better late than never!

"Good heavens no," I said.

I parked the jeep in the street below the castle, and walked the remaining fifty yards slowly, drifting along, the standard, sensible pace for this climate. It was the hottest day so far, and early afternoon the hottest part of it. The only wind was that from passing cars, full of dust and exhaust fumes.

"Hel-lo." With the lazy smile.

"Hello, Eléni. Does this look too ridiculous?"

She stood back for a better look. Most shops were shut, but I'd seen one selling tourist goods, stopped, and bought a baseball cap.

"No-o-o," she said critically. "No, it is all right."

"I had to get something. Jesus, it's hot!"

"We will go upstairs and have a cool drink. Will you like that?"

"I think I'd die without it. How can you live in this climate?"

She led the way up to the sitting room overlooking the street and the castle. Even there it was stuffy. But the sun was off the balcony: out there, there must be some air movement. I moved past her, meaning to investigate, but she put her hand on my arm and stopped me.

"What is it?" I said.

She inspected my face in the light from the window. "Not too bad. Just a little, on the neck, here, and here." Her fingers touched me lightly. I said:

"I don't strangle easily."

"Aha. But it was not a joke, I think."

"No. I think he would have gone all the way."

"But why?"

"It was war. And there was nothing to stop him. It's an experience, to kill a man."

"You know this?"

"Yes."

"Oh."

"It was in self-defense. But I found I could do it."

"And afterwards?"

"Afterwards . . . I threw up. But to be honest, I think that was as much from shock, from relief, as from remorse."

She had dropped her hand, and stood looking at me. "I did not know this," she said. "I am surprised. Also sorry."

"You mean, you don't serve cold drinks to killers?"

"No, I . . . Oh!—these so-British jokes."

"I'll try to avoid them."

"Please. And I will get you some fruit juice, with ice. Orange? Grapefruit?"

"Grapefruit, if you've got it."

"I think so. Sit down, and I will bring it."

I watched her leave the room. "Surprised," she had said. What did that mean, exactly? That I don't look like a man who can pull a trigger? No, but statistically, the streets are thronged with ordinary men who have had to do that in some war or other. In my case, it hadn't been a war but a Frenchman called Jean-Louis interested in emptying his automatic into my face for financial gain. I hadn't felt at all bad about preventing him, but I had been shocked, afterwards, by how horribly easy it had been, and how lucky we all are that most people believe in not pulling triggers.

I walked towards the balcony, and looked out of the french window, over towards the castle. Even in this heat, figures were strolling the battlements, in full sun. The trees below the castle wall were beginning to look tired and yellow: it was that time of year. Soon, the leaves would—

What's *he* doing?

He's standing there, looking down at something. Ah yes!— stopped to let his dog have a pee. That must be it.

No. No dog.

He's got a notebook out, flipped it open, is writing a note. A traffic warden's gesture—but he's not in uniform. He's got short fair hair, dark glasses, is wearing a lightweight, cream-colored suit . . .

"Would you like to have it on the balcony?" Eléni said from behind. I'd been so engrossed I hadn't heard the glasses tinkling on the tray.

"Wait," I said, "just a moment . . ."

"What is it?"

"There's a man by my jeep. He's just written down the

number in a notebook. Now he's bending down, doing something at the back . . . Eléni, have you got binoculars?"

"No, I am sorry."

"Never mind. I think it's too late, anyway—he's walking
away now."

"You don't know him?"

"Never seen him before . . . Does it mean anything to you?
Short fair hair, lightweight cream-colored suit?"

"I don't think so."

"Police, perhaps?"

"In a suit? It is possible, but usually, they wear . . ."

"Casual clothes, yes, not so formal . . . Look, keep the drink
for me. I'll be back as soon as I can."

"Where are you going?"

But I was already starting down the stairs.

I sprinted across the dark, shuttered hallway to the street door,
and eased it open enough to see out. There he was, already
almost a hundred yards away, heading towards the harbor. I ran
carefully, quietly, keeping my heels from slapping the pavement,
ready to switch to a walk, but he didn't look round. The gap
narrowed to seventy yards, fifty, forty. I slowed, began walking.
The prospect of boats and blue water at the end of the street
grew wider, wider. He was almost there. I anticipated that he
might turn to look back as he reached the end of the street, and
ducked almost out of sight into a doorway. He did! I felt a surge
of delight—*I can handle this!* He went round the corner. If he was
really smart, he'd wait a few seconds and then look back, but I
decided to risk it, and sprinted the rest of the way, braking just
before the corner. I could hear a hum of conversation from the
waterside cafés, until a clatter of pans being washed up burst
from a nearby window and drowned it. I slipped round the
corner, and stood, searching for my quarry over the heads of
tourists sipping cool drinks . . . *Cool drinks!* Where was he? None
of the standing or walking figures was him. The next street was

too far—he couldn't have gone that way. He's inside, in one of the bars or hotels, or sitting at one of the tables. But which?

"Mr. Warner!"

He's got to be here . . .

"Mr. Warner . . . William! Over here . . ."

What?

Oh my God—it's Maggs and Dottie. Waving fit to break their wrists. Well, I'll have to pretend I haven't seen them, I can't possibly . . .

On the other hand . . .

I eased between the tables, under the Heineken umbrellas.

"Hello. Shall I join you?"

"But of course," they cried. "I say, it really is hot today, isn't it!" Dottie said, flapping her disintegrating straw hat. "And you look just about at boiling point. What *have* you been up to?"

"Nothing special," I said. "Heat like this doesn't agree with me, I'm afraid."

"No, it's a bit much for us poor old Brits. Maggs has come out in a rash since breakfast."

"Nothing serious," Maggs said with annoyance.

"Oh well, I'm glad to hear that . . ."

Where is he? I'm looking for short fair hair, and dark glasses . . . He could have taken them off, once in the shade of an umbrella . . .

". . . more of the northern type. Sunburn is the most frightful problem, if I run out of the special goo I have to use. So of course I always take care to stock up at Boots before I . . ."

Could have taken his jacket off, too, so I'm looking for a man with short fair hair, with or without dark glasses, and with or without a cream-colored jacket . . .

". . . really too hot to eat, so we've been making absolute pigs of ourselves with ice cream. Oh good, here he comes. Now look here, this is on us. Yes, absolutely, we insist."

"Very kind . . . if you're sure . . . a beer. Yes, Heineken, thank you . . ."

That could be him! Seven or eight tables away, in the next restaurant's bit of waterfront, in fact . . . Already got his drink, and is taking a first long pull at it, dark glasses flashing as he tilts his head back. Now he's looking round, looking this way, I'd better—

"So, how's the sketching going? Or have you decided against it for today?"

"Oh yes, it's *far* too hot for watercolor, I'm afraid. You just try laying on a wash in this heat! We work under umbrellas, of course, but even so, you're no more than halfway down the sheet before it's dried, and you've got a hard edge."

"Disaster."

"Oh absolutely. All you've done is ruin a sheet of expensive Whatman. Here's your beer."

"Thank you very much." I began, lovingly, to pour it out, tilting the glass to avoid froth. There were icy beads on the green bottle . . .

"I made some pencil notes from the hotel window," Dottie said, "so the day won't have been entirely wasted. But poor Maggs, with her rash, has been rather *hors de combat . . .*"

I took my eye off him for a moment, and he's standing up, slipping on his jacket as he moves away . . .

"Damnit! There goes a friend I simply must catch." I said, taking a quick swallow, and catching my knees on the table as I leaped up.

"But you've hardly touched your beer!" Dottie cried.

"I'm very, very sorry. Please forgive me. I'm dying to drink it but if I miss him now, I'll never . . ."

I was away, weaving through the tables, dodging umbrella rims. Where was he now? *There*—just about to turn into the next street. Quick—*sit down!*

"I'm afraid this seat is taken," an English male voice said loudly, with determination. A large red face interrupted my field of view. Beyond it, I saw my quarry complete his quick rearward check and move on round the corner.

"Sorry." And I was off again.

At the corner I slowed and made a show of looking for the street sign while I located him. He was thirty yards away, walking unhurriedly on the right-hand pavement, the cream-colored suit easily distinguishable among the semi-clad tourists and blue-jeaned fishermen. I followed. He slowed, reaching into his coat pocket. There was no doorway to duck into, so I stepped the other way, into the street, between two parked cars. Over the roof of a Renault 5 I watched him cross to the offside, and unlock the driver's door of a medium-sized, white saloon car. He had the door partly open, but had to wait, flattening himself against the car while a battered pickup truck loaded with wooden crates roared by, emitting clouds of blue smoke. Then he opened the door fully and got in.

He's going to get away . . . All I could do now was to get the make of car, and the number. I stepped back onto the pavement, and strode rapidly down the line of parked cars which now shielded me from where he sat in the driver's seat. He would look in the mirror before he pulled out, but that, too, would be on the offside, along the street: I'd have to hope he didn't bother to look in the nearside mirror, along the pavement . . . anyway, I was near enough, now. Into the line of parked cars again, then.

It's a Peugeot 404. Left-hand drive—that's normal. I can't see round the two cars between me and it to get the registration, but should have a chance when he drives off. Until then, best to duck down and watch through the car windows. Cup hands and pretend to be lighting a cigarette. He's starting the engine. And there he goes . . . The number is:

HP 1002.

Simple enough, these local numbers. HP 1002. Can hardly forget that, but I'll write it in my pocket book just the same. Just watch him out of sight, first . . . Oh, soon over, he's taken the first right. That must connect with Eléni's street, where the jeep is.

"Probably dirt in the carburetor," I said. "In any case, I didn't
want to take the risk of breaking down in traffic again, so I left
it for you to collect. Luckily, it's only a short distance away—ten
minutes' walk."

I could see what he thought: *another idiot tourist* . . . "I've
checked the petrol," I said, "and the tank's half full. Doesn't it
say in the hire agreement that you deal with breakdowns?"

"Okay," he said with resignation, "we collect. Where do you
say?"

"Melissinou. The street by the castle that leads down to the
harbor."

"Okay. I am sorry you have this trouble."

"Could have been worse. I still have a problem, though. I was
on my way to Heraclion to meet a friend at the airport. I'm
already late."

He shrugged. "A taxi . . ."

"All that way? Are you going to pay for that?"

"No, sir. Oh no, we are not able to . . ."

"I thought the easiest thing would be to transfer to another
jeep. Or car."

"All cars are out. I am sorry."

"*All?* You must have *something,* surely? I don't mind what, as
long as it goes."

"All cars are out. We have left only motorbikes."

It was a stroke of luck, I soon realized. In a car, I'd have had to
stay well back, and might have lost him in traffic, or by being cut
off by a red light. On the Honda 125, I could keep up with ease,
and the concealing helmet and overalls were a useful bonus.
Provided, of course, that I could manage the thing—it was years
since I'd ridden a bike.

I wobbled away from the hire company trying to avoid hitting anything at least until out of their yard, but five minutes later old skills had begun to revive, and I rode gently and with growing confidence up a side street into the harbor end of Melissinou. I chose one of several spaces (all of which would have been too small for a car), maneuvered into it, and cut the engine.

The Peugeot was still where I'd last seen it, facing away from me, and he was still in it, watching the jeep, waiting for me to return and drive off. A boring job, and I suspected his heart wasn't in it: a more conscientious sleuth wouldn't have paused to snatch a cool drink on the way back to the Peugeot in case I drove away meanwhile. But he'd only lost three or four minutes, and he'd have been hardly human to have passed up that opportunity in this heat. All the same, he must have been relieved to see that he'd got away with it, that the jeep was still there, and therefore I was still in Eléni's house . . .

It felt good, sitting there watching him watching for me to return to the jeep. I took the helmet off: it was cooler without it, though not much. It was safe enough, he wasn't expecting me to be behind him, and the top of my head, which was all he could see, would be invisibly small in his driving mirror.

It was a quiet, residential street, with no shops and few passersby. The Honda seat was reasonably comfortable, and I hoped there wouldn't be too long to wait—the hire company had agreed to try to get the jeep back into working order for me to collect later this evening, on the way back from Heraclion.

Ten minutes went by, then fifteen. If they didn't collect the jeep, I'd have to think of a change of plan. I could go to a kiosk, ring Eléni, and ask her to—

No, it's all right. A man in overalls is walking purposefully up the street from the far end. He stops by the jeep, unlocks the door, gets in. A moment later, I hear the engine start . . . I'm too far to hear him cursing me, but I can imagine. Now the Peugeot has started up. It's my turn: on with the helmet, zoom, zoooom. The only snag with bikes for a job like this is the noise, but I'm only one among many.

And we're off. Cursing mechanic, puzzled sleuth, cautiously celebrating wine merchant.

Half an hour later, at the cost of a wobble, I looked at my watch. Ten to four, and we were well on the way to Hania, the most western of Crete's three large towns, at the head of Suda Bay. Everything had gone according to plan: the jeep followed to the hire company's yard, a pause while the sleuth went in and was told I'd gone to Heraclion, and then this drive on the main road west, which I hoped was the return home, or to headquarters. *Now* he'd be cursing that four-minute pause for refreshment, without which, he must be thinking, he might have got back to Melissinou in time to see me leave, and so not have lost me. It wouldn't feature in his report, that's for sure.

Ahead, the Peugeot slowed, indicated a right turn, and turned off the main road. I followed. To my right, a broad lozenge of blue water had appeared, with more land beyond. If this was Suda, it was more like an estuary than a bay. The road was well surfaced, but minor: the Peugeot slowed again, and kept to a steady forty. A sign appeared ahead; I just had time to see the symbol on it, a camera with a red cross superimposed, and underneath: PHOTOGRAPHY FORBIDDEN. Soon I saw another, and more followed with increasing frequency.

Buildings began to line the road, houses, a barracks with gate guarded by sentries in Greek naval uniform, and then, the now intermittent glimpses of the bay were closed off altogether behind a high wall.

Half a mile further, and a dockyard began where the wall finished. A car ferry was at a terminal, loading. It looked innocent enough, but holiday snaps were still FORBIDDEN.

The road began to curve to the right, reconsidered it, then curved right again. There was an open view to the right, down the bay: near the water, the white rectangularity of a cemetery. The traffic had been thinning out: I was glad of a Mercedes taxi which overtook me and stayed between me and the Peugeot, giving cover.

Now we were climbing, and turning back along the northern shore of the bay. Through a village. Along a ridge, with mountains visible to the north. What had Eléni called it, this great knob of land, almost an island, projecting into the sea?ʼ

The Akrotiri . . .

She'd said something else, too. There was a NATO base, rockets . . .

Round the intervening bulk of the Mercedes, I saw the Peugeot slow again. Against the blue water of the bay, I could see a young pine plantation, neat huts and bungalows, all enclosed by tall fencing. In there, at the edge of the trees, was an open watchtower: a uniformed figure was silhouetted against the sky, lounging but alert, the butt of his submachine gun propped against his thigh.

The Peugeot pulled up at an entrance barrier, between white picket fencing, by a freshly painted guard hut. I followed the Mercedes past, but had time to see a marine in dark blue uniform and white gaiters step forward to the car window, holding his hand out for a pass, and to see a white board with black letters which read: NAMFI.

I couldn't make it out. Two miles further on was Hania airfield, with an airbus coming in, presumably to deliver several hundred more tourists from London Airport, Gatwick, or wherever, each one strung around with loaded cameras. And yet, along the perimeter, there were more prohibition notices, more colloquial this time: NO PHOTOS. What was it which was bound to be seen by so many people but *must not be photographed*?

More curious: there was a military signpost at each road junction, a painted regimental shield incorporating a star, a rocket, and a mountain goat. THIS WAY TO THE MISSILES, it clearly announced. So why should the Warsaw Pact part with good rubles for forbidden photographs, when the target is so politely pinpointed for them?

While trying to work it out, I followed the signs. Nobody stopped me. I rode past the airfield, over some open scrubland, towards the central mountain, Mount Hordaki, on which I could see radio masts. The signs made sure I didn't lose my way. The road climbed, skirted a vast quarry. What had all that stone been used for? Then I turned a corner, and braked. Here, at last, was a barrier, another guard hut, manned by Greek soldiers. Beyond, the hillside was scarred by a series of earth-covered mounds, as though a giant mole had been at work . . .

A soldier stared out from the roadblock towards me. I turned, and let the bike coast away down the hill, thinking, *If those aren't missile silos, I'm a KGB agent . . .*

"I'd like to talk to the member of your personnel who came in about twenty minutes ago. White Peugeot 404, fair hair, dark glasses, lightweight pale cream suit."

"You would, sir, huh?"

"That's what I said."

"You gotta pass?"

"I'm not asking to be let in. I'd like it if he would be kind enough to come out."

"You gotta appointment?"

"No."

"Whadda you wanna see him for?"

"It's confidential."

His dark glasses were darker than mine. He was taller, too. And broader. The holstered automatic on his hip looked, close to, about the size of a grand piano.

"You British or sumthin'?"

"Yes, I am."

"Yeah, I thought you were."

The dark glasses considered me a little longer. Then he said: "Okay, sir. You wait right here."

"Thanks."

He crunched over the clean white gravel to the guard hut, went in, and picked up the telephone, standing where he could see me. I waited. It took time. Eventually he put the phone down, and crunched back.

"He's comin' over."

"Thanks. What's his name?"

He thought about it, then said: "Maybe he'll tell you. Maybe he won't."

"Tight security you've got."

"Yessir. It's tight."

"Can you tell me what NAMFI stands for, on your board there? Or is that a secret?"

"That's no secret."

"Oh, good."

"NATO Missile Firing Installation. Okay?"

"Yes, thanks."

"You're welcome."

I left him, and went to sit on the bike. Two or three minutes passed. Then my quarry arrived. I got up and went to the barrier to meet him. He slowed when he saw me, then took his dark glasses off, and blinked. I said:

"So. We meet at last."

"I don't think I know you, Mr. . . . ."

"You know me," I said. "I drove a hired Suzuki jeep into

Rethymnon this afternoon, parked it in Melissinou where you
were keeping watch on a house. When I went into the house,
you took the number and wrote it in your notebook. Then you
walked down the street to the harbor, snatched a quick drink at
a waterfront restaurant, walked on to your white Peugeot 404,
registration number HP 1002, which was parked in the next
street, drove it through to Melissinou and parked there, where
you could watch the jeep for me to return. Only I didn't."

"All right."

"You know me?"

"I know you." He hesitated, frowning. Then he said to the
marine:

"Let him through. I'll sign for him."

"Okay, sir."

We walked up the drive, in through the first of several doors
in a long administration building. He led the way along a corridor, and into a small office. It had a polished wood floor, steel
desk, and two chairs, a square of carpet on the floor. It didn't
look like home. A computer terminal squatted blankly on a side
table.

"Take a chair," he said, going behind the desk. "Then tell me
what this is all about."

"That's what I want you to tell me," I said.

"Oh, now, my job is to *collect* information, not hand it out."

"I can be very cooperative, given a modest incentive," I said.

"Such as?"

"Such as who you are, for a start."

He sat back in his chair, put his fingertips together, and gave
it some thought. Then he nodded, and said:

"Okay, I'll buy that much."

He reached into his jacket, withdrew a slim folder like a
passport, opened it, reversed it so that it was my way up, and slid
it across the desk. I looked.

"Thanks," I said. "So you're CIA, and I'm a—"

"Wine merchant," he said. "Though frankly, we have a credibility problem on that."

"I know," I said. "You don't meet them every day, do you."

Throughout the whole Island there are a world of Caverns. Doubtlefs fome Shepherds having difcover'd thefe fubterranean Conduits, gave occafion to a more confiderable People to turn one into this marvellous Maze, to ferve for an Afylum in the Civil Wars, or to skreen themfelves from the Fury of a Tyrannical Government: at prefent 'tis only a Retreat for Bats and the like.

I wasn't happy about it. As I'd told Maud, the chances of finding him this second time were less than the first. He'd have gone to ground more thoroughly, must have. And Maria's brothers who, Maud said, had been seen in the village over the weekend, would soon hear about my departure if they weren't already behind me, and would stick close, hampering the search. The more effort I made to shake them off, the more convinced they'd be that I knew where he was. Sooner or later they were likely to lose patience, and demand to be taken to him—and the phrase book wasn't strong on "You're making a big mistake/I do *not* know where my friend is hiding/Look, I'm as much in the dark as you are." No, they'd assume I was holding back on them, and act accordingly—an experience I preferred not to imagine in detail. They'd have to catch me first, of course, and the one good thing about this expedition compared with the first was the considerable armory I'd acquired: the Smith & Wesson, with six rounds loaded and a dozen spare; the vintage Mannlicher rifle (the sight of which would deter even if some or all of the ten cartridges proved to be dud); and the remaining cigarette tin bomb.

All of which would be needed if the Gyparis brothers lived up to their portrait in *Macho Man*. It was bad enough trying to understand urban Greeks doing business, less interested in the transaction than in a complicated exchange of personal favors and obligations. Even more foreign to my way of thinking was the shepherd lifestyle, an extreme and frequently lethal form of oneupmanship—they call it *eghoismus*—in which success is what counts, and honor is satisfied by a bullet or knife in the back. Points are scored for trickery, ingenuity, shock effect . . . Definitely not cricket, and I wasn't encouraged by reading that. While on the subject of Greek mentality, I've never understood why people are so respectful about *The Iliad,* either, several hundred pages of gruesomely detailed hand-to-hand fighting on the lines of *swift-footed Achilles thrust with his sharp sword at the groin of glorious Hector of the shining helmet and with a woeful groan noble Hector sank down in the dust at the feet of invincible Achilles clasping his bleeding entrails with both hands and darkness covered his eyes* . . . All that egocentric, murderous masculinity. It's a tradition I'd like to think had softened over the centuries, but *Macho Man: Field Studies of the Mediterranean Male* warns otherwise . . .

My hands are slippery on the wheel. It's the heat, mostly. But I'm afraid there *will* be a confrontation. Afraid, yes. No shame in that: in these circumstances I'd be a fool if I wasn't. And anyway, fear is a survival mechanism: sharpens the wits, sends get ready messages to the muscles.

Too late to back out now, but I'll be glad when it's all over.

In the *kafeneíon* at Kalikrati, the old man was in the same place,
just as I'd hoped. He'd changed his waistcoat for a scarlet sash,
which gave him a piratical air, but otherwise was as before,
turbanned, whiskered, in full patrigroup costume. But today he
was the only customer, his splendor wasted on an empty room.
Until now.

"*Kali méra!*"

"*Ah, Inglis! Kalós orísate!*"

I held out my hand, and he shook it firmly. Then he offered
a drink. A beer? Of course. I sat on the bench next to the old
man, and said:

"Have you seen Nikolaos?"

"Nikolaos . . . *ne.* He come."

"Oh good! . . . is he still here, in the village?"

"Not here."

"Where did he go to?"

"He does not tell."

"I am looking for him. It is very important."

"Important?"

"Yes."

The proprietor brought the beer on a tray. I took it gratefully,
raised the glass to the old man, who bowed his head ceremoni-
ously in return. The proprietor said something. I looked up to
find he was pushing an envelope at me. I took it, turned it over,
and read: *William.* I tore it open, and found a scribbled note on
a page torn from a notebook.

Car is in Kalikrati—proprietor will show you where. Map and
directions under driving seat. Tell no one, and make sure you are
not followed. Rely on you.

N.

It was plain, peremptory. No entreaties, or apologies for deserting me—at high speed—to fend for myself in Arcadés. But that was Nick, who belonged firmly to the never apologize, never explain brigade. I looked up at the proprietor again, pointed to the note, raised my eyebrows . . . Maybe the lousy phrase book could rise to this occasion . . .

No, he understood. But it was my round, a ceremony that I'd be unwise to ignore. I ordered hastily, the *rakí* and the little dish of *mezés* came, we clinked and drank. Then I shook his hand again, and at last could go.

The proprietor led me to the jeep, and indicated we should get in. I started up, and he pointed—back down the old street, with its semi-ruins, wire chicken runs, and overgrown gardens. We came to a turning, and drove left, up a narrow lane. Here, the houses were all ruined, but a hundred yards up, at the point where the lane petered out into open ground, and next to a house which had been largely rebuilt, was a hideous concrete block shed or workshop.

I understood I was to stop. The proprietor pointed at the house next to the garage, and then to himself: *mine*. Then he got out of the jeep, undid a padlock on the double steel doors, and dragged one open far enough to let me see in. I looked. It was dark inside, but at the far end was a rectangular whiteness—the Hyundai pickup! Now, the note had said—

But the proprietor was making urgent signs that he needed to get back to the *kafeneíon*. We got back into the jeep, and I drove him there. On arrival, he presented me with the padlock key, and got out. I thanked him warmly, and then drove back, scattering chickens, to the shed. This would be the worst possible time, with the mystery about to be explained (*please!*), to run head on into the Gyparis brothers in hot pursuit . . .

But I didn't. I drove up the lane to the garage, jumped out, strode to the door. Some defensive instinct made me look round before going in. The proprietor's house, first. There were no windows in the side facing the shed, and nobody was looking out from the door. I looked down the lane. A solitary stray goat browsed among the ruins. *All right, then* . . .

I pulled the shed door open, and went in. The Hyundai was unlocked, and there was a folded piece of paper under the driving seat as promised. I opened it.

> Leave car in shed, and come on foot SAP. Map on back. Bring torch!

Hmm. As blunt, telegraphic, as his first. I turned the paper over.

There was a sketch. At first glance it seemed that he'd left an anatomical diagram in place of the intended map. These curls, whorls, branchings, and dead ends could be a surgeon's notes, made in the course of tracking down some intestinal horror—an ulcer, or bowel cancer. No map I'd ever come across was as complicated, as tortured, as this.

I looked more closely, and saw an arrow at the bottom, marked ENTRANCE HERE.

Entrance?

Then I realized. *Bring torch!* "Intestinal" was right. *This map was underground* . . .

There were also some scribbled directions to the arrow, or starting point.

> On leaving the shed (don't forget to lock and bring key!) turn right, go up old track across scrub to olive trees, keep going uphill until you reach oaks . . .

He always was a madman. Or, more precisely, he'd never grown up . . .

Did I want—was I prepared to play this game? Would he actually *be* there, at the end of this labyrinth, or was his real intention that I should get lost in it, while he could get clear away? As a precaution against being followed a second time, it made perfect sense . . .

In short, could I trust this map?

I sat in the Hyundai, looking through the windscreen at the interior of the shed, lit only by the open door. There was a pile of unplaned planks, a half-finished packing case, and a number of large flat objects wrapped in plastic, stacked against the wall . . . Well, I don't know. I suppose I'll go, find the entrance, look inside, see what I think, then . . .

I got out of the Hyundai, unbolted the second steel door and dragged it open, then drove the jeep in. There was just enough length to spare. I dragged one door shut, and bolted it. I put Nick's torch on top of all my other gear in the *sakoúli,* hoisted it onto my back, then fished the Mannlicher out from behind the front seats, and slung it over my shoulder. I wiped the dust off my dark glasses and put them back on, and adjusted the new baseball cap, pulling the peak well down over my eyes. Then I was ready.

I walked to the door, and took a last look round the shed. Those planks—was that something to do with Nick? And the packages wrapped in plastic? I walked back to take a closer look.

Something crunched underfoot. I looked down. Loose nails, spilling out of a brown paper packet. I'd seen those, or similar, in Nick's hideout at Arcardés. Near them was a hammer. Could well be the one missing from the cellar at Maud's.

The packages, then?

I pulled one away from the stack, pulled the plastic wrapping away from one corner, and looked inside. A wooden frame, painted canvas . . . It must be Maud's. I unwrapped it some more. Yes, definitely Maud's . . . Just check one other . . . Yes, also hers. It's a sizeable stack, there must be . . . twenty, twenty-five, twenty-seven. Twenty-seven of Maud's paintings, waiting, presumably, for shipment. Like the ones I've already seen

they're large, up to about three feet by four . . . She said it took
her two months, sometimes more, to complete a large painting
. . . That's a lot of work, stacked up here.

I put the wrappings back, carefully, and replaced the paintings
against the stack. With these in stock, and assuming they all sold,
Nick and Maud would be quite comfortably off for some time
to come, given their economic life-style. So whatever Nick was
doing, it wasn't because he was hard up, except in the sense that
people always want more than they've got.

But why does he keep the stock *here,* in this out-of-the-way
place? It's dry, and probably cheap. Is that all?

Perhaps, in an hour or so, I'll be able to ask *him* that question.

It was a different kind of discomfort up here in the White
Mountains from that of Rethymnon yesterday. The air was cool
and dry, a relief after the steamy heat down on the coast. But that
was the good news. The sun was something else . . .

Jesus! That sun! It hit me out of a spotless sky, with not the
slightest, most vaporous wisp of cloud to soften the blow. In
Rethymnon I'd been boiled: today I was still on the menu, but
boiled was *off,* grilled or barbecued was *on.* I thanked God and
my foresight for buying me the cap; even wearing it, I felt my
brains must be shriveling. Any idea that I might do some useful
thinking on the way to Nick's labyrinth had to be abandoned.
In heat like this, you don't think, you *can't* think, all you can do
is switch to auto-pilot and wait for the shade.

The first shade was in the grove of oak trees, not splendid
giants such as stately homeowners are proud of, but little stunted
things, dwarfish and underprivileged. I stood in amongst them,
breathing the delicious air, while the sun scratched impatiently
at the leaves overhead and waited for me to come out, like a cat
at a mouse hole.

There was movement down in the village. I watched a red

open truck arrive from further down the valley, and jolt along between the ruined houses at the head of a dust cloud. It disappeared behind rebuilt houses, emerged again to pull up in the parking area before the *kafeneíon*. Two men got out, looked about them, went into the *kafeneíon* . . . The distance was too great to see any detail, but I decided to assume the worst, that they were the Gyparis brothers. In which case I'd been lucky to get as far as I had before they turned up. They should have guessed I'd be coming up, had the truck ready . . . well, they hadn't. More important was what they'd do next. Was the *kafeneíon* proprietor in Nick's confidence, or would he tell them I'd been through, direct them to the shed? Even if he did, they wouldn't know where to go next: Nick had covered our tracks well by putting the note in the locked shed. In English, too, so they couldn't read it . . . No, I didn't see how they could get after me, unless they saw me . . . In which case, I'd better step into the jaws of the sun again, and make tracks.

> When you get above the tree line, watch for a gulley off to the right, curving up between the smaller hill on your left and the big mountain . . .

The glare off the stones was dazzling. Above the tree line, the vegetation thinned out, letting the bare limestone grin through, bone white. Thistle, prickly pear, and cactus clung on in the crevices, fighting for moisture. There were occasional isolated shoots of sea squill, useful, I'd read somewhere, for cough mixture, chapped feet, sheep wash, rat poison.

> Where the gulley comes to an end, strike off north, directly up the mountain. After fifteen minutes of steep climb, you'll come to a depression with an overhanging rock . . .

Steep climb, he said. He didn't exaggerate. I planted the rubber soles with care to avoid slipping back, choosing each

foothold. The sun on my back was trying to flatten me into the
rock. I thought: if this goes on much longer, I shall melt, and
pour down the slope.

> . . . a depression with an overhanging rock. I've marked this
> on the map with an arrow. Go in under the rock, then follow
> the map—but be careful not to lose your way . . .

Nick's torch was one of those long jobs which hold several
batteries, quite powerful if the batteries are okay. I stood for a
moment under the hanging rock, enjoying the cool draught
which the cave was breathing out, and letting my eyes readjust
from the glare outside. Then I switched the torch on.

The beam was good. I could see clearly up to the first bend
ten yards away. It was a limestone cavern, the walls worn
smooth where rainwater or melted snow had penetrated and
trickled down, as rough as a cliff face elsewhere. The floor was
a mixture of mud and small stones, apparently untrodden. Then
I noticed one footprint, half in and half out of a patch of mud.
Tread on the stones and you'd leave no trace.

I shone the torch on the map. There was no indication of
scale, but by the number of turnings and junctions it could be
several hundred yards to the place Nick had indicated I was to
go to and where, I could only hope, he would be waiting. I
wondered how new the batteries were, and how long they
would last. If it ran out, I'd still have the lighter bought in the
hotel at Frangocastello, but it wasn't an appealing prospect to be
in the depths of this underground system with only a lighter
between me and total darkness.

Be careful not to lose your way . . . Easier said than done. Theseus
had a ball of thread: more recently, potholers have unraveled
sweaters, made paper trails. What shall I do?

Something, certainly. I *have* got Nick's map, and I don't think he'd deliberately mislead me, but he's unpredictable, and I'd like a sure way of retracing my steps if I want *out* . . . It should be legible by lighter flame if need be, and from the other direction.

Cretan small change, then. I've got a pocketful of the stuff, due to a lazy tendency to hand over a note rather than bother to work out the coins. And they'll reflect the light nicely. Here goes, then:

Five drachmas as I come to the first corner, placed to show the way as I come out.

Five more at the next corner.

The next is a junction. I'll give it ten, to show up better.

Now there's a low section, which I have to crawl through. The Mannlicher muzzle knocks a chip off the ceiling—hope I haven't disturbed the foresight.

Then a fork, which gets twenty drachmas. According to the plan, I'm a third of the way in, and still have plenty of coins. Must mark *all* junctions, though—one wrong turn could lead to disaster. The place seems *endless*! And, after frying in the sun I'm now shivering with cold.

It was hypnotic, this slow burrowing through the mountain, watching the torchlight shining off the rock, creating shadows that seemed to take on a life of their own, flitting like bats away from the light to hide again in the surrounding blackness. The cavern changed its shape constantly, would grow from a passage-way to a room, to a larger room, and then shrink down to a narrow passage again. Several times I heard running water, but it was always distant: there were nearer noises, sounds like sighs, and echoes of my footsteps in places where the floor was solid rock.

I couldn't say how many times I consulted the map: thirty, certainly, maybe as many as fifty. I felt extremely glad I'd marked the way. Not that I'd lost confidence in the map, which had several unmistakeable landmarks marked on it—a pool, a misshapen rock—which had always (so far) turned up more or less when expected. But I was beginning to feel enough was enough: I had seven coins left, and the torch light seemed less bright than it had been, unless it was my eyes that were getting tired.

Six coins left.

Five.

I looked at the map once more. If it was correct, and if I was on course, I was three-quarters of the way there, maybe a little more.

I'd used up three more coins when I rounded a corner, and thought that the blackness seemed slightly less impenetrable. I stopped, switched off the torch. It was. There was something else, too. The sound of a *voice* . . . It was too faint to distinguish words, but by the cadences I thought it might be speaking English. Then I heard something else—*music* . . .

I hurried on to the next corner, marked it with a fifty drachma piece, rounded it.

". . . *concerto in A major, K 488, recorded at a concert in the Royal Festival Hall last February and conducted, from the keyboard, by Daniel Barenboim.*"

I stood, and let my eyes follow the torch beam. I'd seen the whole labyrinthine range of caverns on my way through, and this was one of your small, homely models. The beam passed over a camp bed with rugs, a stone-built fireplace with an iron pot suspended over it, a camping gas stove and two saucepans, a suitcase, a folding canvas chair, and a packing case on which the radio stood, next to an unwashed plate, a mug, and a small pile of books. Beyond the packing case, the effect of daylight against the cavern wall was stronger, though I couldn't see out. The radio had started playing Mozart. And the mug beside it was steaming.

"Let's hope you can manage a better welcome this time," I said to the nobody who was there.

There was movement to my left. I swung the torch, and saw him emerge from a side tunnel, the torch beam flashing off his glasses and throwing a monstrous shambling shadow on the wall behind. *The Minotaur . . .*

"I expected you *yesterday*," he complained, frowning.

*Tho this Alley divides itſelf into two or three Branches,
yet the dangerous part of the Labyrinth is not there, but
rather at its Entrance. If a Man ſtrikes into any other
Path, after he has gone a good way, he is bewilder'd
among a thousand Twiſtings, Twinings, Sinuoſities,
Crinkle-Crankles, and Turn-Again Lanes, that he could
ſcarce ever get out again without the utmoſt
danger of being loſt.*

$\mathcal{N}$ick lit a paraffin lamp, and then stood watching as I
unslung the Mannlicher and inspected it. There was a scratch on
the end of the barrel where it had struck the cavern roof, but no
apparent damage to the foresight. I stood it against the packing
case, and then unloaded the *sakoúli* from my back. The steaming
mug caught my eye: I picked it up and tasted it. Tea—Earl Grey
probably.

"You have it," Nick said, coming forward. "I'll make some
more. Care for a biscuit?"

He proffered a packet of Huntley & Palmer digestives. I took
one. He picked up the Mannlicher, snapped the bolt open,

noted the full magazine, closed it again, reapplied the safety catch. He said:

"So you found the ammunition, too."

"I had a hunch there might be some where you found the gun."

"And so there was." He hunched over the little gas stove, which lit with a pop, then balanced a tin kettle on it.

"You knew that, surely?"

"Oh yes."

"Anything else?"

"Why do you say that?"

"There was plenty of space up there, between the beams. And one thing often leads to another."

"Oh, is that all . . . Have another biscuit?"

"Thanks." I watched him spoon tea into a second mug. "How did you find this new, deluxe hideout?"

"You saw the old boy in the café? In the *pallikári* outfit?"

"He showed you?"

"He used to bring food up during the war, run messages and anything else they needed."

"They?"

"This was where our radio post was. No one could hear the charging engine from outside, and you could see the Germans coming from miles away. In fact, they never found it."

"Bloody cold in winter."

"They could have a fire—when there was any fuel."

I imagined it: the snow outside, the meager, standard rations . . .

"Was it worth it?"

"Why not?"

"Well, they couldn't have had much of interest to radio back, buried away up here."

"Runners brought information," Nick said. "And coming in the back way, you won't, of course, have seen this." He walked to the far side of the cavern, where I'd noticed a faint lightness before Nick lit the paraffin lamp and killed it. I put down the mug of tea and followed.

The cavern narrowed to a narrow passage, which turned left, then right, all the time getting lighter. We came to a rockfall, with daylight coming from above. Nick led the way up, fifteen or twenty feet. Then . . .

"Fantastic!" I said.

Nick had stopped a few steps short of the entrance. But framed in the mouth of the cave was a panoramic view. Hanea was over to the left. To the right of Hanea, a white ship was steaming eastward along the bright blue strip that was Suda Bay. And beyond Suda, a conical mountain rose to a dominating height above a jumble of smaller hills. *The Akrotiri* . . .

"So I've come right through, and we're now on the *north* face of the White Mountains," I said. "Why the hell didn't you direct me here, and save me the labyrinth?"

"You'd have had to climb over," Nick said, "and you'd be grumbling about *that,* believe me—it's exclusively for mountain goats and shepherds. Also, if you were followed again, they'll still be blundering about in the south entrance, not being provided with my excellent map."

"Hmm." Perhaps he was right. "I've got one or two other questions as well," I said. "Like, for instance—"

"My kettle will be boiling," he said. "Let's get back inside."

I took another look at the Akrotiri. With good binoculars, or better, a high-powered telescope on a tripod, you could . . . I turned to follow him in.

The difficulty was knowing where to start. Perhaps it didn't matter. It was all going to be lies, anyway.

Or was it? In my bedside reading, I'd come across a reference to the problem of the Cretan Liar, a logical contradiction which had given many a wise man a headache, Bertrand Russell among them. It goes: "Epimenides the Cretan says that all Cretans are liars . . ."

So what? Well, Nick was a habitual liar. So if he said he was telling the truth, that should also be a lie, ergo, he wasn't. But did it follow that, if he admitted to a lie, that that in itself was a lie, ergo that particular lie wasn't a lie, but the truth? To put it another way, as Nick knew I knew he was a liar, he might use this fact to tell me something that was true, knowing that I would disbelieve it. So anything he said might be 1) a normal lie, 2) a truth which he wanted me to think was a lie, 3) an abnormal truth which was true . . .

Look, I'll try to explain that more clearly . . .

Well no, perhaps not.

I sat on the edge of the packing case, Nick on the camp bed, sipping his tea. I said:

"I imagine it wasn't just my company you wanted?"

"I count you among my oldest friends," he said, waving his tea mug in a circular gesture to express emotion, solidarity . . . It might have been Spyro speaking. Nick had found his spiritual home in Crete.

"You mean," I said, "you've got others?"

"That's a bit hard, isn't it?"

"At the last count," I said, "at least five separate people and/or organizations were passionately interested in contacting you, and I have the impression that it isn't friendship they're after, but money, goods, justice, or in at least one case, blood."

"Five," he said thoughtfully. "Are you sure? I thought it was four."

"Perhaps you've omitted the CIA. They only got on to my list yesterday."

"You're joking!" he said. "And I must say, this isn't the time to—"

"Greg Barnes. He showed me his ID. After signing me in to the NAMFI base on the Akrotiri. Pressed a button and all your personal details came up on his computer terminal. I didn't know before then that you'd actually been done for drug peddling; I thought you'd always managed to—"

"I was never inside," he said indignantly. "A fine and a year on probation, that's all. It was only hash, you know that. In those days, we were all—"

"I know that. And I don't think he was much interested—it was flashed up to impress me, more likely. To show they mean business. So, what *are* they after?"

There was only a minute pause before he answered. I might not have noticed if I hadn't been listening for it. The pause that betrays calculation. He said:

"Blundering idiot."

"Him, or me?"

"Oh, sorry, it's him I mean."

"He didn't strike me as amazingly competent," I said. "I had no trouble tailing him back to base."

"Exactly! My God, he could blow the whole thing!"

"What thing?" I asked cautiously.

"The operation," he said. There was no pause this time—but that could just mean he'd had time to work it out.

"The operation. What operation would that be?"

"Well, good God, I'm not up here for fun," he said.

"No?"

"You've seen how bloody uncomfortable it is. Of course I'm not."

"Ah. Tell me more."

"I suppose, as I need your help, I'll have to. But it's against the rules: you'll have to guarantee absolute confidence. Not just for me, but for the others who'd be put at risk if this gets out before they're ready."

"What others?"

"Other people like me who've agreed to help."

"Help who?"

"Oh. William . . . the *police,* of course."

I stared at him, and he met my stare. The lamplight shone off his glasses, hiding the pale eyes, but it didn't matter, I'd seen it all before. I said:

"You . . . are helping the police?"

"It'll be the biggest bust Crete's ever had if it comes off as planned," he said.

"But *you*—"

"I'm the poacher turned gamekeeper," he said. "You know I never touched the hard stuff, I was always against it. Smoking the occasional joint, well, too much fuss made about that. But smack, coke, and the rest—no, I've seen too much to have any illusions. So yes, when they approached me, I agreed."

Once agan, I was reminded of Spyro: *I hadda friend . . . ,* the friend who died of drugs, over whose grave he'd sworn, etc. . . .

On the other hand, it was true that Nick had never shown any sign of the drug baron mentality, the cold inhumanity of *never mind the bodies, count the cash.*

"Have you sold pot to Eléni?" I asked.

"Oh, Eléni . . . so you met her. In Moustaki?"

"Yes. Have you?"

"Isn't this a bit ridiculous? I say yes, I say no—where does that get us?"

"It might explain how her friend Stavros got to hear of you."

"Stavros!"

"You know him?"

"I know of him. Where does he come in?"

"I had dinner with him and Eléni on his boat, at Frangocas-tello."

"Did you now!"

"He asked after you. Seemed to think you had an interest in common."

"What was that?"

"What do you think?"

He scowled. Yes, it was a cross-examination, and I was treating him like a hostile witness. He said:

"What are you getting at?"

"I want some answers."

"I've given you some."

"I want some more."

"Why, for God's sake? Why not just accept what I've told you, and leave it at that? I didn't ask you to come to Crete."

"No, but you asked me up here. You want something, and I'll give it if I can. Once I know what's going on."

"Oh Christ. What, then?"

"I was asking what Stavros and you have in common."

He thought. Then he said:

"You want to be careful of Stavros, you know."

"And Eléni?"

"She's in with him. I'd steer clear of them both, if I were you."

"His main passion seems to be antiquities," I said.

Again that tiny hesitation before he said:

"That's an expensive hobby."

"He doesn't seem short of money."

"He isn't. Look, this is getting too close for comfort. I'm afraid I can't say any more about Stavros. Just stay away. If you took that as a warning, you wouldn't be wrong."

"Does his money come from drugs?"

"What makes you think that?"

"The money comes from somewhere. Plus, he's got a personal bodyguard of three trained men, so there's risk involved. And he was very keen to know of your whereabouts."

"Was he?"

"My guess is you're treading on his toes, Nick, perhaps without realizing it. Now tell me you're not bringing in pot, if nothing else. You wouldn't see anything wrong with that, I'm sure. But Stavros is *trading on the same route* . . . How about that?"

"You think so?"

"It wouldn't just be pot for him—not enough money in it. It would have to be hard drugs: that's where the big money is. And you're in his way . . . Am I right?"

"My God!" Nick said. "I suppose you could be."

"Ah! So you *are* . . ."

"No! But he might *think* I was."

"Why?"

Nick blinked. Then he said:

"As you reminded us, a few minutes back, I have a record . . ."

"He could find that out?"

"If you've got enough money, you can find anything out."

My turn to think about it. I thought it made the most sense of any idea so far. The fact that Nick denied it, might, on the Cretan Liar principle, make it more likely to be true than all that stuff about the Great Crack-Down. If he *was* bringing anything in, he might very likely have limited himself to pot. That, of course, would still bring the authorities on his tail . . . And explain why . . .

"Greg Barnes didn't sound much like an ally," I said. "And why wouldn't he know where you are, if you're part of this crackdown?"

"You might well ask yourself that," he said.

"Me?"

"Of course. Who brought the Gyparis brothers down on my neck?"

"I know, I'm sorry . . . So you had to move from Arcadés . . ."

"Left that route wide open," he said accusingly. "And I don't have regular contact, it's too risky. So we'd temporarily lost touch, and he was trying to trace me. Made a balls-up of it, but I suppose he felt he had to try."

"Good old Greg."

"Never met him. But he does at least seem to have kept the wrappers on the operation, as far as you were concerned."

"Oh, he was hot stuff on secrecy. Gave nothing away."

"Glad to hear it," Nick said with approval. "Well now, shall I tell you what I'd like? Assuming that you're ready to cooperate?"

"Hang on," I said. "I'd like to talk about the view, first."

"The view? William, there's isn't all that much time to—"

"The view of the Akrotiri. From your back door, here."

He sat up, took his glasses off, began polishing them. "The view of the Akrotiri," he repeated. "The view of the . . . Oh, yes, right, I'm with you."

"This was an observation post in the war," I said. "From here, they could see the German ships and planes come and go, and radio it all back to base in Cairo."

"London," he said.

"Wherever. Now there's this NAMFI, which I'm told means Nato Missile Firing Installation. I drove round, obeyed the No Photography notices, but kept my eyes open. It's extensive, the biggest base this end of the Mediterranean, Greg Barnes said— he knew I could read it in newspapers. You've got a splendid view of it from here."

"Every Tuesday at between ten and ten fifteen, there's a test firing," Nick said. "You hear the roar, and can actually see the rocket when the visibility's good."

"Ah—"

"Not only from here, but from our terrace in Moustaki."

"Oh."

He put his glasses back on and inspected me sorrowfully through them. "So, it's not information that would be worth a great deal, is it. Even if I—"

"*I* didn't think you would. Only that *Greg Barnes* might think so. As I said, he didn't speak of you as an ally, but from the point of view of an opponent. So, of course, I ask myself why."

"I got it right the first time," Nick said. "He's a menace."

"He's paranoid, probably. Many of them must be, in the CIA. Mind you, sometimes it's justified. But at other times they go right over the top. Greg Barnes could, I feel sure. He probably has a combination lock on his deep freeze."

"I wonder if you're right," Nick said, sounding stunned. He wasn't used to other people floating ideas, and the novelty had taken him off balance.

"I got the impression, driving round, that the top brass were slightly unhinged," I said. "On the one hand, they expect coach loads of tourists to obey restrictions on photography. On the other hand they've put up prettily painted regimental signs which all but say *'This way to the missiles.'* What else can you conclude?"

Nick considered it. "We always used to say that the military mind lived in a world of its own," he said.

"When you were a paid-up member of the Campaign for Nuclear Disarmament? Yes, Greg Barnes had that on computer, as well."

"Oh, *shit!*" Nick muttered.

"Well, it's a non-starter, isn't it," I said. "You're not the most straight-up character I've ever met, but nobody's going to believe you've been selling microfilm to the KGB . . ."

"Oh for Christ's sake, no, of course not . . . That isn't what I meant. What worries me is the thought of this CIA enthusiast managing to drop a spanner in the works, by accident. Just what I could do without at this moment."

"What works?" I said suspiciously.

"Oh . . . the operation, the crackdown."

"Ready to go, is it?"

"Yes, yes . . . ready to go."

"When, exactly?"

"Oh, well . . . I can't tell you that. Very soon."

"You can't because you don't know?"

"I haven't been told."

"Waiting for instructions?"

"Yes, that's it."

"How will they come?"

"What do you mean?"

"What I say—*how will they contact you?*"

"Why do you want to know?"

"It'd be a convincing detail."

"I thought I'd already—"

"Convinced me? No, Nick, you haven't."

"But *why* . . ."

"Why don't you save time and energy, and just tell me the truth?"

His glasses flashed as he moved his head this way and that, a fish being drawn to the net. I said, to ease him in:

"What do you want me to do?"

"Do? Nothing. Well, not much . . . I suppose you've still got the hired jeep I saw at Arcadés?"

"Yes."

"I'd like to borrow it. You could go back in the pickup."

"Why do you want the jeep?"

"I have to get to Hora Sfakion, on the south coast. I can't go out through Moustaki—someone would recognize the pickup. The only other way is over the mountains, along the track they're working on. But there's a section still unfinished; the pickup wouldn't make it."

"Nick, that's a hired jeep—I'm not even supposed to drive it off the tarmac road!"

"Oh, the old track goes through. There's just this one narrow section where they've been held up. They're having to blast the rock away to get the bulldozer in, and of course the locals keep stealing the blasting granules to sell down on the coast. They use it for—"

"Fishing."

"Yes, right."

"How will I get the jeep back?"

He thought about it, then said: "I don't want the pickup seen in Hora Sfakion, either. And you know Frangocastello. So I'll drive your jeep there early tomorrow, get a lift back to Hora. You can collect it at any time to suit yourself. Leave the pickup outside the hotel, and the key with Apostolos."

"Who?"

"The owner. He'll be in the bar: tubby chap with curly black hair—"

"I know."

"Well, that's fine, I knew I could rely on—"

"I didn't say I agreed."

"Oh, didn't you? I thought—"

"Why are you going to Hora Sfakion?"

"Oh Christ, William, not *more* questions! I've told you I—"

"Why?"

"We've already been through this. I've got to make contact urgently. I told you—the thing's ready to go. I've got to confirm what they want me to do."

"Your instructions."

"My instructions, yes, of course."

I shook my head. It was sad, like watching a high-wire artiste falter, wobble, scrabble to regain balance . . . The effortless perfection is gone, and instead of a glittering god you see a frightened, fallible thing of tearable flesh and breakable bone . . . I said:

"Sorry, Nick, but that's it."

"What?"

"A couple of minutes ago you didn't know how you were going to get your instructions."

He was silent. I said:

"I wasn't trying to catch you out. I *wanted* to believe you. And I'll lend you the jeep . . . *if* you'll come clean."

The Mozart was coming to an end. I realized I hadn't heard any of it until now. There was a blast of applause like static interference. Nick crossed to the radio, and stabbed at a button. There was silence. Then he said:

"Why does it matter to you *so much?*"

"I've been here a week. I've met a lot of people. I've endured a lot of trivial discomfort and some real danger. It's been a full week."

"So?"

"I want to know what all these people and all these events add up to."

"Is that all?"

"You know what the truth is worth. That's why you hoard it like a miser's gold. Well, now I want a share. The key to the mystery in return for the keys of my jeep."

"Ha ha."

"Yes, ha ha. So come on, Nick—*give.*"

He sat on the camp bed, and leaned forward with his elbows on his knees, looking at the ground. I listened to the hissing of the paraffin lamp, and thought: *he has to tell me, now.*

He raised his head and looked directly at me. He took his glasses off, exposing the pale eyes. I thought: *this time, I really believe I'm going to get the truth . . .*

"All right," he said. "It's like this—"

—*and here it comes!*

"I've discovered the lost city of Atlantis," he said.

The Dogs of Candia are all a Baftard-Greyhound;
mif-fhapen, thin flank'd, and look to be all of one Breed:
their Hair is ugly enough, and they feem to be between a
Wolf and a Fox. They ftill retain their antient Quicknefs
of Scent . . .

*T*here must be a lingering boyishness and naïveté about my appearance that encourages car salesmen, vineyard owners, and the man with the Eiffel Tower for sale, all to think they're on to a good thing. It's no less annoying when someone you've known a long time makes the same assumption—in fact, it's worse. *Much worse . . .*

Well, of *course* I exploded. The cavern rang with words and phrases I'd forgotten I knew, uttered in a voice last heard on the parade ground at Aldershot. Eventually I regained control, and sat down again. It took some time for the noise to die out in the connecting chambers and passageways, but eventually there was silence. In which Nick said:

"It's true, you know."

He never gives up! "Just drop it, Nick," I said wearily. "It isn't going to work, no way. You've lost your touch; it's gone, kaput, finished. I used to have a certain admiration for your ability as a piss artist, but now I'm afraid—"

"No, *really*," he said.

I looked at him. He still had his glasses off, and there was something in his eyes which . . .

"Oh *Christ!* Go on then—let's have it."

"It's a fascinating story if you're interested in archeology. Which I know you're not, but bear with me." He paused to clear his throat and peer at me myopically.

"I'm still listening," I said.

"Right. Well then, the legend of Atlantis originated in Plato's lost island civilization, which he refers to in the Critias. He says it was located beyond the Pillars of Hercules—which has always been thought to refer to the Straights of Gibraltar. In other words, that the island lies submerged in the Atlantic. But there are now grounds for thinking this a misinterpretation, and that Atlantis was, in fact, Crete."

"Oh, right. So sitting here, we're under water? I hadn't noticed."

"It pleases you to be jocular," he said. "But I don't believe you've been to the eastern end of Crete, where there are ruins under water? No? Well, there are. How did that happen?"

"I guess you're about to tell me."

"I am. According to Plato, the island of Atlantis disappeared 'in one terrible day and night'—in other words, there was a disaster. The destruction was on too great a scale to have been caused by war, so it was a natural disaster. There's a rising theory that the cause was, in fact, a huge tidal wave from the earthquake on the volcanic island of Santorini, only sixty miles north of Crete. That occurred circa one thousand five hundred B.C., the

period when the Minoan palaces on eastern Crete are known to
have been destroyed. So it all ties up."

He was talking fact. It might be wrong, but it wasn't flannel,
bullshit. I'd had plenty of that, and I could taste the difference.
I let him go on.

"That earthquake was unbelievably vast," he said. "It's been
compared to the one at Kraratoa in 1883 which, of course,
there's data on. That was heard three thousand miles away,
blew five cubic miles of material out of the island, and caused
catastrophic air and sea waves. You can see the crater in Santorini—the sea broke in and it's now a bay—and judge the
scale of the explosion from the depth of volcanic ash many feet
thick. The tidal wave created would have been equally vast. It
must have been horrific. And, because of the dust, it happened
in the dark . . ."

"Santorini!" I said. "I've had some wine from there, at the
dinner with Stavros. An excellent dry white."

"Am I boring you?" he asked.

"No no, sorry. Go on."

"It's not the means of destruction, or even the fact that eastern
Crete is almost certainly the Atlantis referred to by Plato. *It's
what I've found there, underwater . . .*"

"Minoan?"

"Yes. Pottery with the characteristic spiral designs, seal stones
with the typical subjects—lions, ships, dolphins, scorpions, spi-
ders. Figurines—"

"Goddesses . . ."

"One, and not a very good example."

"But still worth—"

"—a lot, yes."

"I see."

He put his glasses back on. "I doubt if you do," he said.

"Oh, but surely—"

"Not if you think it's the money."

"Isn't it?"

He was silent. Then he said:

"Don't think much of me, William, do you."

"I keep trying, Nick, but you don't make it easy."

"Hmm. Well, now that it's cards on the table, I'll admit I can see that. But I had a reason. I've been fighting for the most important thing in my life. And it isn't money. It's . . . well, here's your chance for a laugh. It's immortality."

He had the floor. I didn't say a thing. I didn't laugh, either.

"Thanks," he said. "But I wouldn't have blamed you. It's going to seem unreal, my name in all the standard works beside Heinrich Schliemann, Arthur Evans, Michael Ventris . . ."

He was serious. I was sure he was serious. "My God," I said, "as big as *that*?"

"Yes."

"A palace?"

"Yes. Submerged before the ash got to it."

"How did you find it?"

"A hunch. Other people have looked, but I went further out, and struck lucky . . . That's not what I shall say in my memoirs, of course. No, I'll find some data to extrapolate from—that's more respectable."

"I noticed a wet suit in the cellar at Moustaki."

"Yes, I did my own diving. I had to hire scuba gear: it's at a hundred and twenty feet plus."

Something was niggling . . . ah yes. "The ash," I said. "Doesn't ash preserve rather than destroy, as at Pompeii?"

"That was lava. This is tephra, highly acid. Above water level, nothing could be grown, the land was ruined."

"I see." There was something else, surely? Yes!—of course there was! "So you're planning to get this stuff out of Crete?"

"Yes."

"But not for money?"

"I may have to sell a few things to cover expenses, but basically, not for money. As I said."

"As you said . . . It's illegal, of course, to export antiquities."

"Correct."

"Then why not hand the stuff to the Cretan authorities?"

He shook his head. "I knew you'd bring that up. And of course, it would be the proper thing to do. But I've got to establish my discovery first."

"How do you mean?"

"It's technical," he said. "Do you want to hear it?"

"I think so."

"Right. It's pottery we're talking about. So it can't be dated here in Crete—they've only got radiocarbon equipment."

"Why won't that do?"

"Only works on organic material. For pottery, you need TL—that's therminoluminescence dating. What you do is, you heat a fragment of the object until the uranium and thorium in it emit alpha particles which are absorbed by impurities in the clay, causing ionization and releasing electrons which are measured as light. Then you—"

"All right, all right. You heat the thing, it gives off light, you measure the light."

"Exactly. For this, I have to get the pottery to the University Museum, Philadelphia. Until that's done, and the findings published, I'm at risk in two ways. There are plenty of so-called respectable academics who'd like to claim my discovery for themselves, and plenty more honest villains who'd happily cut my throat to get their hands on a hoard of this value."

"Once it's all over, and you've published—"

"Then I shall freely admit to having smuggled it out, and have it sent back to Crete."

"Or most of it."

He smiled. "All right. I may keep a few of the duplicated items. I think that's fair, don't you?"

"Maybe. I'd certainly be tempted myself."

"Right."

I hesitated. If he'd made all that up, it was a masterly performance. Could anyone do so much on the spur of the moment? It fitted with his character, too—always a bit of a buccaneer, liking to live on his wits, making a profit but not too much, basically harmless, entertaining even . . . Who was I to cast the first stone?

"Take the jeep," I said.

"William, I appreciate it."

"If you're still conning me, I'd rather not know. The tale's too good to be spoiled."

"I assure you—"

"Please don't. Here are the keys."

He rose from the camp bed, came over, and took them from me. I said:

"We haven't talked about Maud. And that's a lot of her paintings you've got in the shed at Kalikrati—what are they doing there?"

"Doing? Waiting to be sent off, of course."

"What? All twenty-seven of them?"

"Oh no, not all at once," he said. "I'm holding some back—you don't want to flood the market. Meanwhile, it's a nice, dry place to store them. I hope when she . . ." His voice trailed off.

"What is it?"

"Shh!"

I listened. There was a sound, like the wind in a chimney. Nick said:

"Can you hear it?"

"Wind across the cave mouth, perhaps?"

"No, it's coming from the other direction. Listen!"

We listened. It sounded the same, perhaps a little louder. Nick frowned. I said:

"What do you think it is?"

"I don't know, but when you've been in a place for three days, you get to know the sounds. This I haven't heard before."

He picked up the lamp, and moved to the passage that led into the mountain, the start of the labyrinth, and stood listening, his head bowed. I heard the sound again. It was eerie, almost as if some animal had got itself trapped in there. But an animal would always be able to find its way out, by retracing its scent . . .

"What?"

Nick had been into the passage, had returned, and said something.

"You're losing your cash," he repeated. He held up a fifty drachma piece. "I'm sure it wasn't me. Better check your pockets for holes. And that sound—"

"I put it there to mark the way," I said, "one at each turning. By the time I got here I was nearly broke and using the big ones."

He stared. "You *what*? Why?"

"In case your map was wrong and I had to find my way out."

"There was nothing wrong with the map."

"No, but I couldn't *know* that, could I . . ."

He continued to stare. His mouth opened, then shut again. I realized then what he was thinking. I said:

"You could have warned me not to. Though in that case, I don't think I would have—"

"Shhh!" he said again, flapping his hand palm downward for silence. *There it was again . . . and louder.* I said:

"Let's face it. That's a dog."

Hunt followers have been heard to claim that the fox enjoys the chase. It's natural for animals in the wild to hunt and be hunted, all in a day's work. And, not being conscious of injury and death in the same way as humans, they're not so frightened of the consequences of being caught.

Maybe it's not so bad, then—if you're a fox. As a self-conscious human, I was suddenly aware of sweating palms, a racing heartbeat, an urgent desire to be somewhere else, any-where else, and *fast* . . . Panic, in short. My brain seemed to be on strike, and blind instinct was taking over . . .

Then the moment passed, and reason took control again. All right, so there was a dog running down my scent through the labyrinth. There must be men following. But we should be able to handle it. The dog's howls were scary in this confined place, but had given us useful warning. We would not be taken by surprise.

I reached for the Mannlicher. Nick said:

"It's me they're after. If you could hold them here . . ."

"Thanks," I said. "Last time, at Arcadés, you said that, as a friend of yours, I was also a legitimate target. I propose to go on that assumption."

"If you hadn't been so bloody stupid, pointing the way with those coins—"

"They'd still be on their way, following the dog."

"Yes, but you made it easy for them. And seeing the coins, they'll know they're on the right track."

"Anyone could have put the coins down. They're *Greek*—not a penny piece amongst them."

"But they're clean, obviously recent . . ."

The howling again—much nearer, now . . .

"No point in arguing," Nick said. "The question is, do we stand or scarper?"

"Suppose we scarper—where to?"

"Over the mountain, back to Kalikrati and the cars."

"Steep, you said. And exposed. Also, these shepherds can cover the ground like mountain goats. They'd catch us."

"You could easily hold them off with that," he said, pointing to the Mannlicher.

"*If* they haven't brought rifles this time, instead of shotguns. And *if* the ammo isn't dud—it must have been there since the war, maybe longer."

"All right," he said angrily, "all right. *You* suggest something."

I'd been working on a plan. But, as I opened my mouth to tell him, there was a hellish howl from close to, followed by a scuffling. We were both watching the passage mouth when the beast appeared. It skidded to a stop, and then began to advance slowly. It was a huge, black mongrel, with rough, unkempt fur and a long, mangy tail. It drew back its lips and snarled, showing big yellow teeth . . .

"Shoot the bastard!" Nick urged.

Goes against the grain to shoot a dog. Man's best friend . . . On the other hand it was creeping nearer. The snarling had a frightening, mad ferocity about it. Nick shouted:

"Go *on*, man! What are you waiting for?"

I raised the Mannlicher, aimed between the beast's eyes, squeezed the trigger.

The report seemed loud enough to split the cave. The dog tumbled in a heap, didn't stir. I lowered the rifle.

"That's two things less to worry about," Nick said, sounding relieved.

"Two? Oh yes, two. It doesn't mean all the ammo's good, of course."

"Bloody pessimist," Nick said, pulling on a windcheater and slinging his binoculars round his neck. "Well, let's get going. Hearing that shot may slow them up but, as you said, they'll catch us on the mountain soon enough. Better make tracks. I'll abandon the rest of this stuff . . . Well, come *on,* then!"

"Just a minute." I was reaching into the *sakoúli.*

"Bring it, if you must. But for Christ's sake *get a move on.*

I ignored him. *Somewhere in here is . . . Yes, that feels like it.*

"William! You're wasting *time . . .*"

"Saving it, I hope," I said, showing him the cigarette-tin bomb.

"What's that? A fishing bomb? How did you—"

"Stole it. I had two: only this one left now. Worth a try, I think."

"Right . . . but *hurry!*"

"I'm hurrying. You bring the lamp."

I skirted the dead dog and led the way into the passage which led from the labyrinth. Ten yards should be enough . . . The rock was layered, soft in places. I found a loose chunk halfway up the wall, prised it out with a stone from the floor, tried the tin. It slid in easily. I said:

"The last one had a fifteen second fuse, but I wouldn't count on this being the same. Get ready to run."

"I'm ready," Nick said.

I flicked the lighter into life, applied the flame. The fuse spluttered, then settled into a steady hiss . . .

"That's it!"

We ran back down the passage and through the cavern, Nick dropping the lamp in the fireplace. It broke, and I was aware of flames leaping, the reek of paraffin smoke . . . Then we were out of the cavern and sprinting down the tunnel to the exit. I was counting . . . *nine . . . ten . . . eleven . . .* Nick was scrambling up the rockfall, he was in the open, lucky bastard . . . *thirteen . . . fourteen . . . fifteen . . .* Oh Jesus! And I'm not clear yet . . . *seventeen . . . eighteen . . . nineteen . . . twenty . . . twenty-one . . .* Well, I'm clear now, but there's not much point if it doesn't—

There was a thud from inside the cave, followed by a long, leisurely rumble. A few seconds later, a cloud of dust streamed from the tunnel mouth like smoke. I breathed out, felt my muscles relax.

"I hope it *was* the Gyparis brothers," Nick said reflectively.

"Oh my *God!*"

"Don't worry," he said kindly. "I'm fairly sure it was. Who else would bring that dog into the cave?"

Fairly! "Something worried me," I said. "If they were tracking with it, wouldn't they have kept it on a leash, not let it go streaking on ahead?"

"I thought that. Then I realized that they might have let it off, once they were sure your coins were on the same track. Sort of 'Go boy! and get 'em.' It's their style."

"I hope you're right."

"Sure I am. Let's go then, shall we? I'll lead, and you watch our rear, in case the passage wasn't completely blocked."

It was good to be out in the open. The heat had gone out of the sun, too. I looked at my watch: ten to six. I suddenly realized I'd had nothing to eat since breakfast. The thought as much as the feeling brought complaints from my neglected stomach: there were sandwiches in the *sakoúli,* but now wasn't the time. I tramped after Nick, turning every couple of minutes to perform my allotted duty as rear guard.

But there was nobody else on the bare, rocky mountainside we were traversing, climbing diagonally to a dip between peaks. The view to the north was becoming more and more dramatic: I could see the naval dockyard in Suda Bay, the built-up area further west that was Hania, and the array of radio masts on the Akrotiri that marked the position of the missile launching base . . . Well, surely I could stop speculating in that direction? I glanced at Nick's back, bobbing ahead of me over the rough ground, imagining what label he would choose for that blank space where building workers carry the name of their firm. Wheeler-dealer, con man, spy . . . Spy was the least likely: for that you had to be patient, unobtrusive, political—he was none of those. He *was* a con man, he told tales, wove spells . . . and a dealer, in goods because they were the raw material, but primarily in dreams, or (you could say) in *futures,* one in particular—his own. Odd that I feel sympathetic, as I'm not included. But I do. I want to see this bird *fly* . . .

I stumbled, and was rudely shaken back to reality. Are we really going to climb up *there*?

Nick was already on the first of the ledges which barred the way. I turned, studied the mountainside below. A hawk sailed out from behind a rock outcrop, turning its head as it searched for prey. On the ground, nothing moved. I turned back, and started to climb.

"Kilikrati," Nick said, pointing.

We were on the saddle between the two peaks. The rest of the way was down, but it looked rough.

"About time too," I said. "Five minutes to get our breath back, right?"

"If you must."

"I've been carrying the bag *and* the rifle."

"Okay—give me the bag, then . . . My God! What have you got in here?"

"Sandwiches, cheese, some apples. A bottle of wine . . ."

"For Christ's sake! Can't you go anywhere without a full-scale picnic?"

"The trouble with you, Nick, is that you live for tomorrow. Meanwhile, you're happy to starve. I'm not."

He gave a contemptuous snort. I got out the sandwiches and started on one. He looked away. After a while he said:

"I wouldn't mind an apple. To lighten the load."

"Help yourself."

He reached into the bag, groped, frowned, brought out the Smith & Wesson. "Where'd you get this?"

"Stavros," I said, through a mouthful of lettuce.

"*Stavros?* You didn't tell me that!"

"You're not that free with information yourself."

"Perhaps not, but . . . *Stavros* . . . Why did he?"

"Considerate of my welfare," I said. "You'll find that hard to understand, but there it is."

He stared at me suspiciously. "What did you promise in return?"

"Nothing."

"Well, what did he ask for?"

I shook my head.

"Oh come on, William! He *must* have, he's a *Greek* . . ."

"I told you, he wants to contact you."

"But you didn't—"

"No, of course I didn't agree. Damn it, Nick! I'm helping *you*! God knows why, but I am. Can't you see that, feel it?"

He went on staring, then nodded. He bit into the apple, munched, swallowed, and said:

"Sorry. Lost my cool."

"Forget it . . ." I spoke absently, my attention distracted by a movement below. Nick said:

"What is it? Can you see something?"

"Some*one*. Down there, at the entrance to that gulley."

Nick reached for his binoculars, pushed his glasses up to his forehead, and put the lenses to his eyes, began focusing . . . I said:

"If there's only one, it may just be a shepherd."

"There are two," he said tersely. "The second's sitting down, partly screened by a bush." He lowered the binoculars, began to scramble down to the shelter of a rock. "Keep low," he called back. "I'm pretty sure they haven't seen us yet."

I seized the *sakoúli* that he'd left behind, and scrambled down after him, abandoning my second, half-eaten sandwich. "Is it the brothers?"

Nick was training the binoculars again from behind the rock. "Yes, it's them. *Shit!*"

"Shotguns?"

He fine-focused. "Think so. The one standing certainly has a gun, not a rifle. Not sure about the other."

"Let's hope." I slung the *sakoúli* on my back again. Nick said: "Here! I said I'd carry that."

"Don't bother, it's lighter now. Let's get going."

He hesitated, nodded, and started off across the slope. I imitated him, moving swiftly behind cover, bending low when forced to cross a patch of open ground. There was no point in being overly careful: speed mattered most, to get between the brothers and the village. Once in that position, we could expect to hold them off while we retreated to the cars.

It was hard going: the rocks were in crumbling, jagged rows like waves, with sharp edges and spiny bushes in the interstices. I slipped and, trying to save myself, put my right hand on one, cursing as the thorns bit into my palm. Nick looked back:

"What's up?"

"Thorn bush."

"Is that all."

"Thanks!"

"No, I mean—don't twist an ankle."

He was right—that would be a disaster. But I wished he hadn't said it: things seem to go wrong precisely when you're trying to avoid them, probably *because* you're trying to avoid them . . .

I decided not to risk a careless slip by glancing back while in flight, but to stop and do it thoroughly, deliberately. First stop, that bush there . . .

By some strange empathy, Nick halted right there, turned, and began to sweep the hillside below and to our right. If the brothers had seen us, they'd be legging it that way, trying to cut us off. I said, breathlessly:

"Anything?"

"No . . . What d'you think they're up to?"

"Still waiting—didn't see us."

"Why just there?"

"I've been asking myself that. I don't think they went into the cave, but sent the dog in to try to flush us out. *That's* why it was loose."

"Why wouldn't they follow?"

"No light," I said, pleased with myself.

"Ah! Yes, you could be right. They wouldn't have had a torch."

"Not unless they *knew* you were in there."

"So they're at a loss. They must have heard the explosion, the dog didn't come out, but they couldn't go in to look for it without light. So they decided to wait at the entrance to the gulley, on the way back to the village, hoping that we and/or the dog would turn up. But we slipped past behind them . . . So let's keep going, take advantage."

"We stop about every five minutes to check for them, right?"

"Right."

And we were off again. The village had disappeared from sight behind a low ridge, but Nick seemed to be confident of the direction, with only an occasional glance at the sun for confirmation. We stopped, checked, went on again. Then Nick slowed, and cursed.

"What's the matter?"

"I was trying for an alternative route all the way back to the village," he said, "but we're being squeezed by the mountain on the left. We're bound to go over that ridge, now, and drop on to the route I gave you. If they've given up and are on the way back, we'll not only be on a collision course, but we'll be

exposed as we cross over—they can hardly fail to see us. What
do you think?"

"If we wait until dark, we'll lose the long-range advantage of
the rifle. And I don't fancy the final approach to the cars in
darkness, do you?"

"Just what I was thinking. So, we go over, then?"

"I'm with you."

It was deceptive, this rocky landscape. Seen from a distance,
there appeared to be plenty of cover. In fact there *was*—so long
as you didn't have to move. Going cross-country, as we were,
you were constantly having to climb over rocks to get from one
concealed position to the next. To an onlooker, Nick and I must
have resembled a pair of performing seals, or dolphins, constantly bobbing into view and out again. It was tiring, very hard
on the hands—the rocks were hot from the sun as well as
scratchy—and dangerous. But there was nothing we could do
about it, except to hope that if there were any onlookers, the
brothers weren't among them.

Nick was still in the lead, reached the top of the ridge first,
and started a sweep with his binoculars. I panted up beside him,
and frankly flopped. Down there to the left was the oak grove
where I'd enjoyed a short relief from the sun. The cars were less
than half a mile beyond. I said:

"Your direction's good."

"Further to the left, above that grove, would have been
better," Nick said. "But I don't feel like going back, do you?"

"No. And they may well be behind us."

"Yes. And furthermore, I've had enough of this mad scramble
to avoid two young half-wits. We've got the rifle—I say we just
go straight on down, out of these sodding rocks, and turn for
home."

"Agreed."

We moved on again, climbing down over the thinning rocks

to emerge on to scrubland. The relief at being able to walk normally again! I said:

"The labyrinth was as *nothing* compared to that. You said it was a shortcut—and how!"

"Not far now," he said.

"Good sun today. Should be enough hot water in your roof tank for a bath."

"Should be."

"We must settle what I'm to tell Maud."

"I don't want you to say anything, yet."

"Nick, I just can't go back there, all knackered, hands torn to shreds, and say nothing. It's not possible."

"Hmm. Can't you?"

"Of course not."

"Pity. Now that I'm so close to—"

"Nick—sorry, but I can't."

"Oh. Well look, tell her you've seen me, that I've just got a business matter to settle tomorrow, after which all will be explained. Tell her . . . no, that'll do. Please."

"Why not more?"

"For the same reason I've had to cut myself off so far. She's very short on worldly wisdom, William—you must have noticed. She hasn't the first idea how to keep a secret. If she ran into Spyro, for instance, he'd have the whole thing out of her in thirty seconds. That could easily blow the whole thing. Listen, you've got to promise me this! I trusted you, and—"

"All right, all right."

"You mean it?"

"Yes, yes. Don't worry."

"Well that's a relief! I thought for a moment, there, that you . . ."

He went on about it, quite unnecessarily, as I'd already decided it was his decision, and had agreed. I was tired, and I just switched off. Automatic functions kept going, like the mental clock which prompted me to look behind every five minutes. Time was up. I glanced behind, and of course, once again, there was nothing—

I blinked, looked harder. *Not nothing, no* . . .

"Nick!"

"—but Spyro's the one to watch, he's really up shit creek with that hotel he's building, and he'll . . . What?"

"Look behind."

"Oh Christ! I really thought we were in the clear."

"So did I. Into the trees, then?"

"Right."

Whatever our other differences, we seemed to think as one in military matters. We moved fast into the wood, each chose a tree for shelter, and turned as one. The brothers were a hundred yards away, and closing. If I hadn't turned round just then . . .

"That's close enough," Nick said urgently. I threw up the Mannlicher, aimed at the ground between them, squeezed the trigger. There was a satisfying bang and whine as the bullet ricocheted off stones. The brothers stopped dead, seemed to confer, but instead of running for cover or dropping flat simply shouldered their guns and opened fire. We had time to take cover behind our two trees, but it was chilling to hear the rustle of shot through the leaves near us.

"These burks mean business," Nick said with what sounded like indignation. *Hadn't he been telling me they did?*

"Pump-action shotguns, three to five shots to a loading," I said. "Plus a belt of maybe twenty spare. Each."

"How many rounds have you got left?"

"Eight." I chanced a quick look round the tree, and ducked back again. More shot brought a shower of leaves down from over my head.

"Is that all?"

"There were ten, minus two I've fired, equals eight."

"Well, better not waste any more."

"Not a waste. They stopped."

"But they're still there. Didn't even bother to take cover."

"Perhaps to a Cretan, that's chicken. And they know I didn't aim to hit—that was an obvious warning shot of mine they're being brave about."

I looked round the tree again. Both men were reloading. I'd counted the shots, and knew they'd fired six. So the guns each held three, not five. That was something, though not much. Nick said:

"They're not backing off. William, you're going to have to shoot in earnest next time."

"If they come on, perhaps. Trouble is, I like shooting people even less than shooting dogs."

More shot blasted through the leaves. Nick said bitterly:

"This is terrific. You swagger round armed to the teeth, and when the time comes to pull the bloody trigger, you *can't do it.* Any moment now, these nuts are going to rush us and I, at least, am going to get my head blown off. What's the matter with you?"

"I thought you were a pacifist."

"Oh, very funny. Look, if you're not going to shoot, I'd better start running . . . Well?"

"I'm not sure," I said.

"Why the hell not?"

"They don't seem to be in any hurry to get to grips. I think they're firing over our heads."

He stared at me from the safety of his tree. I stared back from behind mine. "If so, why?" he said.

"Because, to be blunt, if they kill you, they'll have lost what their boss is after—the location of the Minoan treasures. So they want you alive."

"No," he said, "no . . . we can't bank on that."

"You mean, there's more you haven't told me?" I risked another quick look round the tree. The two were in conference, but they still hadn't come any closer. What *was* going on?

"I mean, there's someone who knows where the stuff is, but knows I would shop them if they took it," Nick said, taking a turn to look round his tree.

"Who?"

"I can't tell you now, for reasons which are . . . Oh Christ! *Look out!*"

If I've never heard a true word from Nick before, I know he's genuine now. I drop flat, poke the rifle round the tree, and realize with a chill of fright that I may already be too late—they're only fifty yards away, forty, and coming on fast. Nick must have shown himself, because both fire from the hip, simultaneously. I aim, fire, and the one on my side yells and tumbles. I work the bolt, aim at the other, fire again . . .

Or think I have. It takes a second or so to realize that there'd been no report. A dud cartridge—*now*, of all times . . . I work the bolt frantically, but now the tree's in the way, I have to jump up, swing the rifle round to the left, it catches on branches, Nick is yelling, and now there's a crashing as the man charges right into the wood and Nick grapples him, the shotgun goes off in the air, oh good, and he can't work the pump to reload, but there's a mad struggle going on and they're rolling on the ground, I can't shoot because I might hit Nick, and now the idiot's managed to pull a knife, I've got to *do* something, well if I can't shoot there's still the other end, the butt . . .

I leave Nick sitting on him, and go cautiously to look at the other. He's sitting on the ground a safe distance from the gun he dropped when I shot him, holding his thigh with both hands. I keep him covered with the rifle, and he glances up at me along the length of the barrel, hardly more than a boy in spite of his big black boots and big black moustache, his face frozen in an expression of heroic stupidity, or stupid heroism; anyway, it makes me want to shoot him all over again . . .

17

As for their Morals, in fpite of all the Care their
Legiflators took to mould them, they have been found
tardy in many things. Polybius writes, that of all
Mankind the Cretans were the only People that thought
no Lucre fordid.

*I*t was almost dark by the time I got back to Moustaki in the
Hyundai. And I was glad about that. I was going to slip quietly
into Moustaki, give Maud Nick's message, collect my bags, and
drive on to one of the many hotels on the main road to Rethymnon; tomorrow, I'd drive round to Frangocastello and collect
the jeep as arranged with Nick. That was a better plan than
spending the night in Moustaki, where the Gyparis household
would soon be in a turmoil over the return of the brothers.
We'd done the best we could for the wounded one, binding up
his thigh with a torn-off shirt tail, fetching the jeep, transporting
him and his brother to their pickup in the village, even handing
back their guns—though not until we'd confiscated their car-

tridge belts and searched their pockets for spares. It was meant to show what misunderstood and decent chaps we were, prepared even after such provocation to forgive and forget, but as it all had to be done Smith & Wesson in hand for fear of losing control, the message must have come across a bit mixed. There was nothing in their black, unrelenting eyes except a burning desire to bite chunks out of the hand of friendship at the first opportunity. But what else could we do? Nick worked in silence, obviously feeling that persuasion was a waste of time, and I only had the phrase book, which for once could hardly be blamed for not including "My Friend Did Not Violate Your Sister" among its everyday messages. So I handed the Mannlicher over to Nick, got into the Hyundai, and set off down the track to Moustaki. He was to hold the brothers up for twenty minutes before he threw them their car keys and took off himself in the opposite direction, over the mountain track to Hora Sfakion.

I drove as fast as I could, wondering whether I'd been stupidly altruistic to ask for a mere twenty minutes. The boy's leg was bleeding, and needed attention, though . . . In any case it was still Nick they were after, and they knew he wasn't with me . . . On the other hand, these people operated on a code so different from anything I'd encountered before, it was hard to tell how they would react . . . Sentences from *Macho Man* sounded in my head: "the shame, when a family member is killed, of 'failing to take the blood back' " . . . What obligation of revenge applied to a wounding, and by a foreigner?

Best not to wait and find out. That was one reason for not tarrying in Moustaki. The other was Maud. I wasn't looking forward to that interview, and the shorter I could keep it, the easier it would be. My job's done, I'd tell her; I've found Nick, helped him out of his present difficulty, all of which he's going to explain to you in person after a final business transaction tomorrow . . . She wasn't going to be content with that, and I

didn't enjoy the prospect of having to fend off her questions
while knowing all the time about the shipment he was sending
out. Though it made sense that she should get the details from
him, not from me.

No, my time is up, the *p'tite escapade* over—and I'd better not
tell Claudine what a misnomer *that* turned out to be! I'd have
preferred to leave in sunshine, with smiles all round, instead of
secretly in darkness, but that's what associating with Nick does
for you—wraps you in his own atmosphere of twilight and half
truth. I've had enough, and I'm going back to Claudine while
my skin is still unpunctured. Mustn't forget the flight schedule,
on the bedroom chair . . . Can telephone a booking from the
hotel at Frango . . . Think that's all.

Concentrate now on *driving* . . .

I'd remembered correctly. There *was* an old archway just above
Maud's house, leading to a patch of wasteland. I got out,
removed a fallen stone which was in the way, and backed the
Hyundai in. It could still be seen, but it was in shadow, away
from the street light. It was the best I could do.

I'd been lucky coming up into the village, and had only passed
one old woman, who'd shown no interest. There could have
been unseen eyes at windows, though: the village grapevine
could already be stirring into life . . . But—see Maud, collect
gear, get out. That was all. Ten minutes should do it, if I
managed to be as brutally brief as I intended.

Old doors have their own built-in alarm system. The street
door into Maud's courtyard groaned as I opened it. Cursing
under my breath, I slipped through and closed it behind me,
failing to avoid a clank of the worn iron latch . . . Well, it
wouldn't matter as long as Maud was on her own.

Which, unfortunately, she wasn't. There was light coming
from the terrace upstairs, and voices. I decided to wait in the

shadows below while trying to make out who she was with. A man—Oh Christ, *no*! It sounds like *Spyro* . . . Just when I least want to run into him . . .

"Who's down there?" *Maud, leaning over the railing, having heard the goddamn door.* I hissed:

"Me."

"Who?"

"William," I said, showing myself. "Look, can you come down for a moment?"

"Oh, it's you!" she said. "Oh, I'm so glad. Spyro's here— come on up."

"No, listen—" *Damn! She's gone.*

It's unavoidable then. I climbed the stone steps to the terrace.

"Hi there!" Spyro said with loathesome enthusiasm. "Well, this is great! I just call, you know, to see what is the news, and here you are!"

"Hello," I said. "Yes, here I am. Hello, Maud."

"I expect you'd like a drink," she said.

"No thanks, haven't time. Spyro, I hope you'll forgive me, but I've just got to have a word with Maud."

"Of course, my friend," he said without hesitation. "You just go right ahead. Good news, I hope?"

"I meant, in private," I said.

"Sure, sure, I understand." But he didn't move.

"We'll go inside, then," I said to Maud.

"You go right ahead," Spyro said. "I wait for you here. But, you know, there is no need to go inside. I never repeat what a friend tells me if he don't want that—no, never."

"Thanks," I said, "but all the same . . ." I drew Maud after me into the living room, closed the door, and turned my back on Spyro. "Let's go over there by the bookcase, he'll be doing his best to lip-read."

"Oh dear," Maud said with a shiver, "you're terrifying me,

William. And what have you done to your hands? They're all scratched and bloody . . ."

She stood, shoulders hunched, prepared for bad news. I said: "Don't worry, it's all right. Well, not all, but mostly. I did find Nick again, that's the first good thing, and he's fine. Of course, knowing Nick as we do, we knew he was going to be in some sort of trouble, and he is, but that's no surprise, is it."

"You're preparing me," she said, "you're *preparing* me . . . What for? What's he been doing?"

"He's going to tell you himself," I said. "Tomorrow . . . or very soon."

"Tomorrow? Can't you tell me now?"

"He was very insistent he must tell you himself. I'm sorry, Maud, but I don't really know all the ins and outs, and it would be better coming from him."

She made a face, then shook her head. "No," she said, "no, I'd much rather hear what he told you, now. He can fill in the details tomorrow. Please, William."

"I'm sorry, I think I must do what he asked."

"Why?" she said angrily. "What's he done that's got to be a secret from me?"

"It's not like that, it's just that he wants to tell you himself. To make amends, I expect—"

"Make amends! What you mean is, he's hoping to talk me round, and thinks he can do it better than you can."

"No, I—"

"Well, I don't accept that, I'm not prepared to sit here with my hands folded doing nothing until he chooses to come swanning home full of whatever tale he's decided to tell me. I want to hear it from you, William, *now*."

"Yes, well of course I knew you'd feel that, say that . . . But look, Maud, there's another side to it: he wants to keep the pressure off you just for one more day until this project he's involved in has got past a critical stage. There are people who want to upset it, and he wants to protect both you and the project. If they found out now—"

"What people?"

I gestured over my shoulder. "There's one of them, right there. Don't tell me this was a social visit. He knew where I'd gone, he's determined to catch up with Nick if he can, force his way into the action. He needs money to complete that hotel he's building, Nick said."

"Nick said! We both know what that's worth, don't we!"

"I've seen the hotel, you go past it on the coast road to Rethymnon, half finished, but no builders at work. It's the classic road to bankruptcy: undercapitalized project, cash and credit all used up, but no income yet. He's got to get it open, making money, or the bank will call in their loan and he'll have to sell for peanuts. It makes sense, Maud—you never liked him, and you were right. He's after Nick, to squeeze him for what he can get. But what you don't *know* he can't trick out of you. Can he?" I turned to check that the trickster hadn't crept forward to press a shameless ear to the window, but he hadn't. He was watching, though, and smiled and waved at seeing me. I turned back to Maud.

"It's easy to tell you've been spending time with Nick," she said sharply. "The pair of you together, deciding what I should and shouldn't be told . . . I thought I could rely on you, at least."

"It's true I decided to do what he asked," I said. "I'm not happy about it, Maud, but I do think it makes sense."

She shrugged. I said:

"Look, I'm sorry, but I've got to go now."

"Go? You mean you're just going to drive off and leave me here, not knowing where Nick is, what arrangements you've made, or *anything*? William, you just can't *do* that!"

"Maud, I *have* to go. Listen: I loaned Nick my hired jeep so he could get out of the mountains on the old track without coming through Moustaki. So I'm in the Hyundai, and if people see it they may turn up here demanding to know where Nick is. The sooner I get it out of the village, the better, and I'm going to drive on and stay somewhere else tonight, maybe bed down on the road to Frangocastello where I'm to collect the jeep tomorrow. There's something else you'd better know: the Gyparis brothers attacked us as we were coming back to the cars at Kalikrati, and I had to shoot one in the leg—"

"Shot one? Oh, William, you *didn't!*" Maud was aghast.

"So it's best if I don't hang around."

"Oh my God," she said. "So they really think—"

"Having seen them close to, how young and mad they are, I think they see it as a sort of game, a test of manhood, all that crap. Anyway, I'm afraid it finally came to the crunch, but the bullet doesn't seem to have hit anything vital, so there's no permanent harm done, thank God. He may even be pleased to have a bullet hole to show off."

"Sometimes I really *hate* men," Maud said emphatically.

"I can understand it. We've all got identity problems, you see, which women don't seem to have, or not so much, and—"

"Several times, since Nick went off, I've asked myself if I really want him back. You said I didn't seem as worried or upset as I might be, and that's why."

"It did cross my mind. But could you live alone? Or with another woman?"

"Not with another woman, no, I'm sure of that. I tried to imagine living alone, but couldn't. I still seem to be stuck with the idea that a woman has to have a man in her life. I always have had. Then there are all the practical things Nick does that I really miss, getting me taken on by the New York agent, for instance. That's the best thing that ever happened in my life, so I suppose, yes, I do want him back."

"The best thing? Really?"

"You said something about identity," Maud said earnestly,

"and I don't mind admitting to you, as an old friend, that being an accepted painter matters to me more than I ever imagined it would. It's what, it's *who* I am, now. Maud Aspinall, Painter. That may seem ridiculous, but all I had before was being a so-called beauty, and I hated that, counting the crows' feet and wondering how long I'd got left. I don't care if I get old and ugly, now. Because I've got *that*, haven't I."

"You certainly have," I said.

"You sound as if you mean it."

"I do mean it. I feel sure of it," I said firmly.

I was watching her face, and saw the smile appear on it. I thought: she *is* good, and if Nick lets her down, as I have a feeling he may, she's established now, home and dry.

"—always used to trust your judgment," Maud was saying. "And as people say, you've either got it or you haven't—it's not a question of training, but of having a seeing eye."

"Mmm," I said. "Well, maybe. In any case, you've got expert opinion to give you confidence. And whatever else Nick has been up to, he's managing your sales brilliantly, isn't he. Like keeping some paintings back and not flooding the market all at once. That's the sort of thing he's really good at."

"Keeping some back?" she said, frowning. "What do you mean?"

"He just mentioned it. I thought he was right—don't you?"

"I don't know anything about that," she said.

A sudden chill settled round my spine. *He couldn't, could he? And if he had, why?* I said:

"How many paintings have you done, now? Apart from the ones you've got here?"

"How many?" She looked at me. "Why do you ask?"

"I wondered . . . how many sales it took to make a painter feel secure," I said, forcing a grin.

"Oh." She considered. "Between twenty and thirty, I suppose."

"Oh, really. Well, that's a lot of work, isn't it . . ."

"William," she said nervously, "you're trying to tell me something. I know you are . . . I can feel it."

"No," I said, "no. I'm not."

There was a long silence—or it seemed long. Then she said in a small, shaky voice:

"What has he done? What have you seen?"

I thought: *I don't have to tell her. But if I don't, she will have to be told later, perhaps by someone less sympathetic to her, and to what this means to her . . .*

"Twenty-seven of your paintings in a shed in Kalikrati," I said in as matter-of-fact a voice as I could manage.

I didn't have to drag Spyro with me when I left, ten minutes later, after hurriedly piling my clothes into the suitcase. Oh no! He trotted at my heels, panting with excitement. When he saw Nick's Hyundai, I had to physically prevent him climbing in beside me. As I maneuvered the car through the archway into the lane, his eager face bobbed along by the window mouthing new and more frantic offers of friendship and cooperation. Money was in the air: he sensed it with a lover's intuitive certainty, and my resistance confirmed it. In the driving mirror, I saw him trot a few steps more after the car, falter, stop, and stretch out his hands in supplication, a last appeal against exclusion, illuminated in the red glow of the taillights. Then I turned a corner, and lost him.

How could he be so sure? Simple intuition couldn't be enough—he had to have facts. He and Nick could have been working together, perhaps on more than one project. "*My very good friend*"—but then, he claimed that of everybody. A waste of time to ask him what he knew, and in any case I had to get away, I'd already spent far longer than I meant in Moustaki—it was nearly half past eleven. But I was clear of the village now, apparently unpursued, and every minute put more concealing darkness between me and that asylum of homicidal lunatics.

And so, about Maud . . . I'd offered to stay, of course, but her refusal was immediate, and forceful—sent me packing, in effect. Several reasons: one—she'd be safer on her own than with me, an object of resentment and possibly revenge, in the house; two—I'd been the bearer of bad news, and earned the usual ingratitude for it; three—I was a member of the race of men, the whole of which, in her present mood, she would happily see exterminated. Unfair, yes, but understandable. I didn't try to reason: I did my best to console, reminded her to bolt the door as soon as I was through it, and left.

Which brings me to Nick. How could he *do* this to her? It's too late now, but I really would have liked to come face-to-face with him one more time, and . . .

Too late?

Ah!—*perhaps not!*

The petrol gauge read a quarter full, so I made a detour to an all-night garage I'd noticed on the main road to Rethymnon. Which was a lucky decision because the road I'd expected to take was far too rough for the pickup, and I had to drive a long way further east to get round the end of the White Mountain range before turning south for the coast. The road was narrow, and lonely—no place to break down or run out of fuel. It took this tour in the starlight to emphasize what hadn't been entirely obvious when I'd come over the mountains on foot—the isolation of the south coast.

The road to Frangocastello is squeezed between the mountains and the sea. Mosquitoes ruled here until DDT dented their numbers, and mankind still hasn't got much more than a toe-hold. Add to the mosquitoes the *meltimía,* a steamy, sometimes violent south wind loaded with sharp Saharan sand, and it's not hard to see why Cretans have always preferred the north coast, leaving the inhospitable south to pirates, smugglers, and assorted malefactors. Now including Nick Cruickshank.

I didn't get to Frangocastello until half past one, by which time I was almost asleep at the wheel. But a familiar sight jerked me awake: the jeep was already there, parked outside the hotel. *Collect it any time tomorrow,* Nick had said, and I'd assumed that meant from the morning, not from the night before. Damn the slippery bastard!—he's done it *again*! Now I've lost what is almost certainly the last chance of catching him—just what he intended, you bet.

Unless, and it's possible, *he's spending the night in the hotel*! Now that's an idea! Peaceful oblivion on a proper bed, then rise early, rested, to be the skeleton at his breakfast table . . . But the place is in darkness, it's too late to disturb them. Nothing for it, then, but to sleep in the pickup.

I drove quietly past the hotel, parked facing the harbor, hugged my jacket tight for warmth, and dozed off to the sound of waves subsiding gently on the beach.

*Hannibal thought himſelf safe here againſt the very
Romans: but the vaſt Treasure which that fam'd African
carry'd hither, rais'd him a great many Enemies . . .*

*oo bad, it's too bad! Maud's driftwood bed has collapsed com-
pletely this time. I'm doubled up between the parted planks . . .*

Reality dawned slowly, painfully. I wasn't in bed, I was in the
Hyundai. I'd slid down the plastic upholstery and my knees were
wedged against the dashboard.

I struggled back onto the seat, shivering. Not only cold, but
still dark. What time is it? Five in the morning—the hour before
dawn . . . If I had the jeep keys, I'd get in, drive away to warmth,
food, and the plane home. At five in the morning, interest is
firmly focused on creature comforts: at home I'd be slipping my
arm round Claudine, sleepily encompassing her female luxury of

shape and softness. Nobody should be awake at five in the morning unless under dire compulsion: for work, for war, for execution . . .

I yawned, rubbed my eyes. Through the steamed-up windscreen, blurry stars swam overhead. They seemed less bright than I remembered from the night before . . . But no!—of course it was the sky being lighter that made them seem so: the first indication of approaching dawn.

Huddled against the cold, I watched a paleness appear in the east and spread gradually across the horizon. Soon there was enough light to see the shapes of boats on their moorings in the harbor, against the dark outline of the sheltering ring of rocks. I would have enjoyed it but for the thought that, at half past five, breakfast was still two and a half hours distant. Now a chill mist was forming over the water, and the boats beginning to sink into it, losing their waterlines, their mooring buoys and chains, their once-so-solid hulls plank by plank.

But why suffer? I had the car heater, and these were fishing boats—the crews slept ashore. The quiet hum of the car engine wasn't going to disturb anybody.

I slid across to the driver's seat, reached for the ignition key, and switched on. After the first clatter and surge, the engine noise sank to a gentle purr. I fumbled with the levers of the heating system, and sat with my hand over the outlet, waiting for warmth.

Through the windscreen, I saw that I'd miscalculated. A figure was visible in the wheelhouse of a caïque, moored alongside the tiny ramshackle jetty. Damn!—so I'd woken him up, and was due for a shaken fist or maybe an earful of Greek curses through the car window. Now he's opening the wheelhouse door . . . All right, all *right,* so I'll switch off. And *freeze* again.

Switching off hasn't stopped him, though. Jumping on to the jetty, marching towards me, looking almost British in his duffel coat and peaked cap. Well, fair enough—once woken, you might as well relieve your feelings before going back to bed, or rather, bunk.

I began to wind the window down, resigned to pacify, apologize, as required. Then, when I looked up again, he was near enough for me to see the glasses . . .

I stopped winding, and waited for the angry face behind them to appear at the window. He spoke first:

"Christ, William. I wish you'd get off my back!"

I felt a surge of rage, but icy indignation seemed more to the point. I said:

"I came to collect my hired jeep, which I let you drive off in at some risk to myself."

"This early? Don't give me that!"

"It's true I wanted to be here when you delivered it. I've got one or two things to say to—"

"Here are the keys. Thanks and so forth. So now kindly get in and bugger off, back to where you belong."

I said nothing. His face under the peaked cap was looking less and less like a face, more and more like a target, round, fleshily vulnerable and tempting. I felt my fists clenching. *Why don't I just get out of the car* and *do it . . .*

The keys landed in my lap. He turned away. I reached for the door handle, wrenched the door open, closed the distance with three, four paces, grabbed the shoulder of his duffle coat and spun him round. I was taller, I realized. Probably heavier. Certainly angrier. Violence suddenly seemed a wonderfully simple solution . . . I drew back my fist.

"What's the matter?" he said, surprised.

"You are," I said through my teeth.

"What? *Me?*"

I breathed out. If he didn't understand *why,* there was no point. The moment was lost. My fist seemed to sink of its own accord. I searched for words . . . Oh, it was useless.

"Why?" he said. He seemed genuinely puzzled.

"Because you're an unspeakable shit," I said.

He blinked. We stood, face-to-face, trying to read each other's faces in the dawn light, the dueling hour. I rallied my anger hopelessly, felt it recede further. "If you mean Maud," he began.

"Of course I mean Maud. *All* her paintings are in the shed at Kilikrati, every single one she thought was sold. There *isn't* a New York dealer. Is there?"

"Oh *Christ!*" he said. "How did this come up?"

"Ironically, because I was telling her what a good job you were doing, keeping some back, not flooding the market, etcetera. How the hell could you *do* this to her?"

"Because I had to."

"Oh, *bollocks* . . ."

"Yes I did. Look—it's illegal to export antiquities. So I had a problem: how to bring the money in from the States without attracting attention. I needed a legitimate form of export, and Maud needed to feel a success. So I put the two things together, and came up with the New York dealer."

"Brilliant. Did you never pause to think what it meant to her?"

"She wanted her work to sell," he said. "So I made out it had. She was happy." He paused, became indignant that I couldn't or wouldn't see it. "My God, I did more for her than she ever did for me! She took it for granted that I would do her dirty work as salesman and general dogsbody, for all the hours it took and for as long as she wanted. Have you thought about *that*? In return for which, I made her *happy*."

"Oh, for Christ's sake, Nick!"

"What's wrong with it?" he said. "And there's more, which I know you can't deny, because you must have found it out for yourself when you lived with her: she's a cold fish, totally disinterested. So, what do I owe her? Much less than she's been getting, if you ask me. Now you've wrecked all that."

"Don't you understand?" I said. "It wasn't *true* . . ."

"Oh, fucking metaphysics," he said. "Listen, William, one more time—*she was happy!* What does it matter that the New York dealer doesn't actually exist?"

"You really don't understand, do you," I said slowly. *Or was it possible, just possible, that he was right?*

"Was she pleased with you for telling her?" he asked.

"No, of course not . . ."

"Well, there you are then."

No!—of course he wasn't! "You have to know the truth, even if it's not what you want to hear," I said stoutly. "Or nothing makes sense. Does it."

"That's childish crap," Nick said. "In real life, everybody believes what suits them, and then they look for facts to prove it. If you haven't found that out by now—"

It was then I hit him. It wasn't so much what he'd said that finally provoked me, but the expression of worldly superiority that was on his face when he said it. Plus, I'd better admit, an uneasy feeling that I wasn't doing too well with the argument in words . . . Anyway, I hit him, and felt better.

He sat up on the stony ground, and touched his mouth. "All right," he said, "you've done what you came for. *Now* will you kindly bugger off."

"No."

"Oh Christ. Look, if I stand up and let you do it again, will you go?"

"Where did the antiquities come from?"

"Oh no!—not more questions . . . I told you, anyway."

"From the Lost City of Atlantis, you said."

"And so they did."

"Nick!—I think I'm going to—"

"Wait, wait. They did, actually, genuinely come from what

most people now agree was Atlantis—the eastern end of Crete. But it wasn't underwater, and I didn't discover it—that was just to make it easier for you to help me. In fact the stuff was hidden in the ceiling of the cottage, by the owner's son, who stole it. I found it, with the rifle, when repairing the ceiling."

"That would be the boy who was working on the dig at Zakros, and got sacked. Who then crashed a car, killed another boy, and had to go into exile in Athens. Where he's now a taxi driver."

"Right, so Maud told you all that. He broke into the site hut one night, but they could never prove it. I went to Athens, found him, did a deal on the stuff, was hoping there might be more but if so, he wasn't telling. There were only about a dozen really valuable Minoan items, in fact, but it started me off, and I added more ordinary bits and pieces from later periods, Roman, Byzantine, there's plenty once you know where to look, often sitting unrecognized in village houses . . . Will that do?"

I looked down at him, and sighed. He still sat, brushing off his cap, diminished, deflated, demystified . . . Already, it was hard to remember why I'd gone along with the dreams, the glorious tomorrow, the bird about to fly . . . Oh Jesus! How could I have fallen for it? All I could see now was the dust under the conjurer's table.

Talking seemed to be over. I said:

"How far do you expect to get in the boat?"

"Exchange offshore," he said.

"You've got the stuff on board, then?"

He hesitated. "Yes."

"Show me."

"Oh, must I? Time's getting on . . ."

"Just one piece. Then I'll go." I offered him my hand. He shrugged, accepted a pull to his feet. Then he led the way to the caïque.

"You're in a hurry."

"I was waiting till dawn," he said. "The rocks . . ."

"Yes."

We stepped over the heavy gunwale onto the short afterdeck, and down the ladder into the cockpit, past a row of steel drums which reeked of petrol, to the wheelhouse. He opened the door and gestured me in. Down another short ladder was the two-berth forecabin. Both bunks were stacked with sacks. I walked forward, stooping to avoid the low beamed ceiling.

The sacks looked familiar. More, they *smelled* familiar. I said:

"This is how the stuff came down from Arcadés?"

Nick was pulling open one of the sacks. He nodded, smiled and said:

"I thought it was rather neat. There's an old woman who—"

"I know," I said heavily. "I helped load them on to her donkeys. And the carob beans, of course, make—"

"—excellent padding against damage," he said. "Yes, she told me a tall foreigner helped her in return for food. And then left, leaving her grapes half trodden. So I thought it probably wasn't you. What happened to your professional pride?"

"They were perfectly well trodden," I said. "In fact, I was worried that the skins and stalks—"

He was holding out a small, oval object. I took it, and held it to the porthole to see better. It was embossed with a ship: single row of oars, stumpy mast, and squaresail.

"Seal stone, four thousand years old," Nick said. "As Philadelphia will no doubt confirm."

I handed it back to him in silence. I ought to shop him, but . . . Oh, let someone else do it.

"Satisfied?" Nick said. He was peering through the porthole. I glanced out, across the harbor to the hotel. I could understand his nervousness—it was getting light. I said:

"All right, I'm off."

"Thanks."

He followed me up to the wheelhouse. "Listen, William, I know you're sore at me—to put it mildly—but you wouldn't—"

"I just decided not to," I said, stepping out into the cockpit, "or, to be more accurate, that I couldn't. Don't know why, but . . ." I was passing the smelly fuel drums lined up there, and something was wrong. A moment later I realized what it was. "Don't these boats have diesels?"

"The fuel's for the boat I'm transferring to," Nick said.

"Transferring?"

"The goods . . . One other thing—as you're going, please don't hang about. They've got plainclothes customs men in this area, and if one of them sees you—another Englishman—near the harbor, they might put two and two together."

"All right."

He nodded at me, stepped back aboard. I started to walk along the jetty, back to the Hyundai to collect my suitcase. So that was it.

And how was I going to feel, as the plane accelerated down the runway, lifted off, and Crete sank out of sight? Not good, I suspected. Not good at all. I'd come to help, and succeeded only in making Maud's situation worse. I didn't see how she and Nick could get together again after this. Then there were the paintings . . . I could offer to show some to the London dealers who were already clients of mine: the personal contact at least meant that they would look, if not buy . . . But *was* she good enough? Well, they'd tell me that, and she'd get some high-level opinion without having to hawk the things round herself, which she hated so much. Yes!—I'll do that, I'll call in and suggest it.

I reached the Hyundai, and lifted my suitcase out. Behind me was the splutter of a diesel starting up. I turned, and saw puffs of black smoke rising from Nick's caïque. Was it his, or hired?—I hadn't asked. There were other questions, too, which would never be answered now. They didn't matter, not anymore. He was late getting under way: the mist was clearing, and a yellow glow on the eastern horizon was the beginning of sunrise . . . People were stirring, two men in jeans and sweaters coming down the beach opposite to a rubber dinghy hauled up there, an early riser coming onto the hotel balcony. And a car arriving, just coming round the end of the hotel: a white Mercedes taxi with a single passenger. I looked at my watch: just coming up to six. Nick had better get a move on if he wants to slip away quietly to make his rendezvous. I suppose that's my fault too, that he's delayed. If he'd trusted me more, of course . . . but he couldn't. The Cretan Liar, in person. Always and everywhere.

The taxi passenger is coming towards the jetty, so we'll pass. It's a girl, carrying a suitcase in one hand, a bag slung over her shoulder, and in a hurry. Young, pretty, and obviously Greek, with that raven hair. And in a hurry . . .

He was consistent, you have to give him that. He'd lied about everything else, so why not about this? I hadn't the energy to be annoyed all over again, and in any case, I'd already decided that Nick and Maud were finished. I stopped, put the suitcase down, waited for her to come past, to see what this aspect of Nick's double life looked like close-to. She hurried past, the black eyes darting a worried glance at me, but without faltering in her pace. Oh yes—a very tangible dream, this one, this Maria. Or motive. Yes, a lot more things made sense now.

I looked along the jetty. Nick was on the foredeck, slackening the final mooring line. He wouldn't be coming back, of course. So I'd have to see Maud, break it to her, collect another load of Nick's cast-off troubles. I'd have to, because there wasn't any-one else.

Might as well get on then. I don't feel much like waving good-bye.

I turned away, and picked up the suitcase. There was another car arriving at the hotel, breaking sharply, skidding on the gravel. I looked up. A red pickup. And the doors were being flung open—two men jumping out . . .

With shotguns, of course. Though I didn't spend any time gawping. I was making for the edge of the jetty, dropping over it, onto the rocks, away from the harbor. Once there, I looked over the edge and saw the two men running to the Hyundai. One was much faster: I recognized the unwounded brother. He glanced into the car, shouted back to the other, who was pounding after him, an older, heavier man. The father, it must be the father: about fifty, tall boots, baggy trousers, fierce black moustache, and a shock of black hair—he was shouting too, deeper, more roughly than his son. Now they were running onto the jetty, rattling the planks as they came . . .

I ducked as they passed me, but their attention was on the caïque: must have seen Nick on deck. As soon as they'd passed, I put my head up again. Maria was out of the boat, standing on the jetty, screaming at the two men and making warding-off gestures. I could see Nick behind, still in the cockpit, shouting to her—probably to get back in, so that he can motor off, put some water between them and her menfolk. She isn't taking any notice, hasn't understood, or feels that the drama has got to come to a head . . .

A car horn blasted several times by the hotel. I glanced across, and saw a dark blue jeep pulling up. Two policemen in uniform jumped out, followed by a girl—it could be Eléni—yes, it *is*. Another figure is running down the outside steps from the hotel balcony to join them—Leather Jacket, with what is probably a walkie-talkie in his hand. They're all running towards the jetty, the police fumbling at their holsters . . .

I scramble back onto the jetty, and run to meet them, away from the caïque. I've gone maybe ten yards when there's a loud bang from behind. I drop flat, uselessly, because if it had been aimed at me I'd have already have been shot or not. The police and Eléni have taken cover behind the Hyundai, and suddenly that seems a most desirable place to be, rather than where I am now, on the bare jetty exposed to fire from both sides. The police are opening up with pistols, and it's as good a time as any to get up and run for it . . .

"Hello," Eléni says. I don't reply for a moment, being somewhat breathless, but that's only natural when you've just broken a world sprint record. One of the policemen says something to me, but he isn't smiling and it doesn't sound like congratulations. Eléni says:

"He asks, who is in the boat besides your friend?"

"Tell him, Nick isn't my friend, not anymore. And there's no one else in the boat: apart from Nick, there's Nick's girlfriend—Maria from the village—"

"Yes, I know. And?"

"Her father and brother."

"I thought so, of course. This is very bad."

"I agree . . . Oh Christ, *look!*"

Along the jetty, beside the caïque, Maria had dropped to her knees in front of her father, and we could hear shrill cries of misery and appeal. We could see his back, his shoulders hunched like a bull about to charge, and the butt of his gun. He was threatening her with it . . . I said:

"He won't, will he? I mean, it *is* just for show?"

"I don't know," Eléni whispered. "I really don't know . . ."

Facing us, the brother stood guard, shotgun at the ready. *While his murderous father worked up his rage . . .*

"Tell your police *they've got to rush them!*" I said urgently. "Or if they won't, sod it, give me a gun . . . I can't stay here and watch this . . ."

I was suddenly aware of an ear-shattering clatter from behind, and a helicopter burst over our heads, turning to make a slow return pass. It slowed further, and hung over the harbor, the downdraught shredding the mist, lashing the surface into waves and sending small boats tugging at their moorings. As it turned, it showed US ARMY in large white letters on its camouflaged flank . . . Now what?

But through the racket of engine and rotor I could still hear the roars and screams of father and daughter arguing out their personal quarrel. It couldn't go on, something had to give . . . And, oh God! —*the maniac is putting his gun to his shoulder* . . .

I heard the report, but I had anticipated it, and was looking away. There are some things . . . a cold-blooded murder of a daughter by her own father . . . Oh no, no, *no*. Beside me, Eléni screamed. The policemen were shouting . . . *Too late, you bloody fools!*

Well, it was over, then. I raised my eyes, and saw—

What's this? The girl, Maria, is still on her knees, not screaming, but with her hand across her mouth. *And it's her father who's lying there, on his back, arms outstretched, his gun a yard away* . . .

I looked across the caïque and saw Nick behind the wheelhouse, still covering Maria's father with the Mannlicher . . . I'd forgotten he still had it.

His mouth is opening and shutting—I can only just hear his voice through the racket of the helicopter. It's Greek, directed at Maria . . . now he's signing to her, urgently, to get aboard . . . But she's still on her knees, bent over her father . . . She's straightens up, is screaming again, shaking her head about, the hair flying . . . Grief, tragedy, it's all there, you don't need the words . . . Nick is still shouting, but she's ignoring him. The brother is indecisive, twisting nervously between Nick with the Mannlicher on his right, and the police on his left . . .

Maria's getting up. She's on her feet now, still by the body of her father, who hasn't moved that I could see . . . She's tearing her hair, throwing the arms about—I've never seen anything like this outside a theatre. Well, I shouldn't say so at such a time, but she's giving it all she's got. She's virtually making a speech, the sort that winds up to—

A denunciation. Oh yes, someone's for it, someone must pay. And here comes the closing gesture: her arm descends from above her head—you could say with the consent, the approval of the gods—and she points, she's pointing at . . .

Well of course it's Nick, who else. Nick just shot her father, never mind whose fault that was. Nick shot her father and now her equally maniac brother has had his duty pointed out to him by his sister, of course he's got to take the blood back and shoot Nick . . . And so on, and so on, and so on.

But now the police have seen the shotgun point away from them, so they're up and bravely opening fire again. Don't blame them all that much, it'd be a lucky pistol shot that brought the brother down at this range. And they're doing some good, they've distracted the brother, who swings round suddenly and fires his third shot in our direction, shattering the windscreen, but now he's having to reload . . .

Meanwhile, Nick has disappeared. No, there he is in the wheelhouse, and the diesel is thumping as he opens up the throttle. The boat is too tight against the jetty for a clean pull-away: it surges forward, hits a pile and rebounds off, shaking the jetty, but winning the shove off that Nick needs. Now he's pulling away fast, there's a yard of swirling mist between the boat and the jetty, two yards. He's got steerage room: the boat begins to turn, making for the harbor entrance, he's twenty yards out . . . thirty.

The helicopter has turned away and is making for the beach, hovering, descending. Does that mean that Nick is going to get away? In spite of everything, I hope it does . . . If ever there was a justifiable homicide, that was it . . .

The caïque is going flat out, a huge bow wave setting the moored boats lurching, and splashing up the rocks. It's coming up to the entrance . . . in it now . . . and through, into the open sea. The helicopter has landed on the beach, and the din is subsiding, the rotor slowing, stopping, drooping. At last we can speak. Eléni nudges me.

"What?"

"Stavros," she says, pointing.

And there's the sleek white beast racing out of the misty sunrise with all the speed that money can buy, on course to intercept. Which he will, no trouble: Stavros has a Ferrari to catch a farm cart. So Nick isn't going to get away . . .

Unless . . . *unless Stavros is the exchange Nick was talking about.* Does it make sense?—yes! —*that's it!* They were in it together all the time: Nick collected the stuff, and Stavros is the dealer. That's why he wanted to contact him—not a rival in any way, but a *partner* . . . Of course, of *course!*

The brother has given up, and throws his gun down with a disdainful gesture—policemen not worth the shooting it seems to imply. Eléni goes forward with the police to see what she can do for Maria, who is keening over her father. Let's not forget she's pregnant with Nick's baby, so there's plenty of tragedy in stock for the long winter evenings, oh yes, knitting little socks and weeping over them. Well I'm sorry, but as *Macho Man* puts it, "the egocentric cannot see that his pride must always be at the expense of another's." They worked hard for this result, the Gyparis family, so I'm going to give up on trying to understand them, and close the book.

"Mr. Warner." A voice from behind. It's the CIA, just descended from the skies, or maybe clouds. "What do you think of life on earth?" I ask him. "Personally, at this moment in time, I think it's pretty shitty."

He looks at me suspiciously. Nothing to worry about: he looks at *everybody* suspiciously, does Greg Barnes. "You're not injured?" he enquires.

"No, just sickened. Tell me, how did you manage to arrive so precisely at zero hour?"

He extends his right hand. On it is, guess what, the proverbial little black box. "Gee whiz," I say. "You guys have all the latest technology . . . What the hell is it?"

"Trace transmitter," he says solemnly. "I've just recovered it from the rear of your hired jeep."

"And I saw you put it there," I say, "that day in Melissinou. Except that I didn't *know* I was seeing it. In my world, such things don't come into one's everyday calculations . . . You mean, you've been able to follow the jeep's movements ever since?"

"Pretty largely," he says. "We lost you a while in the mountains, but we knew there were only two ways out: all we had to do was wait."

"But listen—you're not going to tell me my ex-friend Nick was running dope after all? I'd just made up my mind for sure that he wasn't."

"You can relax on that, Mr. Warner. True, we thought he might be, with his record, his disappearances and all. But no, he's now wanted for a customs infringement."

"Then why—"

"Oh, we like to give our Greek friends a helping hand when we can."

"And that man over there, in the leather jacket—"

"—is their local customs officer, that's correct."

Friends . . . gifts . . . I recognize the pattern. It only takes a moment to think of the return obligation. "You make yourselves useful. And they let you keep your missiles on their territory."

"Let's say, they may take a little less notice of their peaceniks."

He nods and potters off. I look offshore. Stavros's yacht has caught up with the caïque, but seems to be standing off some yards, not closing to take Nick and his merchandise on board. I can hear the quack and howl of a loudhailer. So, what *is* going on? I'm going to tackle Eléni about it, but she's still busy with Maria, putting her own coat round heaving shoulders, and mopping tears, so it'll have to wait. Across the jetty, the brother squats in silence, the morning sun sparkling off handcuffs.

There's a lull. Greg Barnes is now back on the beach by the helicopter, chatting to Leather Jacket, reinforcing the *entente cordiale*. Think I'll go over.

Then I remember my suitcase which is still beside the jetty where I'd abandoned it. I collect it, and take it to the jeep, which sits waiting, has quite the same air of patient resignation as a donkey. There's a carob bean on the backseat. I suppose he collected the sacks from the old woman last night—her cottage is only a mile from here. How many were there on the boat? Eight, I think it was. He'd only just have got them all in, with two beside the driver's seat . . . Can't stop these calculations, it's become a habit. I take the carob bean off the backseat, replace it with the suitcase, and put the bean in my trouser pocket. Now I'll join Greg Barnes and Leather Jacket.

The hotel terrace is peopled with onlookers roused by all the noise, speculating on events. They look at me, decide I'm part of the show, and someone calls a question. "Sorry, don't speak Greek." This provokes the usual chorus of interrogation—but I shrug and walk on. The chorus dies down, disappointedly.

Behind the hotel, the sound of car engines, tortured tires. I turn: a police car appears, closely followed by an ambulance. They look at a loss, so I trot back, and point out the way to the casualties. Then on to the beach.

The helicopter is smaller than I thought, and emits an electronic humming: the pilot is sitting inside looking thoughtful, and Leather Jacket is hanging about looking superfluous. I push through a row of teenaged Greek boys with their mouths hanging open, and go towards Greg Barnes, who is standing by the open door with a microphone in his hand and a heavy expression. He sees me, beckons, says into the microphone:

"Okay, Mr. Papadoyannis, wait in, sir, please. He's here now, and I'll ask if he has data on that."

"Who are you talking to?" I ask.

He eyes me doubtfully, then says: "You see that yacht out there, Mr. Warner? I'm talking to the—"

"You're talking to Stavros?"

"Oh, so you do know Mr. Papadoyannis."

"Up to a point," I say. "What's he doing out there?"

"He's trying to persuade your friend Mr. Cruickshank—"

"My ex-friend."

"—to surrender the valuable contraband he has on board."

"And you believe him?"

"Do I believe Mr. Papadoyannis? Why sure, of course I do. Mr. Papadoyannis heads a governmental department, with special responsibility for the prevention of illegal exportation of antiquities . . . You seem surprised, Mr. Warner."

"An illusion merely."

"Okay sir. Now, here's how it is. Mr. Cruickshank declines to play ball. Not only will he not play ball, he threatens to blow his boat and himself to hell if Mr. Papadoyannis interferes with his passage."

"Including the valuable contraband."

"We've got upwards of thirty fathoms out there, Mr. Warner, and I understand the items are small. Can you confirm?"

"The fathoms, no. The items, yes. Scattered at thirty fathoms, it would be, er, a needle in a haystack situation."

"Okay. Now, how would you rate the chances of Mr. Cruickshank doing a thing like that?"

"Psychologically, he's just shot his prospective father-in-law and had to abandon the girl he was eloping with. Physically, he's got several large drums of petrol on deck, and a Mannlicher rifle with maybe six rounds of ammunition . . . Of course, he could just use a match."

"Mr. Warner, I greatly appreciate your providing this data.

Shall I confirm to Mr. Papadoyannis that you rate the event as possible, going on probable?"

"Affirmative, Mr. Barnes."

I said that, but of course I didn't believe it. Nick had always managed to stay one jump ahead of reality, and I didn't believe he would let it catch up with him now. It had caught up with Maud, but Nick was already on his way by then, leaving me to pick up the pieces if I could. It had caught up with Maria's father, now on his penultimate journey to a hospital mortuary with a white sheet drawn up over his face. It had caught up with Maria, now leaving the scene in the wake of her father, weeping, supported by Eléni. And with both her brothers, the one present in handcuffs, and the one absent with a bullet wound— my contribution to the bottom line of disaster. It had caught up with all these, but Nick had made his jump ahead. Stavros had decided not to risk a boarding, and the white yacht sat on the opalescent Libyan sea, almost motionless, while on shore all eyes strained to follow the caïque as it puttered steadily towards the horizon, fading into the haze; became a blur, a phantom, and was gone.

One jump ahead, yes. That's what I thought, and that's why I was as surprised as anybody when, a few minutes later, waiting for coffee on the hotel terrace, I saw the flash light up the mist, followed, some long seconds afterwards, by a sound like a distant drum roll. On the terrace, there was a shocked silence, and then a chorus of sighs, like the last echoes of a requiem.

Postscript

"**W**hy do you not *open* it?" Claudine suggested impatiently, reaching for my coffee cup. "You think, perhaps, it is a bomb?"

I ignored this. A personal letter deserves better than a careless ripping: there's a ritual to be performed. I'd admired the foreign stamp (Greek), examined the postmark (Rethymnon), gone on to identification of the handwriting . . . I'd never seen Eléni's, but imagined it would be small and neat. This was large and distantly familiar. I sighed. No escaping the fact: it was from Maud.

I slit it open. Claudine waited three seconds, then said: "*Et alors?*"

"You were right—it's a bomb."

"From Maud?"

"She's coming to London, with the paintings, probably to live. Wants me to line up some galleries."

Claudine chuckled, not without malice. "You have a chicken coming home to roost, *mon cher*."

"My idea was that she should *send* the paintings, not come herself . . . I wonder where Guy lives these days?"

"You don't want to help her yourself?"

"Oh, of course I *will*, but . . ." The image rose up again of Maud's face: bleak, hostile, spitting out short sentences between her teeth. I didn't ask: she *wanted* me to know what had happened. I could picture it as if I'd been there myself: the Gyparis father and brother, home late from the hospital and finding Maria gone, storming down to Maud's house, hammering on the door, bawling for Nick. *And Maud had told them: try Frangocastello* . . . "I can't forget what she did. I mean, she *knew* they were after his blood, literally."

"I understand it," Claudine said, her black eyes glittering as she imagined it. There were still moments, even after all our years together, when I was reminded that she was a foreigner, pulled by invisible strings from hotter, more violent climes. In her native Bordeaux, the police keep order with machine guns . . . "First he tricks her about the paintings, and then she realizes it is all true about the girl. So she thinks, 'No!—I will not let him get away with this!' "

"Yes, darling, but if it had been you—God forbid—by the next day and after a sleepless night—which is when I saw her—wouldn't you have been feeling a little less sure of what you'd done, a little less vindictive? When you'd had time to reflect, to cool off?"

"Perhaps."

"I'm sure you would."

"But it is more serious to betray a woman of a certain age than a young girl."

"Ah. You mean, more dangerous." *Women begin as Juliet, end as Lady Macbeth . . . where had I seen that?*
"It is a thing all men should remember. Your coffee."
"Thank you, er, very much."
Breakfast regained priority. After a while, Claudine said:
"One thing more."
"Yes?"
"No one saw Nick's boat explode, did they? It was hidden in the mist, you said."
"No, but they sent the helicopter out soon afterwards, and found some floating wreckage. There's no doubt he blew it up."
"Yes, but—"
"He'd shot a man dead, admitted the antiquities were on board. He'd have been tracked on radar, arrested as soon as he tried to get ashore, sentenced to several years in a Greek jail."
"Mmm."
"So he blew himself up . . . Alternatively, he took off in the dinghy, having left one of those tobacco-tin fishing bombs to explode the petrol when he was a safe distance off, motored to his rendezvous in the mist, got picked up, and is now alive and well and selling Minoan seal stones to New York collectors."
"That is more likely," she said, "knowing Nick."
"Oh, but there are several other possibilities. Do you want to hear them?"
"Well . . ." she said.
She was right. Time to exorcise the beast.